THE ODDEST LITTLE CORNISH CHRISTMAS TREE SHOP

Beth Good

Thimblerig Books

Copyright © 2024 Beth Good

All rights reserved

The characters and events portrayed in this book are fictitious. Any similarity to real persons, living or dead, is coincidental and not intended by the author.

No part of this book may be reproduced, or stored in a retrieval system, or transmitted in any form or by any means, electronic, mechanical, photocopying, recording, or otherwise, without express written permission of the publisher.

THIMBLERIG BOOKS 2024
ISBN: 9798341116603
Imprint: Independently published

You might also enjoy this festive romcom by Beth Good...

THE ODDEST LITTLE CORNISH CHRISTMAS SHOP

Artist Marjorie comes back to the tiny Cornish fishing village where she was born to take over the running of her ailing grandmother's Christmas shop, selling everything from Christmas trees to snow globes to inflatable elves.

The last person she expects to see back in the village for Christmas is her old adversary Jack, whose high-powered career has taken him all over the world. But Jack's sister is sick too, and he's come home to be with her... right next door to the Christmas shop!

Marjorie and Jack clashed permanently back in the day, culminating in a kiss and a slapped face when they parted. Yet she's never got over his crooked smile and ironic one-liners. Can she handle his prickling proximity for a few festive weeks until her gran's better? Or is Marjorie in danger of making a fool of herself all over again?

CHAPTER ONE

Late September, present day. Penrock Downs, North Cornwall coast

There was no other place on earth Susie would rather be than in her family's wonderful Christmas tree lot. Though it was more of a nursery, her family having always grown the trees themselves on the adjacent land and sold them neatly netted up, either cut down or with rootballs, along with the usual seasonal accoutrements and a range of other plants, shrubs and trees. Some fir trees took anything from seven to fifteen years to grow to maturity, depending on species, so cultivating them was a labour of love and commitment. Over the years, she would build up a relationship with individual trees, even giving them names, and it was always with a severe pang that she had to cut the dear things down or dig up the rootball for a customer at journey's end.

Lovell's Christmas Tree Shop and its adjacent tree nursery stood on a corner of a long winding road between the moors and the rugged coast, just outside the small Cornish town of Penrock Downs.

It was a special place, and everyone who came here said so.

A *magical* place, in fact.

Susie loved it.

She had always thought she would be here forever, not merely the one growing and nurturing the trees, but eventually the owner. For this was a family business, in every sense of the phrase. Not merely because her lovely mum – until her tragic early passing – had built it from nothing with her dad, with Susie herself playing a key role as she grew up, but because many of their regular customers and long-term employees had become 'found' family over the years too, all sharing their love of everything festive.

So she couldn't contain her disbelief and sense of betrayal on the fateful day in September when she'd discovered her father had other plans for the rest of his life.

'Sorry, maybe I'm being dense. But I don't understand. What do you mean, you're *selling the business*?' Susie demanded, staring at her father, hands on hips, instinctively adopting the same position she'd often seen her mother take up when furious over something he'd done. 'It's a family business. You can't just *sell* it.'

Her father groaned, putting down the tablet he'd been studying. 'Susie, darling, I don't need to be a mind-reader to know you hate the idea. But I have to get away. I can't stand being in Penrock Downs anymore.'

'So take a holiday.' She flung her arms wide. 'Take as long as you need. I'll look after the place until you're back.'

"No, I've made up my mind. I need to cut loose,' her dad told her, adding with a shamefaced look, 'and besides, I couldn't afford to leave without selling. You know that as well as I do. When we first opened, business was booming. We were the only place for miles around selling Christmas trees and paraphernalia. But now we're competing with online retailers and big out-of-town garden centres… We barely make a profit over Christmas these days, and maintaining the nursery over the rest of the year soon eats that up.'

'Dad, you can't give up on the shop and nursery. Think of the trees!' She felt physical pain at the thought of abandoning her tender young charges. 'We made Mum a promise, remember?'

Though even if they hadn't promised to keep the place going after Mum had gone, it would still be a horrible idea to let it go…

She'd grown up on the plot since babyhood, after her parents had bought the land and built a nursery, shop and adjacent house there, brick by brick, using money Mum had inherited from her own parents. Her smart, capable mother had homeschooled Susie for much of her school years, often in between dealing with customers. Which had meant spending most of her 'school days' wandering free, strolling through row after row of fragrant fir trees, each year helping with the growing and harvesting of

Christmas trees for people's living rooms or store displays. Oh, and occasionally filling out a maths or science worksheet at the kitchen table with her dad, or reading one of the classics in a dusty, sunlit corner of the fir tree nursery, while her mother baked or crocheted or entertained local ladies at her book club.

It had been an idyllic childhood, and having gone into school for sixth form to take Mathematics and Science A-Levels, she'd been thrilled to get a university place, knowing she would be able to spend her life growing and caring for fresh green things.

They'd been so happy in their own perfect family paradise.

Until her mother had become sick, that is.

Jackie had struggled bravely against breast cancer for some years. But her disease had proved stubbornly resistant to treatment. It was over two years since they'd eventually lost her, and she and dad were still reeling with grief. Susie had come back from university to work alongside her dad in the plant nursery, and would be turning twenty-five in the New Year. But it seemed being 'grown-up' didn't make the loss of her big-hearted mother any easier to bear.

It brought tears to her eyes on getting out of bed and pulling on one of the outsized sweaters or cardigans her mother had laboriously knitted, and when sitting down to supper with her father and looking at the empty place opposite that Jackie had always occupied.

Her mum had run the shop and chatted with the customers, something Dad wasn't so good at, but increasingly these days that role had fallen to Susie instead. Never a chatty person, she had learned how to listen at least, and now felt as comfortable behind the counter as out in the greenhouses.

Two years since her mother's passing, and her heart still ached. There was a hollowness inside that would *never* go away, she knew. But a steely resolution had taken root there too. Susie had promised her mother on her deathbed that she and dad would carry on with the family business after she was gone, and that was precisely what she intended to do.

'I know, love,' her dad was saying, trying to excuse the unforgiveable decision he'd apparently made behind her back. Without even *asking* her, for goodness' sake. 'But I can't stay here anymore. Everything here reminds me of your mum.'

'What's wrong with that?' A tear squeezed out from under one eyelid.

'Because it's time to move on, love,' he said plaintively, his face contorting as though he too was going to cry. 'Susie, sweetheart, please try to understand. My heart is broken, and I can't go on *remembering...*'

His voice tailed off and he bent his head, as though in defeat.

Abruptly chastened, Susie hurried forward and buried her face in his chest. His arms came about her, holding her tight.

'Oh, Dad,' she said indistinctly against his dark fleece work hoody, the one he wore both to tend the Christmas trees and man the shop, 'I know it's horrible, trying to get by without Mum. But we can't just give up the farm. She loved it. She begged us to keep going. Leaving and selling up… This isn't what Mum would have wanted.'

She pulled back and gazed up at him hopefully. But she could see he had no intention of yielding.

'I'm not giving up the farmhouse, love,' he told her gently. 'But I'm selling the shop and nursery.'

She stared up at him in horror. 'You can't,' she said thickly, choking on the words. 'Mum loved the Christmas shop. You know how much she adored the festive season. She'd have had Christmas Day every day of the year if she could.'

His crooked smile gave way to a half-laugh and he nodded. 'Yeah, Jackie was like that about Christmas. Crazy for it. And you're fast becoming the same way.'

'So why sell up?'

'Because I need to release some capital,' he admitted sheepishly. 'I've decided to go backpacking in Australia. Find out who I am without your mother. I may even try and get a job over there, if I can get a short-term visa.'

Susie was horrified. 'Backpacking? In Australia? Are you kidding?'

But of course he wasn't.

Her dad shook his head. 'I'm afraid not. In fact, I've already sold the Christmas Tree Shop as a going concern, and the land over the road.'

'What? You've already *sold the shop*? But it was our family business.' Her eyes bulged as she took in the rest of what he'd said. 'Wait, you've sold Twelve Tree Acres too? But… But we were going to use that land to extend the business,' she exclaimed. 'That was Mum's dream.'

'I know this must be hard to hear, love, but I don't have the energy to follow her dream anymore.'

'But Dad –'

'Listen, this doesn't have to mean much change for you. I still own the house and the tree nursery,' he went on, his tone as matter-of-fact as though discussing the weather, not the upheaval of her entire life, 'and I've made sure you'll be kept on as nurserywoman and manager. It's all written into the contract.' Her dad paused, looking guilty. 'The new owner will handle the finances and make most of the business decisions though. So you'll need to work with him quite closely.'

'*New owner*?' Her head was reeling. '*Him*?' She searched his face for clues. 'Who is this new owner you've been doing deals with behind my back?'

'Erm…' Her dad shrugged and thrust his hands into his trouser pockets. 'My crew,' he mumbled.

'Your…crew?' she echoed, confused.

Did he mean Tom, the young man who helped out on Saturday mornings and some evenings? No, that wasn't very likely. Tom and his mum were always hard-up. They couldn't afford to buy a business.

'My crew,' he repeated with a nod, rocking back

and forth with an embarrassed look before his troubled gaze lifted to hers. 'Town mayor. You know who I mean.'

Horrorstruck, she realised what he'd been trying to say...

Not 'my crew'.

Murray Carew, the mayor of Penrock Downs.

'Murray Carew?' Her chest heaving, she gave a few incoherent gasps of outrage and disbelief. 'You sold us out to that land baron? You know how Mum felt about him buying up so much land locally... She'd turn in her grave at the mere suggestion.'

She saw his mouth open and hurriedly said, 'All right, turn in *her urn*, then.' Her mum's ashes stood in pride of place on the mantelpiece in the living room, in an ornate silver urn with a Christmas tree design. 'No, I can't let you do this. Sell the family business? It's out of the question.'

'I signed the papers this morning.'

Susie staggered backwards as though he'd hit her. 'You... You did what? But you didn't even give me a say.'

'I know, and I'm sorry. But this will work out for the best, you'll see.' Her dad caught her as she spun away. 'No, listen, Susie... You love the Christmas trees, all that festive stuff, and dealing with the public. People trust you. Why throw all that away simply because I've had enough? You couldn't have run it alone and I can't afford to leave Cornwall without selling up.'

'But did you have to sell it to *Murray Carew*?' Her

cheeks were hot with fury and disillusion that her own father could have done this to her, and without so much as a word of warning. 'You might as well have made a pact with the Devil!'

'He's not a man with a great reputation,' he agreed uneasily. 'But I've made the contract as watertight as possible to protect our interests. Technically, Murray can't get rid of you. We still own the nursery land. Without access to the actual merchandise, he'd be scuppered.' He paused. 'But he does own the shop premises and the business name now. I tried to make you a partner with equal say but he refused to play ball. So theoretically he's in charge.'

'Great,' she said bitterly, glaring at him. 'The worst man in Cornwall, and you've made him *my boss*. Thanks, Dad.'

Her dad rolled his eyes, looking impatient. 'He's rich, yes, and I know you share your mother's views on wealthy landowners. But Murray's not all bad, don't be so melodramatic. He's trying to do his best by our town, isn't he? And he's a local boy. His dad was a Cornish labourer. Dead and buried now, and his mother too. But he wasn't born with a silver spoon in his mouth.'

'Hardly a *boy* though, is he?' she muttered. 'Anyway, maybe Murray Carew doesn't come from money. But he's got money now. And what does he know about growing trees?'

'Nothing. That's why he needs you.'

'What he needs is to do a proper day's work for once. I bet he just sits in a leather swivel chair in some swanky office all day, spinning round and round...' She shook her head miserably. 'Oh, what have you done, Dad?'

'I'm sorry, love.' He shrugged. 'Push came to shove, and the mayor made me an offer I couldn't refuse.'

'Very Godfatheresque. Very *not* creepy,' she said sarcastically.

'He's just a wealthy man. Like you said, more money than sense. But he's also a canny businessman, and he'll listen to your advice if he wants to make a serious go of the shop. Growing Christmas trees isn't just about Christmas... It's an all-year round job.'

'Don't I know it?'

He gave a crooked smile and held out his arms. 'Come on, Susie, give me a hug and say you forgive your old dad. Then you can sit down and help me plan my Australian backpacking trip over a coffee. How does that sound?'

Susie flung herself into her dad's arms and tried not to weep buckets at the thought of him leaving. Because what else could she do? She loved her father. And he was all she had left. Of course she forgave him.

If her chest felt tight and her nerves were jangling, it was purely down to the new owner he'd lumped her with.

But how could she ever, in a world of adamant, clenched-jawed *never-evers*, put up with an arrogant, smooth-talking man like Murray Carew as her boss?

CHAPTER TWO

Murray slicked back shoulder-length dark hair, put away his wetsuit in the garage closet, and stacked his surfboards against the wall. The glorious Cornish summer was long over, autumn had rolled in with its sea mists and chill winds, and it was finally time to turn his mind to... Yes, to Christmas.

As a regular Scrooge, better known for 'Bah, humbug,' than 'Merry Christmas!' he couldn't quite believe that the rest of his working year would be devoted to the *festive* season. He'd almost rather be doing anything else.

But the good people of Penrock Downs had elected him mayor on a two-year term, and if he wanted to be re-elected in the spring, he would need to fulfil his campaign promises to rejuvenate the coastal area and bring new sources of revenue to the town itself. The masterplan that he had decided upon earlier that year meant commercialising Christmas, and he was determined to forge ahead with it.

Pushing away his memories of the fantastic surf he'd enjoyed that morning, Murray strode through to his home office. There was a project board installed on the wall opposite his desk. He stood to study it, hands clasped behind his back, and mentally walked through the progress he had made so far.

From his list of goals, only three had ticks beside them.

Acquire Christmas Tree Shop business and adjacent land.

Put forward sale of adjacent land (location of Christmas Market) to council for 1 pound.

Put out Christmas Market stalls to tender.

Three major goals.

Three checkboxes ticked.

Not that it had been easy, even getting this far. Louis Lovell had driven a hard bargain over his acquisition of the man's Christmas tree business, forcing Murray to keep his daughter on as store manager. Not ideal, as he had originally intended closing the business and repurposing the land for resale. But he'd grudgingly agreed to keep Susie Lovell on for a year, at least. He didn't know much about Christmas trees – he didn't even like the festive season that much, to be honest, considering it a waste of time and money – but it might be interesting to run a nursery and shop for a year. It would be a learning experience.

So, yes, he was making excellent progress with his plans for the rejuvenation of Penrock Downs. But this was no time to be complacent.

For his list of goals was lengthy, with many other items still uncompleted, and he had yet to finalise the sale of land to the council for a token amount, as suggested by his solicitor. Irritatingly, some councillors had lodged objections to the location, claiming it would overload infrastructure, by which they meant gum up the narrow Cornish lanes for a few weeks prior to Christmas. And a handful of townsfolk were getting together a petition to stop him, a petition that would almost certainly be unsuccessful.

But local pushback was a small price to pay, in Murray's opinion, for an event that was likely to pull in massive revenue for local traders and incomers alike, and put their small town on the map as a place to visit.

He was doing the right thing and, come January, he'd prove that to his Cornish town of birth with pleasing statistics from the Christmas Market.

That was the plan, at any rate.

Against his will, his gaze drifted right and locked.

A photograph had been pinned to the project board frame some months ago, before he'd even started work on the Christmas Market plan. It was a Polaroid of him and Genevieve, arms about each other's waists, smiling as they posed in front of an ice sculpture of a dolphin.

His glamorous ex looked every inch the fashion model she'd been in those days, clad in a figure-hugging gold sweater dress, subtle make-up that emphasized her long lashes, with her dark-blonde hair worn loose, its long, elegant tresses tumbling over her shoulders…

They'd been out together at a boozy launch event

in London for a friend's dolphin-themed business initiative, and one of the official photographers had been going around the room, snapping candid shots of guests with his Polaroid camera and haphazardly sticking the results on the wall like impromptu art.

On their way out, Genevieve had dragged their snap off the wall and thrust it into his jacket pocket. 'You've got to hang on to your memories,' she'd slurred at him, charmingly tipsy. 'Because you never know what's going to happen.' Then she'd stumbled into him, and giggled. 'Oops!'

'I know what's going to happen tonight,' he'd told her, chuckling as his girlfriend swayed back and forth on the threshold, her hand in his. Leading her out into the dark London street, he'd raised a hand to summon the waiting taxi he'd pre-booked. 'I'm going to tuck you up in bed at the hotel and let you sleep this off.'

'No boom-boom?' Pouting, Genevieve had batted mascara-thick lashes at him, her big blue eyes pleading.

That had been almost three years ago, when he'd still been living and working in London. Murray grimaced, his gaze moving slowly over the photograph. They'd made such a great couple. A power couple, in fact. He'd been thinking she might just be The One, and had even considered asking her to move in with him, though he knew her work as a model meant she'd almost never be at home.

Yet only a few months after that evening, he and Genevieve had broken up, following her utterly out-of-left-field announcement that she'd found God and would be giving up her career as a model and entering a convent instead. Since his girlfriend becoming a nun had left little room for their relationship to develop, he'd had no choice but to say his goodbyes and let her go. The Great Split, as he still thought of it, had precipitated his return to Cornwall, the land of his forefathers, and his decision to run for office.

'No boom-boom,' he murmured, and pulled out the pin. The faded Polaroid fluttered to the floor, where it lay face-down. He didn't bother to pick it up, merely trod crisply away, heading for his desk and the reassuringly full work schedule on his computer, ready to make progress on this Christmas Market plan.

Murray had no idea where Genevieve was these days, nor was she any longer his concern. It was time to move on.

About to turn on his computer, his phone buzzed, and he glanced at it idly. A message had popped up from one of the town council's WhatsApp groups. The private group that only councillors could access.

It was a link, accompanied by a message.

Who the hell is Susie Lovell and what exactly did you do to piss her off, Murray?!

Huh?

He frowned down at the link, which appeared to lead to a personal blog, called *Susie Says What*?

Lovell's daughter. The woman he'd agreed could continue managing the Christmas tree business he'd just acquired. He'd been planning to meet up with her soon to discuss how the arrangement would work but hadn't got around to scheduling the meeting. Indeed, he had a suspicion that Lovell hadn't told his daughter yet about the sale...

Before he could click the link, a new message popped up.

Isn't she the crazy woman who spoke against the Christmas Market at the public consultation evening? Louis Lovell's daughter?

He grinned appreciatively, recalling that evening. A short woman with untidy red hair and a distinctly unfeminine air, clad in jeans, boots, and a sturdy fisherman's jumper, she'd spoken heatedly against the Christmas Market scheme, and had garnered quite a round of applause afterwards.

Yes, she had gusto, Susie Lovell. And apparently he'd annoyed her. Not hard to do, he guessed.

He clicked the link to Susie's blog and leant back as the page loaded. Definitely the same woman, he thought, studying her profile picture. Bouncy auburn curls framing a heart-shaped face, a cheesy smile, shapeless hand-knitted sweater in various shades of orange and yellow, no make-up whatsoever. She had a kind of homely charm. But not his style, thankfully. He could do without that kind of distraction right now.

His gaze dropped to her latest blog post.

The headline read, *Mayor Carew Hell-Bent on Ruining Our Town*.

Murray sat bolt upright, all indolence abandoned.

What the...?

Mayor Murray Carew is possibly the worst thing to have happened to Penrock Downs since the Peasants Revolt in 1672, when the medieval guildhouse was razed to the ground and ten townsfolk were hanged for sedition. Just as we've begun our slow fightback against the dual horrors of the pandemic and a cost of living crisis, Vampire Carew intends to subject us to a Christmas Market that will suck revenue from local businesses and destroy the natural habit of thousands of precious flora, fauna and insect life.

Blinking, Murray scanned the rest of the scurrilous article.

Basically, he was a megalomaniac POS who cared nothing for the environment or human beings so long as his evil endeavours turned a profit. Fair comment, some might say. He did tend to ride roughshod over public objections, but only when they were baseless and would only serve to hold up progress on a much-needed project, which they usually were. As for the environment, he cared as much as the next businessman for the natural world. But the people of Penrock Downs had elected him to improve the lives of people, not insects...

More WhatsApp messages continued to buzz on his phone, some worried about the public reaction, others outraged at her tone and asking if he planned to sue for defamation.

Susie Lovell had been silent since her impassioned outburst at the public meeting, so he'd foolishly assumed she'd either given up or had a change of heart.

But something must have happened recently to reanimate her opposition to the Christmas Market and prompt her into posting such a libelous blog post, and it didn't take much detective work to figure it out.

Her father had recently agreed to sell the family business to him, and presumably hadn't even told his daughter until the final papers were signed.

Now Susie knew what Daddy had done, and she was steaming mad.

Running a hand through his damp hair, Murray read more carefully through her online tirade for a second time, and then grinned appreciatively.

Scooping up his phone, he calmly tapped out a reply to the group,

I'll deal with Susie Lovell. Let's not get distracted, people. We've got a Christmas Market to plan. Now, where are we on mobile toilets?

CHAPTER THREE

Susie's favourite time of day was early morning, out on the nursery grounds, tending to the growing trees. At this time of year, in the run-up to Christmas, the fragrance was almost overpowering. She would pull on her trusty old Wellington boots, her fleece-lined jacket and trusty woollen hat, and march out from the farmhouse to the nursery, which lay only a few hundred yards from their back door. Sometimes, she would stop by the greenhouses where they propagated seeds or grafted rootstock to check on her 'babies' in their sheltered, well-controlled nursery beds, waiting to be transplanted into open ground where they could flourish.

It was so peaceful, wandering among the saplings in the mornings. She would walk down row after row of young trees, removing weeds sprouting in the soft, carefully enriched compost, checking the automatic watering and heating systems were working as they should. Sometimes she would have to pause to adjust the vents, for the precious new growth required exactly the right amount of air and water to thrive.

Then, closing the greenhouse door behind her, she would walk on to where larger trees were being 'grown-on,' some of them fully mature now and only waiting to be purchased and dug up.

In the forest lot, the scent of Christmas was at its most intense. She was out there most days too, checking for signs of damage or disease, noting fresh growth, pruning any browning or tattered-looking branches, correcting growth trajectories, to keep the trees looking perfect.

It was always sad, digging up a tree for a client or for the big potted displays in the shop, knowing that tree had probably reached the end of its life. She knew that once dug up for someone's living room or office display, few trees would be planted out again after the Christmas season was over.

Worse yet, to take a saw to a perfectly healthy trunk...

But that was how this business worked, and she'd grown up understanding and appreciating its cycles and traditions.

Some people liked their Christmas trees cut at the trunk and fixed with metal stands and tripods for convenience. Others preferred a living Christmas tree, still with its rootball, and that was how Susie preferred to sell them. That way the tree could enjoy a longer 'life,' besides being less likely to shed needles.

It was silly to be sentimental about the process. These trees had been grown specifically to serve a social purpose. Once purchased they would bring joy to many families, strung with shining tinsel and decorated with bright baubles and fairy lights, putting on a fantastic show for somebody's Christmas. Yet she couldn't help it.

That morning, she'd come out later than usual to check on the trees. First, she had seen off her father on his way to the airport. They had hugged at the door when his taxi arrived, and she'd cried a little. It had been pointless trying to change his mind. Ever since he'd admitted to selling the business, she'd been badgering her father to reverse his decision. But her dad had remained adamant.

Besides, the paperwork was all signed. They still owned the farmhouse and the nursery land, but Murray was now legal owner of the business and she would have to put up with that or resign her job as manager.

Leave her beloved Christmas trees for someone else to care for?

Not a chance.

Dad's taxi had driven away less than an hour ago, and she had stood there for a long time afterwards, glad of her woolly jumper in the damp autumnal air, trying not to despair.

But she did feel a sense of desperation.

In fact, she'd never felt so alone in all her life. Abandoned by her father to run the family business for a man she frankly loathed and despised, her only other option was to walk away.

Walk away from trees she had known and loved since they were tiny saplings?

It hadn't come to such a drastic move yet, surely?

Her best friend would come and work alongside her in the shop as a favour if she asked, though Tansy was a bit of a hippy; she lived in a caravan and preferred short-term gigs over nine-to-five employment, strongly disliking anything that involved four walls. And Tom, their part-time worker, was young but a nice enough lad.

Yes, maybe she could muddle through with a little help from friends...

She was bending over to check a tree trunk for any signs of disease when a voice behind brought her up in startled dismay. 'Mmm, what a charming view.'

Her cheeks flared with heat as she spun around.

Murray Carew.

The mayor looked powerful and untouchable as always in an expensive grey suit and thigh-length coat, which she guessed to be pure wool. She had to remind herself again that he hadn't been born to the wealth he had accumulated, and was aware of a grudging admiration for such shrewd business acumen. For the son of a Cornish labourer, he'd certainly done well for himself. But that didn't mean she had to enjoy working for him...

'I beg your pardon?' she snapped.

His smile flickered. 'All these Christmas trees.' Murray swept an arm in a broad arc. 'So charming, so festive.' He paused, his dark gaze challenging. 'What did you think I meant?'

Susie glared. How to answer *that*?

'So,' he said softly, 'I read your blog.' His smile

struck her sinister.

Her heart beating curiously fast, Susie folded her arms and glared at him. If the mayor thought he could intimidate her, he had another think coming. 'What about it?'

Murray's smile widened, displaying his teeth, gleaming white and perfectly aligned. Maybe they only looked so perfect because they were *dentures*, she thought savagely.

'I knew you were unhappy about my acquisition of your father's business,' he said. 'What I didn't realise was just how unhappy.' He paused, presumably for dramatic effect. 'Understandable, of course. You must've expected the business to stay in the family forever and ever. Instead, I'm your new boss.'

At this, she bared her teeth too. Hers was more of a snarl though...

One of his eyebrows rose in response, crooking at a slant as he studied her. 'But Lovell assured me that you far prefer the managerial side of things, rather than the myriad problems that come with ownership. So I'm taking that burden off your hands. In a way, I've done you a favour.'

'My apologies if I don't fall over with gratitude,' she snapped back. 'Because I know precisely why you bought my father out. The council failed to get permission to use the site originally earmarked for the Christmas Market, didn't they? Interestingly enough though, the land you've just acquired from my father, Twelve Tree Acres, ticks all your boxes.'

His smile grew more appreciative. 'It's true, the

surplus land opposite the shop would make an excellent location for a large-scale event like the market. Well-drained, mostly level, and with plenty of parking and space for mobile infrastructure.'

'Aha!' She jabbed an accusing finger at him.

'But if you think I'm trying to turn an illegal profit,' he went on mildly, pretending to look injured by her lack of trust, 'you're sadly mistaken. The fact is, I'm already negotiating a sale of that land to the council for one pound.' His gaze mocked her. 'My gift to the people of Penrock Downs.'

'*One pound*?' she stuttered, disbelieving.

'There, you see? I knew that would surprise you. My lawyers assure me it's all above board. No profit involved. An act of pure philanthropy.'

That information surprised her. She couldn't help wondering if it was true. But it had to be. Corrupt though Murray must surely be, she doubted he would lie to her face about something so easily fact-checked. Still, she was sure he would be trying to turn a profit somewhere down the line. An act of pure philanthropy.

Huh, whatever.

'All right,' she said grudgingly, 'but what about the environment? If you've read my blog, rather than staffing it out to some flunkey, then you know what my concerns are.'

'I assure you, I have no flunkeys. And I take those concerns very seriously, Miss Lovell.' He tipped his head to one side, regarding her solemnly. The look of a politician in the middle of bamboozling members of the public, she thought, instantly on her guard. 'At this stage, I can tell you that the council will be discussing new protections for wildlife in other areas, as a counterbalance to our use of Twelve Tree Acres for the Christmas Market.'

The way he talked so casually and possessively about land that had been in her family for years made her flush with irritation. 'You think you're so clever, don't you? You think you've got all the answers. But you're just a suit,' she threw at him.

'A *suit*?'

'Just an empty suit. A corporate executive with no soul. Maybe I can't prove how exactly, but I know you're only looking out for yourself and your cronies, and all this talk about protecting wildlife is your way of shutting me up.

'Not at all.' He looked stung at last, and she knew her words had hit home. 'First, *flunkeys*... now, *cronies*,' he muttered, shaking his head. 'Not to mention bringing my suit into this. Like everyone else on the council, I'm simply doing my best for Penrock Downs.'

'You're doing your best for *yourself*, Mr Carew. For your political career. You don't care about this town or the environment, just how far this project will get you. You're probably running for Cornwall Council next. Maybe you even plan to stand in the next general election. Who knows how far your ambitions stretch?'

He laughed, but uneasily. Thrusting his hands into his pockets, Murray Carew regarded her through narrowed, speculative eyes. 'You and I have got off on the wrong foot,' he said, abruptly changing tack. 'What can I do or say to persuade you that I only have the town's best interests at heart?'

'Nothing.'

His smile looked pained. 'You're giving me a headache, Miss Lovell.'

'Oh dear, what a shame.'

'Give me a chance, for God's sake,' he exclaimed, finally sounding exasperated. 'I wasn't joking about the headache. In fact, maybe we should take a raincheck on this conversation.'

As he turned away, Susie couldn't resist throwing after him, 'Or maybe you should get out more, rather than spending all day stuck behind a desk. Touch grass for once.'

He spun on his heel. 'Touch grass?'

'Stretch your legs properly, get out into nature.' Smugly, she looked him up and down. No doubt frequent trips to the gym accounted for his impressive physique, and she'd heard that he was a keen summer surfer too. But they were fast approaching winter now, the beach wasn't the countryside, and the mayor struck her as completely out of place in this green, rural setting. 'A little fresh air would cure that headache in no time, I'm sure.'

He surprised her by saying swiftly, 'All right, challenge accepted. How about you help me with that?'

Taken aback, she blinked in confusion. 'I'm sorry, what?'

'I'm opening the funfair for Halloween on Saturday afternoon. How about you come along as my plus-one?'

'Excuse me?'

'It's a park... Plenty of nature there. Insect life too, I should imagine.'

He was mocking her again. 'Tempting, but no.'

'We could use the opportunity to get to know each other better. After all, I'm going to be your boss. You can air your views on running the business,' he told her, 'and I can try to persuade you to my point of view over the Christmas Market.'

Her eyes widened. Be his plus-one at a mayoral event?

'No, thank you.'

'But you want me to listen to you. That's what your blog post was about, wasn't it? You slagged me off in front of the world in order to bring me out here and listen to your... *concerns*. Well, I've listened, and I've tried to address your fears. That approach doesn't seem to have worked. So maybe a different environment will help. Besides, I hear some of those rides are pretty good.'

His glinting smile left her speechless.

'Be there at two o'clock.' He played with his cuffs, infuriatingly sexy. 'There'll be candy floss in it for you.'

'Now you're just being creepy.'

'Toffee apple, then?'

'I can't just waltz off to the funfair and close the shop for the afternoon. My customers will be rightly annoyed.'

'So get someone else to cover for you.'

'I can't afford it.'

'Then allow me.' He drew out his smartphone and began scrolling numbers. 'I know at least a dozen trustworthy people who might be free tomorrow and who owe me a favour.'

'Seriously?' Susie shook her head. 'What's this all about? Are you trying to find ways to fire me for insubordination? Like, go with me to the funfair or you're sacked... Eat this delicious candy floss or else.'

He threw back his head with laughter. 'You've a powerful imagination, Miss Lovell. Though if we're going to be working together in future, I think calling you Susie would be more appropriate. And you should call me Murray.'

'I'd rather not. And I'm Miss Lovell to you, thanks.'

He smiled, and the perfect teeth came out to play again. She wondered if he kept them in a jar on his bedside table.

His eyes narrowed on her face, instantly suspicious. 'Look, I don't want to fire you, Susie,' he insisted, ignoring her request. 'I want to inspire you.'

'Wow.' She pretended to be amazed, staring at him. 'Where did you get that little nugget of wisdom, Mayor? Fortune Cookies R Us?'

Murray opened his mouth, and his phone buzzed, presumably with a message. Glancing down at the screen, he frowned. 'Let's put a pin in this and revisit tomorrow, okay? I'll see you at the funfair at two.' He walked away, head bent, thumbs working furiously.

Susie swore and kicked a tree stump out of sheer frustration.

'Ow.'

CHAPTER FOUR

'Okay, call me paranoid, but you look a bit cross,' Tansy remarked as Susie jerked open the passenger door of the VW van and jumped in beside her. 'What's wrong? Am I late?'

'You know you're late. I said, pick me up at one-thirty.'

Her best friend had made a special effort for the Halloween funfair, Susie noted. She'd woven her long hair into two thick straw-coloured plaits and was wearing half a dozen friendship bracelets on each forearm, gold hoop earrings and a loose-fitting, tie-dye, below-knee dress with an ancient blue woollen cardigan that smelt rather unfortunately of cat, its sleeves rolled up to her elbows. This unusual outfit was completed by scuffed brown ankle-length boots, thick odd socks showing over the top, one lurid green, one faded pink.

'Well it's only... one-fifty now, admittedly,' Tansy admitted, glancing at the dashboard clock, a little shamefaced. She threw the Volkswagen camper van into first gear, its faded orange panels painted with flowers and heart symbols, and razzed out of the Christmas Tree Shop car park, tyres spitting gravel.

'But I've got a really good excuse. You see there was this sheep –'

'Let me stop you right there.' Susie checked over her shoulder and raised a hand to Tom, their nineteen-year-old part-timer, whom she'd left in sole charge for the afternoon.

Tom waved back from the shop doorway, still looking nervous after the two-hour training session she'd subjected him to on everything from how to work the tills to procedures for dealing with emergencies.

'Honestly, I don't want to hear about the sheep. Just concentrate on driving until we get to town.'

She felt uneasy leaving Tom in charge but there was no way she was accepting Murray's offer of a random shop helper, and Tansy had already declined her request to work.

'Hey, I'm doing you a favour here.'

'Sorry, yes.' Susie sat back, dragging on her seatbelt, which was fuzzy with cat hair. No doubt one of Tansy's many cats had been prowling about inside the van. 'I'm really very grateful. I just wish you could have held the fort for me instead of Tom. He's sweet but he's not very mature.'

'I've told you, I'd love to help you out, Suze, but I'm not great with selling stuff or dealing with the public,' Tansy said uneasily. 'Plus, I'm working at the fairground all Halloween week, and I can't be in two places at once.'

'You're *working* at the fairground? Doing what?'

'I dated the dodgems girl a few times this summer.'

Tansy winked at her. 'She promised me work when the fair came back to Penrock Downs for Halloween week.'

'Why am I not surprised?'

'Hey, can I help it if women find me irresistible?'

'Probably, yes.'

Grimacing, Susie pulled down the visor to check her reflection. Perhaps she ought to have worn a nicer outfit for this trip than dungarees and baggy old work sweater with its Christmas Tree Shop logo. Maybe make-up too. But it had been an exhausting six am start that morning, taking delivery of box after box of Christmas decorations, and after training Tom on the tills, she hadn't had time to nip home to change out of her dungarees, tidy her hair, and put on lipstick as planned.

'Do I look awful?' she asked, rubbing a dirty smear off her cheek.

'Define awful.'

'Wonderful, thanks.' Sighing, Susie smoothed down tangled red curls with her fingers. 'I still can't believe I'm doing this.'

'Dating the mayor?'

'*It's not a date!*'

'Nooo, of course not.' Tansy rolled her eyes. 'Mayor Carew is taking you to the funfair because... reasons.'

'So he can spout rubbish at me while I'm strapped into a ride and can't escape, that's why.' Susie fumbled with her seatbelt, which seemed to have come undone. 'Does this thing actually work?'

'Um, it just needs a bit of this...' Chewing on her lip, Tansy tried to watch the road, steer the van, and fix Susie's seatbelt all at the same time. Not surprisingly, the vehicle veered all over the narrow Cornish lane, oncoming traffic beeping and gesticulating as they struggled to get out of her way.

Susie's eyes widened. 'For the love of God, Tansy, watch where you're going!'

'One second.'

The seatbelt snapped into place, and they both leant back with a sigh of relief.

'So, this isn't an actual date? You're just going to pump him for information?' Tansy waggled her eyebrows at Susie.

'Don't be disgusting.'

'You love it.'

'I really, really don't,' Susie insisted, though she had to admit that the mental image of her pumping the mayor was not entirely unpleasant. He was quite an eyeful. 'This is purely business.'

The old VW van tore into town at a rattling pace, then came to such an abrupt halt that they were both flung forward, Susie almost bumping her nose on the windscreen. But at least the dilapidated seatbelt had done its job.

'Sorry!' Tansy grimaced, pointing to the silver-haired lady carrying a cat box across the road to the vet's surgery. 'But I couldn't crush Pixie into the tarmac just to avoid you being another thirty secs late for your meeting with his mayorfulness.'

'Pixie?'

'Mrs Fletcher's cat.' She waved a greeting at the lady, who smiled back. 'She's a lovely tortoiseshell. Only she slipped into their next-door neighbour's garden pond last week and injured her leg getting out. Mrs Fletcher posted about it on Penrock Downs Pets Facebook Group.' Tansy shook her head, accelerating away again. 'Ever since I parked my caravan by the river, I've been worried about one of my cats falling into the water. But so far, they've kept well away...'

Tansy lived permanently in a caravan beside the river which wound steadily around the outskirts of town on its way to the sea. 'How many cats do you have now, Tansy?'

'Five.'

'You need help.'

'I need kitty litter,' Tansy said flatly. 'Ran out again this morning.'

Susie grimaced.

'Okay, here's the fairground,' Tansy announced. 'You'd better get out here. I'll be parking round the back.' Screeching to a halt in front of the park gates, the driver behind beeping his horn irately, she gave Susie a wink. 'Have fun with the mayor. Don't do anything that I wouldn't.'

'Which leaves me plenty of scope,' Susie muttered. 'Thanks for the lift. I hope you and...'

'Charlotte.'

Susie frowned. 'Not Charlotte the Harlot?'

'The very same.'

'Right.' With a grin, Susie suppressed her

memories of Tansy's drunken 'my summer at the funfair' tales of debauchery behind the candy floss van. 'I hope you and Charlotte have, erm, a great time.'

Tansy raised her brows with a look of dignified affront. 'What does that 'erm' mean? I'll have you know we're both professionals. We'll be working, not smooching.'

'I expect you'll find time for a bit of both,' Susie shot in before slamming the car door and waving her friend goodbye. 'Laters, lovely!'

The park gates had been hung with giant balloons and fairy lights, and a huge banner proclaiming the arrival of the funfair at Penrock Downs. The funfair was held in the park for three weeks every summer and one week at Halloween, catering for locals and holidaymakers alike. Of course, Susie hadn't been to the funfair since her sixth form days. She wasn't a kid anymore. But she guessed an hour or two away from the shop wouldn't kill her.

Nervously, she slung her handbag over her shoulder and sloped through the gates.

A man pressed a green ticket into her hand, marked ONE FREE RIDE, and she thanked him, searching the crowd for Murray.

Susie had barely gone ten paces into the crowd before a heavy hand descended on her shoulder, as though she were being arrested. She gasped, and a deep voice chuckled behind her, 'Jumpy little thing, aren't you?'

Heart thumping, she whirled around to glare at

the mayor. 'Do you have to sneak up on people like that? You could just have said "Hello, Miss Lovell."'

'Hello, Miss Lovell,' Murray drawled.

Mayor Carew looked undeniably edible in a black leather jacket and powder-blue shirt unbuttoned to midway down his chest, sleeves rolled up to reveal powerful forearms – did she *really* have to go weak at the knees over muscular forearms? she wondered with a flicker of irritation – and figure-hugging black jeans that sat rather too indolently on his hips. The perfect blend of political seriousness and beach god.

She'd seen Murray out surfing a few times that summer and knew how well he fitted a wetsuit, damn his eyes. But that wasn't a good enough reason to be *nice* to him.

One dark brow quirked as he caught her looking him over. 'Ready for the ride of your life?'

'I beg your pardon?'

Murray was looking her over in his turn, she realised, and was even more annoyed that his scrutiny should leave her flustered rather than amused.

He nodded over her shoulder, and she turned to look.

The sign in front of the Ferris Wheel read, *The ride of your life. Or your money back.* A huge, hulking man with a forbidding countenance stood beside the sign, cracking his knuckles. Somehow, Susie suspected nobody ever asked for their money back.

'I hate Ferris wheels,' she told him flatly.

'Have you ever been on one?'

'Of course not. I just told you, I hate them.'

'The very definition of prejudice. Hating something without knowing anything about it. Let's make the big wheel our first stop, then. After I've officially opened the fair, that is.' Ignoring her furious protests, he steered her towards a low platform where a crowd was already assembled, awaiting his speech. Applause broke out, and several people she knew shouted, 'Hey, look, it's Susie Lovell... What are you doing with the mayor, Susie?'

Throwing Murray a fulminating look, Susie tried to hide behind a row of burly men in suits arranged beside the podium with their hands crossed below their waists, like footballers guarding against a free kick. Ignoring the questions, Murray waved cheerfully at the onlookers and then hurried up the steps, striding to the podium.

'Thank you all for coming today,' he said into the microphone, deep-voiced, somehow both friendly and authoritative. 'I'm Murray Carew, Mayor of Penrock Downs, and I'm happy to welcome you all to the first day of our Halloween funfair. Between two and three today, everyone gets one free ride, courtesy of the council. You should have received a free ticket on your way in. I hope you all have a wonderful time. And remember, watch out for ghosts and ghouls once darkness falls...' He grinned, turning to the men in suits. 'First though, there are a few people I'd like to thank for making this funfair possible.'

Susie zoned out during the business part of the

speech, her gaze lifting unhappily to the Ferris wheel looming high above the fairground. She genuinely didn't like heights. But she didn't want to admit that. It was a weakness and she hated looking weak.

Besides, she'd just spotted an ex from her sixth form days, and rather fancied the idea of Geoff seeing her with the mayor as his plus-one. Perhaps one ride on the big wheel wouldn't be so bad. She could always keep her eyes closed, couldn't she?

Having finished his speech, Murray turned to shake hands with the suits. 'Thank you for coming,' he told each one, flashing an identical ultra-white smile each time. 'Thank you for supporting Penrock Downs.'

Geoff had broken up with her after a bare few months, and was married now. She'd never liked her ex particularly, not even when they were dating, and was not above showing off that she could pull a local dignitary, despite not being 'girly' enough for his tastes.

Yes, maybe she'd always been a bit of a tomboy. But that didn't mean she wasn't all woman…

'If you loved me, you'd make more of an effort with your appearance,' Geoff had insisted, looking her over critically on their final date, a dismal trip to the cinema. 'I mean, those cut-off denims may be comfortable. But they do nothing for me. No, this isn't going to work out. Sorry, Suze… You're just not feminine enough.'

Reliving this unpleasant memory, Susie's face set

hard and her teeth ground together.

'Are you in some kind of pain?' Murray asked with a frown, having jumped down from the platform to rejoin her.

'Just bored, that's all,' she flung back at him, banishing Geoff and his crass, hurtful remarks to the past again. 'Done pressing the flesh, have you?' She strode off rather too enthusiastically towards the Ferris wheel, calling over her shoulder, 'Come on, Mr Mayor. I thought you were offering me the ride of my life?'

She'd raised her voice to be heard over the noisy pop music blaring from a nearby speaker, but on those last few words, the music cut out without warning and her voice carried across the assembled visitors, several of whom turned to stare at her in wide-eyed amusement, Geoff included, his pretty blonde wife by his side.

'How marvellously indiscreet of you to share that offer with the world.' Murray took her arm, the crowd parting miraculously at their approach. 'Of course, I'd heard things about you before we met.'

'What sort of things?'

'Only that Susie Lovell takes no prisoners.' There was already a queue forming for the Ferris wheel ride, but those at the head ushered Murray forward with respectful smiles, insisting he took their spot. Susie wondered if they were quite right in the head. 'Oh, are you sure?' he murmured with barely a pause, shaking more hands on his way past. 'Thank you, that's so kind.'

Murray held out two green tickets to the hulking attendant, who grinned and led them to the first empty car on the Ferris wheel, jumping the queue.

'I can't believe you did that,' she muttered, her cheeks flaming.

'There are perks to this job,' Murray told her coolly, 'and queue-jumping is one of them. Besides, if it makes someone happy to let me go first, why on earth would I offend them by refusing?'

The car was narrow, decorated with hearts and flowers. Murray squeezed in beside her, and the gigantic attendant fastened the bar across to stop them falling out. 'Don't try to get out until the ride's over,' he warned them.

Susie had an immediate vision of climbing out in a panic at the top and shinning down the metal supports. Yes, and probably breaking her neck in the process.

'Looks like we're stuck with each other for the next ten minutes,' Murray told her.

'Oh, goody.'

Other people were now being seated, their own car swaying as the attendant advanced them into the air. As they left the ground, her hands tightened on the cold metal bar, and she breathed through her nose. She could do this, no problem. Probably.

'What... What did you want to say to me, anyway?' she asked, trying not to hyperventilate. 'I mean, you didn't just ask me here for fun.'

'Didn't I?'

'Well, if you did, it's not working. I'm not having

fun.' She shot him a look of dislike. 'Are you?'

The frown was back. 'Now what's the matter?'

I'm afraid of heights, she wanted to scream. But the desire not to lose her shit in front of this obnoxious man was more powerful than her irrational fear of being too far off the ground for comfort.

'I left a kid in charge of my shop in order to meet you here, and all the things that could go wrong are making me sweat.'

'*Your* shop?' he queried gently.

She ground her teeth together again. 'Sorry, I forgot for a moment that you're my new overlord.'

'Selling up was a smart business move on your father's part. The shop's been barely profitable these past three years, due to people buying cheaper goods online.'

'So why acquire it? Oh wait... Because of your master plan to take over the town, of course. Am I right?'

The car moved higher into the chill late October air, and Susie had to clamp her lips together to stop herself from moaning.

'It's true that a Christmas tree business is unlikely to make me much money,' he agreed, 'but that doesn't mean I'm planning to pull the plug on it. In fact, part of the negotiation included keeping you on to run the shop for at least the next year, bar net income dipping below a certain level. Why would I have signed such an onerous contract if I didn't intend honouring it?'

'And I suppose it has nothing whatsoever to do

with locating the Christmas Market opposite our shop at Twelve Trees Acres.'

'Of course it does,' Murray admitted. 'But I didn't buy that land from your father with the intention of making a profit, if that's what you think. Which brings me to why I asked you to the funfair.' The car moved higher, swaying more violently as they began to clear the roofs of adjacent fairground structures. He glanced down at her whitening knuckles where she was gripping the bar for dear life. 'You okay?'

'Fan-bloody-tastic.'

His brows jerked together at her tone, but he went on, 'Good, then I'd like you to look down at our town, Susie.'

He swept his arm in a generous arc as the car jerked up another few feet, clearing the treetops. Her heart was thudding sickly, her body locked deep in fight-or-flight mode. Except she couldn't flee with a metal bar locking her in place. And punching Murray in the nose, while temporarily satisfying, seemed unlikely to improve her situation.

'I brought you up here to admire the view,' he went on. 'Park, shops, houses, beach, coastal paths, sand dunes, river... Penrock Downs is a beautiful place, don't you think?'

Focusing on the upright metal supports nearest her rather than risk looking down at the blurry ground, Susie somehow mumbled her agreement.

Her chest was tight, her lips numb.

'Yet, despite its natural beauty,' he continued, apparently oblivious to her distress, 'this area has been in a steady decline for decades. Outside tourist hotspots, there's increasing poverty and people in need. Each summer season allows local businesses and their employees to survive another year, yes. But only just. My vision of a Christmas Market is designed to bring a second tourist season to Penrock Downs and generate greater wealth for townsfolk like yourself.'

'I already heard your self-congratulatory speech at the public consultation, thanks,' she burst out, then clamped her lips tight again.

Speaking had been a mistake, she realised grimly, her tummy roiling.

Say nothing, do nothing, keep perfectly still…

'Maybe, but have you considered what your role could be in all this? The unused land at Twelve Trees Acres is integral to my vision, and by getting fully on board with my plans, you'll be saving this town from a slow death.' They were almost at the top of the wheel. Right in the lap of the gods. Murray threw back his head and sucked in a deep lungful of air. 'Do you smell that, Susie? Salt air, candy floss, popcorn, hot dogs… That's the smell of money being made. Look at the visitors and locals down there, spending their hard-earned cash and having a wonderful time at Halloween. Don't you want this to happen all over again at Christmas, and for local businesses like yours to benefit from the extra footfall?'

Her stomach heaved.

Murray glanced at her impatiently. 'You're not looking down,' he exclaimed. 'But maybe you don't care?'

'I care,' she whispered, then swallowed against the urge to barf.

'Then look at your town, Susie. Doesn't it deserve everyone on board for this project?' Murray smiled as she bent her head, staring down past her work trainers with their mismatched laces and his black leather shoes, polished to a high shine. 'That's it,' he told her encouragingly, resting his arm along the back of the car. 'Take a good, long look.'

Peering down from the swinging car, she saw blurry faces far below, heard shrieks of laughter, the ground swaying back and forth…

'Now, tell me truthfully, what do you think of my vision for Penrock Downs?'

With a helpless groan, Susie leant back, muttering, 'Sick.'

His brows shot up. 'I beg your pardon?'

'Eurgh,' she groaned and leant her head on his shoulder, wishing the world would stop spinning.

There was blessed silence for a moment.

Then his arm slipped across her shoulder, and he was looking down into her face, an odd look in his eyes. 'Miss Lovell?'

Susie closed her eyes, blotting him out. Him and the whole terrible sky. Maybe if she sat very still and said nothing, perhaps she would feel a little better…

Then she stiffened in alarm.

Her eyes flew open again, unable at first to comprehend what she was seeing.

The sky had been blotted out all right, but by the

mayor's face. His nose and chin were looming mere inches from hers, a blur of sunkissed skin topped with far too much dark hair, long enough to brush his collar.

'What the...?' she began to splutter.

But it was too late.

His lips brushed hers and she realised with a shock of unreality that Mayor Murray Carew was kissing her!

CHAPTER FIVE

He hadn't intended to kiss her. Not for a single moment. Susie Lovell wasn't his type. Not now, not ever. But then she'd sighed and nestled against so cozily, as though the intimacy of the setting had softened her attitude towards him, and as she'd tilted her head to look up at him with smoky green eyes, a sudden madness had seized hold of him...

But their lips had barely touched when she shoved him away, so violently that the whole car began swinging back and forth, almost threatening to tip them both out.

'How d-dare you?' she spluttered, flushed and indignant, clinging to the bar of the Ferris wheel car as it creaked madly about. 'You're unbelievable. Utterly incorrigible. You're like some kind of wild animal.' She sucked in a breath, glaring at him. 'Who the hell do you think you are?'

The mayor, Murray thought, but wisely kept that retort to himself. Okay, he'd misread the signals. That was obvious. But the woman had leant her head on his shoulder and made soft noises under her breath. If that was no longer an indication of sexual attraction, maybe he'd been out of the dating game for too long.

Still, it was clear she hadn't intended to give him that impression. So he needed to come up with something better before she marched him to the nearest police station for sexual assault. Which wouldn't be funny, given that the nearest police station in these days of public spending cuts was probably a good three- to four-hour walk. He liked to keep fit but there were limits.

'That wasn't a kiss,' he began uncertainly. 'It was a... a...'

Her eyebrows were almost in her hairline. '*Yes*?'

Murray had nothing further, so gave up on that sentence. It hadn't been a very interesting sentence, anyway.

Damn it, why didn't the woman have a sense of humour, at least? Though, he conceded, she was perfectly right. He shouldn't have given into impulse and tried to kiss her. That had been asking for trouble. But he'd been following his male instincts. Her pretty, tousled red head leaning against his shoulder, her warmth and intriguing feminine scent...

Hurriedly, he banished those dangerous thoughts.

'I was attempting to distract you,' he said with authority.

'Distract me? By *kissing* me?'

'Honestly, it wasn't intended as a kiss. More of a peck... Anyway, you were moaning and groaning. Losing the plot, basically. I thought it must be vertigo. I didn't want you to fall out or throw up.'

Backed into the corner of the car, he glared back at her, his own eyes narrowed in accusation. 'I don't know why you're so upset, Miss Lovell. It worked, didn't it?'

'What on earth are you going on about?'

He jabbed a finger towards the ground. 'Look, you maniac.'

'Huh?'

'The wheel has come full circle. We're nearly back at the start. You were so busy being furious with me for that peck on the cheek, you totally missed the last part of the ride.' He felt as flustered now as she looked. 'It's okay, you can thank me later.'

With a look of bemusement, Susie Lovell peered slowly down. To his relief, realization dawned on her face. The wheel had rolled back to the point where they'd got in, and the huge grinning attendant was there, ready and waiting to release them from their prison.

'You could have tried talking to me instead,' she threw back at him, fumbling with the protective bar. 'It's true, I may be ever so slightly afraid of heights. But I certainly didn't give you permission to *kiss me*.'

Naturally enough, the Ferris wheel attendant was listening to this with unabashed interest.

Murray kept smiling, though he was secretly annoyed. 'I apologise sincerely if you somehow misread my intentions, Miss Lovell,' he said, shooting a quelling glance at the earwigging attendant, who entirely failed to take the hint. 'Though I wouldn't call it a kiss... More of a peck, really. Good God, we barely made contact.' Politely, he gestured her to leave the Ferris wheel enclosure first. 'Ladies first.'

'Oh, go to hell,' she muttered and strode away.

Forced to stop and shake hands with a few constituents who'd called out to him, Murray caught up with his new employee near the candy floss stand. He felt a sense of aggrievement towards her, though he thought it better not to voice his opinion. In fact, he should be careful not to behave in anything but a professional manner with her in future. The woman was clearly unpredictable enough to take offence at the slightest thing.

That peck on the lips had been a major mistake though. He'd be kicking himself for being such an idiot for some time, he could tell. But why on earth had she allowed herself to be taken up on a Ferris wheel if she genuinely suffered from a fear of heights?

'Miss Lovell, please accept my apologies. It will never happen again.' Murray ordered them both candy floss and paid with a card, much to the stallholder's bemusement, his gaze barely wavering from her face. 'Not that it happened this time, of course.'

'Oh, of course not.'

'Just a misunderstanding.'

'If you say so.'

He studied her solicitously. 'You look unwell.'

'My legs are wobbly, that's all.'

'I'm not surprised. Do you need me to find a paramedic for you?' He glanced about for the distinctive green uniforms. 'We always have emergency services on standby at the fairground in case of situations like this. Especially at Halloween.' He tried not to sound judgemental. 'Some people can be spooked by the slightest thing.'

Her striking green eyes narrowed on his face. 'I don't need an ambulance, thank you,' she said pointedly. 'I'm not having hysterics or a heart attack. I've got jelly legs, that's all.'

'You can never be too careful after a panic attack.'

She had taken the candy floss from the stall with a muttered word of thanks, but now her gaze swung back to his face. 'I did not have a panic attack,' she insisted, enunciating each word with furious emphasis.

'I see.' He rubbed his chin. 'Well, whatever it was you had, are you feeling better now?'

'Again, I'm perfectly *fine*, thank you, Mr Mayor.' Susie Lovell gobbled down a mouthful of candy floss, hiding behind the huge pink web of goo. Licking her fingers, she added indistinctly, 'This is never going to work, you know. I think it's best that I start looking for another job.'

'Because?'

'Because you say peck, I say kiss.'

Sensing danger, Murray gestured her to a nearby empty bench and sat down beside her, holding his own candy floss gingerly by the base of the stick.

What on earth had possessed him to buy the

horrible stuff? He hadn't eaten candy floss in years. Yet it had seemed like the most natural thing in the world while talking to her. Exactly as he'd reacted to impulse up on the high wheel and tried to kiss her, with disastrous effects. Good grief, she was reducing him to infantile behaviour.

'I hope you don't mean that, Miss Lovell,' he said carefully. 'My vision for Penrock Downs revolves around you and the Christmas Tree Shop. It would be an absolute disaster if you walked out on me now.'

'I can't stay on.' She glared at her over the top of her candy floss. All he saw was a vast wodge of pink goo topped by snapping green eyes and pale, slanted brows. He sat mesmerized, watching those mobile speaking brows flick first one way, and then the other. Like windscreen wipers... 'I've seen the way you operate, Mayor Carew. You're a fake.'

'I am?'

The pink goo wobbled precariously as she nodded. 'You try to make everyone think you're into Christmas. That you're like... I dunno... Santa Claus, or something. But you're the polar opposite of Santa Claus.' She waved a hand wildly, candy floss swaying too. 'Santa is about love and generosity and every child mattering. You don't enjoy Christmas, Mr Mayor. And you're not generous. And you're not in it to make Christmas wonderful for the kids of Penrock Downs, not as far as I know.' Those expressive eyes locked with his over the top of the candy floss. 'You don't *love* Christmas. You just want to be able to *sell* it.'

He had thought her Santa analogy funny at first. Pictured himself in a big red suit and fake beard, chuckling, 'Ho Ho Ho.' But she'd meant it in a cruel way, he realised. She'd meant he was Scrooge, not Santa. And even though he wasn't a big fan of Santa, not since an unfortunate incident in his childhood, that still stung.

His grin faded. 'There's no need to get personal.'

'You kissed me up there,' she hissed, then backtracked when he protested. 'All right, you pecked me. How much more personal can it get?'

'And I apologised for that.'

'I bet you don't even celebrate Christmas,' she went on, gobbling down more candy floss with a compulsive air.

'Of course I celebrate Christmas,' he said irritably.

'I don't believe you. I bet you just treat Christmas Day like any other day of the year. In fact, I bet it annoys the hell out of you that nobody else is working that day, so you have to stay home and pretend like you have a life too.'

His hands had clenched, fingernails digging into his palms. He forced himself to take a deep breath and relax them. It was nonsense. Nothing to feel hurt about.

But she'd hit close to the truth.

'And you're all about the festive spirit, I suppose,' he replied lightly, trying to manage a smile. He took a tentative mouthful of candy floss and grimaced, hardly able to swallow it. Far too much sugar, and all that fake pink colouring... 'You and the Christmas

Tree Shop. No commercialisation there at all.'

'Actually, I *love* Christmas.'

'I bet you do... Ha, talk about selling it,' he bit out, forgetting to relax. His hands were sticky and he had a horrible over-sugary taste in his mouth. 'Can you hear yourself? Miss Lovell, you literally run a shop selling *Christmas* trees.'

'That shop has been a part of my life since I was tiny. It means everything to me,' she declared passionately. 'I don't mean selling decorations. I mean watching the trees grow, tending to them, knowing how much pleasure they'll give to some child when they're standing in a living room at Christmas, wreathed in tinsel and baubles –'

'You can't be serious,' he interrupted her.

'Of course I'm serious.' She devoured the last of her candy floss, munching on it ferociously now, as though eating his head. 'But you,' she muttered between mouthfuls, her words jabbing at him, 'you're never serious, are you? You're always spinning a line, seeing how much you can get for nothing in return.' Munch, munch, munch. 'That's why you can't recognise honesty in other people.'

Murray got up and slammed his barely touched candy floss into a bin. 'Never had much of a sweet tooth,' he muttered when she stared at him.

He stood before her, sticky hands jammed into his pockets, his gaze moving restlessly about the funfair. It was clear that he'd handled this situation very badly. And he would ordinarily have fixed things with a few smooth words and a smile. But she seemed impossible to placate. Or his methods so far had backfired. Maybe both together.

'Look,' he said awkwardly, 'I'm sorry about what happened up there on the Ferris wheel. It was stupid and crass, I admit. I'm not usually such an idiot. Obviously, you bring out the reckless side in me.'

'Yes, it's always the woman's fault.'

He threw her a grim look. 'I didn't mean it like that, and you know it. I'm *trying* to apologise. It was a simple case of mixed messages.' She jumped up and he took a quick step towards her. 'Listen, you can beat me up later for that stupid peck on the lips. Right now, I need you at the shop, and from what you said just now about your trees, I'm guessing you don't really want to leave.' He softened his tone. 'It was your family business, I understand that. Just tell me what I need to do to make things right, and I'll sort it out.'

'No, it would be a mistake for me to stay,' she insisted, tossing her candy floss stick into the bin and stalking away. 'Goodbye, Mr Mayor. I'm sure you and your minions can cope without me.'

He ought to have turned and walked in the opposite direction at that point. *Minions* now… But something about her wouldn't let him drop it.

Plus, he needed to make this Christmas Market work. The last thing he needed right now was a groundswell of local opposition to his plans, and he guessed she could be a seriously difficult ringleader to deal with.

Murray caught up with her beside the ghost train ride. There was a gaggle of giggling teenagers stumbling out of the train. 'How long since you last went on a ghost train?' he asked, close to her ear.

She stared round at him, bemused. 'You want to go on the ghost train now?'

'We still need to talk. I thought the Ferris wheel was a good choice. But you were afraid of heights. Maybe you're afraid of things that go bump in the night too.'

'Don't be ridiculous.'

'We could try the dodgems.'

She curled her lip. 'No thanks.'

'Okay, then. And you're right. It's hard to talk while bashing the hell out of each other on the dodgems. So, you and me on the ghost train. It is Halloween season, after all.' He raised his brows, daring her to walk away again. 'So long as you don't scream too loudly in there, it might provide a good opportunity for us to thrash out a few terms of business.'

Her eyes narrowed on his face. 'Why would I scream?'

'Ghost train? Spooky stuff?' He lifted both hands in the air. 'There'll be no pecking this time, honest. I got the memo.'

'Couldn't we just talk at the shop? Or at the town hall, if you prefer?'

'I don't want either of us to have the home advantage.'

'How chivalrous of you,' she murmured almost conversationally as he paid for their rides and hurriedly steered her onto the ghost train before she could change her mind.

It wasn't as tight a squeeze as on the Ferris wheel. But they were still in close proximity. He felt his heartbeat quicken, aware of the potential danger of offending her again with a badly timed move.

Cautiously, he stretched an arm along the back of the faded leather seat, turning towards her. 'Let me apologise again. And introduce myself properly, so we both know what's what. You're right, Miss Lovell, I am a businessman, not just a politician. And I like to seize a golden opportunity with both hands when it comes along.'

Her gaze moved pointedly to his arm, resting along the back of the seat. 'I'm not a golden opportunity.'

'Duly noted.' To show willing, he removed the offending body part and folded his arms instead, keeping his distance. 'But your shop is,' he told her softly. 'And the land around it.'

Kids were bundling into the ghost train behind them, chattering excitedly and making howling noises that set his teeth on edge.

Susie Lovell was clearly unnerved too. Her eyes had widened, a suggestion of panic flaring again in their green depths. 'You touch a single fir cone on my Christmas trees, and I swear by all that's holy –'

'No, not the nursery,' he quickly corrected her misapprehension. Good grief, this woman was so reactionary! 'I don't intend to go anywhere near your precious tree nursery. I agreed with your father, that is *your* territory. Your responsibility.'

She looked puzzled. 'So, you're talking about Twelve Tree Acres?'

'It's my intention to locate the Christmas Market there, yes, and I don't need your permission to do so. As I told you before, I've already arranged to sell that land to the council for a nominal fee.' The ride started with a jerk, jolting them forwards, and she gasped, clutching the side of the car. 'But I'd still like your blessing.'

She sucked in a breath, her gaze fixed on his.

The ghost train rumbled into eerie darkness, and she turned to face front, looking almost wild again. A looming figure in the shadows ahead chuckled in a deep and sinister manner, and the kids around them shrieked with laughter.

Ghostly 'cobwebs' trailed over his face, and he brushed them away impatiently.

'Susie?'

'I can't give you my blessing,' she breathed, still staring dead ahead and holding onto the door handle with a rigid hand. 'Though I can give you a few swear words if you like.'

'Easy now,' he murmured.

'You're wrecking local businesses,' she hissed.

'For God's sake –'

'The stalls you'll be bringing into the town will mostly belong to big businesses. Roving professional tradesmen. Not small-time locals from Penrock Downs. Our little shops and boutiques will be empty while your market is open. And we *need* that money, Mayor Carew. We need it to survive, not to turn a profit.'

As the ghost train cart rounded the bend, the teenage couple in front of them giggled and clutched each other, and then they too were subjected to a huge dangling spider that danced hairy black rubber legs on top of Susie's head.

She shoved the fake spider away with an exasperated cry. 'We need major Christmas takings, or our businesses won't make it into the next year,' she went on passionately. 'That's how serious this is for us.'

'But the town will benefit as a whole,' he insisted, bending to avoid another barrage of straggling grey cobwebs. 'Everyone benefits by extension. People will come to the town and spend money in your shops too.'

'No, they'll go to the Christmas Market and spend money *there*. The rest of the town's businesses won't get a look in. Frankly, I don't think you've done the maths properly. You need another public consultation on this.'

'We tried that, and most people agreed with us that a commercial market would be a good idea.' Murray ran a hand through his hair, exasperated. 'Besides, it's too late to be stopping everything for a second consultation. The wheels are already in motion and time is money. And I remember seeing you at that first public consultation, anyway.' More sinister chuckling from the darkness drowned out his next words, so he had to repeat them more loudly. 'I said, *you* were at the public consultation.'

'There's no need to shout.'

'Sorry, I didn't think you could hear me,' he told her through gritted teeth. 'You spoke eloquently and at length about your misgivings at that meeting, and I thought the council reassured you at the time.'

'Well, you thought wrong. I wasn't satisfied with your answers that night, and I've written to the council several times since then, outlining my concerns. And received no reply.'

Murray grimaced. He had a vague memory of the clerk forwarding him some emails from Susie Lovell and him telling her to shelve them under Nuisance Mail.

'I'll look into that for you.'

Susie jerked backwards, yelling, 'Mummy!' as an Egyptian mummy wrapped in grimy bandages lurched out of the shadows with both arms outstretched, almost within reach of their car, and abruptly disappeared again.

'Very convincing,' he lied.

She covered her face with her hands, gasping, 'Good grief, what's wrong with me?'

'Good question.' Covertly, Murray checked the time on his phone. He had other people to meet at the fair. 'Look, I'm sorry you felt unheard at the consultation, but you have my full attention now.'

He leant closer in the glimmering darkness, trying to project an aura of protective masculinity. She was such a tomboy, he thought, amused by her tousled hair and lack of make-up. Those dungarees and the work sweater were doing nothing to help. And yet she was clearly all woman too, with hips and bits all in the right places. He recalled catching her bending in the Christmas tree lot, tending to some green thing in the dirt. An odd combination of sexy and grubby. And easily upset by Ferris wheels and ghost trains too, it seemed.

'Tell me what you want,' he murmured, close to her ear.

'What? I can't hear a thing you're –'

'TELL ME WHAT YOU WANT.'

'All right, all right... I told you, there's no need to shout.' The ghost train was bumping through the graveyard section with gibbering corpses on either side, tombstones lit up, skeletal bones rattling out of sight. Her face looked washed-out in the eerie glow. 'Jeez, how much more of this nonsense is there?'

'You said you were left unsatisfied. So, tell me what *will* satisfy you, and I'll try to make sure you get it.'

'Um...'

'Just say whatever you're thinking,' Murray urged her. 'Say the first thing that comes into your mind. Don't worry how it might sound.'

'Okay.' She licked her lips, and his gaze flicked to her mouth. 'You're sitting way too close to me and your breath smells of candy floss.'

Murray blinked. Then sat back, stunned. 'I meant –'

'I know what you meant.'

The ghost train jolted, shooting them through a narrow tunnel draped with cobwebs and strange rubbery tentacles, with light glowing ahead. Then they were out in the daylight again, the car slowing to a halt.

He sat straight, not looking at her, very aware of a photographer a few feet away sneaking quick candid snaps as they emerged.

'Local stalls,' she said abruptly.

'I beg your pardon?' He got out and helped her climb down from the car. He was tempted to sniff his breath in his hand, just to check if she was pulling his leg over the candy floss thing, but she'd be bound to notice.

'If you could guarantee a certain number of locals their own stalls at the market,' Susie told him, 'but at specially reduced rates, that might be acceptable. To be clear, the Christmas stall prices have been set so high, they make it next to impossible for the smaller businesses of Penrock Downs to take part. I want all of us to be able to sell our wares alongside the bigger trade stalls without paying out-of-town prices.'

He took that suggestion without any change of expression. At last, they were getting somewhere. And he'd always intended to cut a deal on prices for Cornish businesses, to keep local commercial interests sweet. Though he wasn't sure how much of a reduction she was suggesting.

'The council has huge overheads to cover,' he began warily, but she interrupted him.

'Take it or leave it.'

He stood watching, arms folded, as the ghost train rattled away with another load of laughing teenagers and parents with young kids.

'And if I leave it?'

'Then you can expect trouble. Organised trouble, and lots of it.' She folded her arms, her chin jutting dangerously. 'I know people.'

'I don't doubt it.' Murray took a deep breath, studying her face. Susie Lovell was fast becoming a thorn in his side and could represent an obstacle to his plans if he wasn't careful. And what did they say? *Keep your friends close, but your enemies closer...* 'Okay, let me take your idea to the council and I'll get back to you.'

'You have one week.'

'It takes at least two weeks to call a special meeting,' he fibbed, playing for time. There was a financial side to be debated, and that wouldn't be a quick process. For every stall they gave away to locals at deeply reduced rates, they would be losing bigger revenue that would have come from external bids. Some councillors would undoubtedly object and need to be persuaded or pacified.

'Ten days tops,' she countered swiftly. 'It's already Halloween. We'll need time to order in extra inventory for the market stalls.'

He nodded slowly. 'I'll set up a meeting and let you know what the council decides. Meanwhile, you won't keep blogging bad publicity about the market. Yes?'

'I agree not to blog about the market again,' she conceded. 'But that doesn't mean I'm on the council's side. And I think you could do with working in the Christmas Tree Shop for a few days.'

Murray was about to turn away, negotiation completed, when her last words hit him. 'I'm sorry, I must have misheard you. Did you just say *working in the Christmas Tree Shop*?'

'Sure.' She looked him up and down, her look scathing. 'It would do a suit like you good to get a taste of the festive spirit.'

'I'm *not* a *suit*,' he muttered through gritted teeth, but she ignored him.

'Halloween is the start of our big pre-season push. We'll have last year's decorations on special offer next week in the run-up to Christmas. Come and work in the shop next week, see what Christmas is all about. You could even help me in the nursery too, if you own a good pair of wellies. Water the baby trees, do some weeding...' Her voice tailed off, seeing his expression. 'What?'

'I'm the boss. You want me to do *weeding*?'

'It would do you a world of good to touch grass for once, Mayor Carew,' she told him, arms folded across her tired-looking work sweater with its Christmas Tree Shop logo, her gaze direct. 'And yes, weeding is a technically undemanding task. Even a *suit* can manage it.' She bared her teeth. 'Given simple enough instructions, that is.'

'Sorry, I don't –'

'This is a deal-breaker.'

He contemplated her in grim silence. Then heaved a sigh. It was obvious he would need to eat humble pie – or humble Christmas pudding – if he wanted this irritating woman to stop embarrassing him publicly through her blog.

Starkly, he demanded, 'How many days would I be working at the shop, exactly?'

'Ten.'

'Five,' he threw back at her.

'Seven.'

'Done.' He stuck out a hand. 'Deal?'

Susie Lovell shook on it with a pleasingly firm grip, then grimaced, releasing him with a frown. 'Your hand is... sticky.' She wiped her palm on her dungarees. 'Ugh.'

Damn candy floss, he thought, watching her stride away. Damn Susie Lovell. And damn *weeding*. He'd rather have his head boiled.

Then found himself wandering in her wake through the fairground crowds, shaking hands – stickily - and exchanging a few words with locals as he went.

Like a damn stalker.

CHAPTER SIX

Susie was in a dream. And a bad one too. Had she just demanded that Murray Carew, her new boss, should come and work in the Christmas Tree Shop next week? To catch the Christmas spirit and look after the baby trees? To do *weeding*?

She must be crazy.

But he'd said yes. They'd even shaken on it.

The thought of the mayor invading her private domain was so disturbing, she felt numb with shock. But perhaps he wouldn't show up. Perhaps she was right, and he didn't even own a pair of wellies. Perhaps, perhaps...

Susie stopped, staring about herself in a daze. Her feet had steered her reluctantly towards the dodgems. She stood watching the kids racing round in the tiny cars, thick bumpers slamming into each other, until she spotted Tansy chatting to the fairground girl she'd dated during the summer.

Feebly, she raised a hand and Tansy waved back before dashing over, grinning.

'That was quick work. I thought it would take you for ages to ditch the mayor.' Her friend elbowed her in the ribs. 'You want a free ride on the dodgems?

I can swing it, you know. Mates' rates. Or no rates, in fact. Tansy's special rates.' She grimaced. 'No, scratch that. It sounds awful. Like I'm touting for business or something. You want a ride or what?'

Ready for the ride of your life? Murray's amused invitation rang in her ears and Susie pulled a face.

'What's the matter?' Tansy stared at her. 'You're upset. No, don't deny it... I can always tell. What is it? Was that horrible mayor nasty to you? Where is he? I'll bash his head in.' She lurched past Susie as though genuinely planning to do the mayor a mischief.

'Woah, don't go crazy on me.' Susie grabbed her by the sleeve, half laughing, still half upset. 'It's nothing... We went up on the Ferris wheel and –'

'You went up on the Ferris wheel? With the mayor?' Tansy's eyes bulged. 'But you hate heights. You're *terrified* of heights.'

'I know.'

'Are you out of your teeny-tiny mind?'

'Very possibly. Though, hey, less of the teeny-tiny, please... Anyway, I had a funny little episode when we were right at the top.'

'A panic attack?'

'It was *not* a panic attack.' She glared at Tansy. Not her too? 'More of a... a flap. But, to snap me out of it, he, erm... Well, he kissed me.' The final words came out in a rush and Susie was aware of her cheeks glowing with heat. Good grief, could she behave any more like a schoolgirl?

'He did *what*? He *kissed* you? On the *mouth*?'

'Lower your voice, for goodness' sake!' Susie glanced around but to her relief the fairground was far too noisy for anyone to have overheard them. 'To be fair, it was more of a... a peck than a kiss. He said so himself, and now I think back, it was barely a thing. All over in a second. But I was completely outraged, of course. So I told him it was over.'

'Told him what was over?' Tansy looked blank.

'My job at the Christmas Tree Shop. I gave him my notice. I mean, I can hardly keep working for a man after he's made a pass at me.'

'Made a pass?' Her friend frowned, looking puzzled. 'But you said he only did it to stop you panicking. Not because he *fancies* you.'

Susie glared at her friend, stupidly aggrieved. 'Oh, I see... No, of course it wouldn't be because he fancies me. Because I am totally unfanciable. I'm like a leg of mutton or something. I am literally so ugly that nobody in the world would want to kiss me in a romantic way.'

'You know that's not what I was saying.' Tansy shook her head pityingly. 'Leg of mutton... People don't even eat mutton anymore. That's straight out of Jane Austen.'

'It means sheep meat, not lamb.'

'I know what it means. I've read *Pride and Prejudice*. And seen *Bridgerton*.'

'*Bridgerton* is based on a book too. By Julia Quinn.'

'Duh... Mutton head.'

'So you think I'm over-reacting?' Brooding, Susie dragged on her lower lip for a moment. 'The mayor fancies me. I'm not imagining it.'

'I would say he must fancy you, yes. Otherwise he would never have asked you to come to the funfair with him as his plus-one. Unless he asked you because you look so dreadful, it goes with the Halloween vibe.' Oblivious to her glare, Tansy peered about, searching the crowds. 'Where is he, by the way? Or did you murder him and stick his corpse in a bush somewhere? Like you do with all the men who try on with you.'

'Shut up.' Susie giggled, though it really wasn't funny. 'I have no idea. He demanded that I stop blogging about him and the council. I told him that I quit.' She paused. 'Then he made me go on the ghost train with him.'

'Oh, this man definitely has the hots for you.'

'No, you don't understand.' Briefly, she explained what they'd discussed on the ghost train and how the mayor had asked what he'd need to do to get her onside. 'So I told him he'd have to work in the shop and nursery next week, maybe do some weeding –'

Tansy gave a shout of amusement. 'I wish I'd seen his face!'

'He agreed.

'No...' Her friend stared at her, awed into silence.

'He's probably gone home by now. To order wellies online.'

'Um, I wouldn't bet on that.' Tansy cleared her throat and made a furtive pointing gesture, gazing over Susie's shoulder.

Susie turned to find Mayor Carew standing behind

her, and blenched. How much had he overheard?

'Sorry to interrupt,' he said smoothly, 'but I'd like a word, Miss Lovell. Excuse us, would you?' He directed this question at Tansy, giving her friend a smile so charming it was practically oily.

'Whatever you like, your Mayorfulship,' Tansy muttered, already backing away. The bell had just signalled the end of that session. 'Sounds like I'm needed on the dodgems, anyway. Have fun, kids.' Giving Susie a final wink, she turned and fled.

'I don't need to order Wellington boots online. I already own several pairs.' Murray folded his arms, regarding her steadily. 'Will you come with me? There's someone I'd like you to meet.'

Susie kept a straight face, trying not to betray her embarrassment at having been overheard talking about the mayor behind his back. 'More of your dreary friends in suits? I'll pass, if you don't mind. In fact, I was just going to take a ride on the dodgems here.'

'I thought you hated the dodgems.'

'I never said that.'

One eyebrow crooked. 'You implied it.'

Susie resisted a childish urge to stick her tongue out at him.

'Anyway, it's not one of my dreary friends in suits,' he went on, then grimaced, shaking his head. 'And those people on the platform with me today are not "dreary". They're philanthropists who support this town. We should all be very grateful to them.'

Silently, she tugged her forelock.

The mayor sighed, his jaw setting hard. 'Just come with me, would you?'

There didn't seem much point resisting.

She weaved after him through the funfair crowds until they reached the hotdog stand, where a middle-aged blonde in camel slacks and a denim jacket over a cream blouse was struggling to eat a jumbo hotdog with a dog's lead wrapped impossibly about her lower legs. The woman was remonstrating with the dog, a tiny yapping ball of fluff with a pink-ribboned topknot who kept leaping helplessly towards her hotdog, while never actually leaving the ground by more than two or three inches.

'Naughty girl! What have you done to poor Cynthia?' Murray Carew bent to release the lead from around the woman's legs, and then scooped up the tiny dog, patting its fluffy head. 'There, there... Hotdogs smell good but they're all kinds of bad for you. How many times do I have to tell you?'

Meanwhile, the woman had finally managed to grab a mouthful of hotdog, though not without losing a blob of tomato ketchup to the ground, a blob followed wistfully by the dog's small black eyes.

Murray threw her a grateful smile. 'Thanks for looking after her, Cynthia. I hope she hasn't been a complete nuisance.'

Susie watched all this in amazement. The mayor had a dog?

The woman was hurriedly swallowing her mouthful. 'Oh, she was no bother, honestly,' she told him indistinctly. She produced a tissue and dabbed at her mouth. 'Any time, Mr Mayor.'

'Please, call me Murray when we're not on duty.' He turned to introduce her to Susie. 'Cynthia, this is Miss Lovell. You may recall I mentioned her the other day? Miss Lovell, this is Cynthia Bloom, Clerk of the Council.'

'Pleased to meet you.' Susie shook hands with the council clerk, sure why he'd so badly wanted them to meet. Surely she wouldn't be expected to get involved with council business, just because she'd agreed not to keep moaning publicly about the Christmas Market? Because that sounded about the most boring thing in the universe...

Her gaze dropped to the dog in his arms. Curiosity prompted her to ask, 'And who's this?'

'This is Betty.' He smiled affectionately at the animal, who was panting and staring up at him in a similarly adoring way, its small pink tongue lolling. 'This is who I wanted you to meet.'

Susie's jaw dropped. 'Oh.'

'Betty previously belonged to an ex of mine,' he explained, shooting Susie a look that seemed to say, *Mock me if you dare, but you'll be sorry if you do!* The tiny dog wriggled, and he set her down to hop about his feet, like an overgrown flea on a leash. 'After we split, I, erm, somehow ended up looking after her dog. It was awkward at first, but we've got used to each other's company. I wouldn't be without my Betty now.' He made a cooing noise at the dog, who responded by standing on her hind legs with her two front paws waving in the air, as though begging. 'Who's a lovely girl, eh?'

His dog was rather adorable, Susie thought grudgingly. She'd always been a cat person herself. But dogs could be cute too.

She did recall seeing him in public once or twice with a beautiful woman on his arm. A tall, elegant blonde. Perhaps she had been the dog's former owner. And she wondered why they'd split up, and whether he was still in love with her... And then stopped herself with a jolt. Why on earth was she even remotely interested in the mayor's love life? Not only was the man a dreary professional suit, but he'd also just become her *boss*, not someone who was ever likely to become a friend.

The little dog yapped at her, as though reading her chaotic thoughts, and then jumped around in a circle, still on her hind legs.

Susie glanced at Cynthia, whose expression snapped instantly from grim disbelief to smiling approval. It looked as though the clerk was not a big fan of dogs herself.

'The thing is,' Murray said, playing affectionately with the dog's lead, 'having agreed to work at the Christmas Tree Shop next week, I forgot to mention Betty.'

'Is this your way of worming out of our arrangement?'

'No, of course not. I agreed to work at the shop, to see what growing these Christmas trees means to you, and I'm willing to do that if it will help smooth my way with the Christmas Market.' He paused. 'But it's just me and Betty at home. And she hates it when I'm out all day. Usually, when I have to be out for any length of time, I go back home around lunchtime to feed Betty and take her for a walk. But your shop's too far out of town for that, and...' His voice tailed off; his brows raised as he looked at her expectantly.

'And you want to bring your dog to work?' she queried.

'She wouldn't be any trouble.'

As though denying that statement, the little dog yapped and danced another circle on her hind legs before subsiding into a fluffy white heap at his feet.

'I suppose that would be okay,' she agreed, though personally it seemed like a bad idea to her. A circus dog running loose among the flashing Christmas tree displays... That was a disaster waiting to happen. 'Since it's just for a week.'

What else could she say?

He was her boss, after all. He owned the whole damn place now. She couldn't exactly tell him to keep his dog at home when he was working there. It wasn't her call. Asking her permission was mere politeness, she felt sure. And Murray Carew didn't strike her as someone who would take no for an answer, anyway.

'Thank you.' He smiled. 'Say thank you to Miss Lovell, Betty,' Murray instructed his dog in an indulgent tone. Or his ex-girlfriend's dog. Or his ex-wife's dog. Susie wasn't quite sure of the ownership situation or even the ex's status in his life, then or now. Perhaps his ex had left the dog behind deliberately, as a conversation starter or to allow for an easier return. Or maybe as a cute thorn in his flesh. Like leaving behind an army of occupation...

Betty wagged her tiny tail with enthusiasm. There wasn't much tail to work with, but the dog was making the most of what she had.

'So cute,' Cynthia Bloom murmured, her gaze on the mayor.

CHAPTER SEVEN

Pulling up outside the Christmas Tree Shop at eight-thirty on Monday morning, Murray released his seatbelt before glancing sideways at the dog sitting in the passenger seat beside him. 'I know what you're thinking,' he told her sternly, 'and I want you to understand, before we go inside, that if you misbehave, I will not have your back. Not today. Not with That Woman. Do we understand each other?'

Betty panted gently, her intelligent black eyes locked to his.

'I'm only here because I let That Woman goad me into working in the Christmas shop with her. Because she thinks I have no festive spirit. And since I have to be here, so do you. Whether you like it or not.' He grimaced. 'I still can't believe I agreed to this. I could have been working in my home office this week, or visiting the town hall, or having a mayoral surgery session. I could have been playing squash with Bob or hanging out in the new golf pavilion bar – which is very nice, by the way. If you're a good girl,' he added, 'I may take you with me next time. Apparently, they allow well-behaved dogs onto the premises.'

Betty said nothing, which was only to be expected, given that she was a dog and had no idea what he was talking about.

'Instead,' he went on gloomily to himself, 'I'm going to be at Susie Lovell's beck and call all week. It will be a nightmare. I bet she doesn't even keep fresh-ground coffee on the premises. And her biscuits are probably value brand.'

At the word 'biscuits,' Betty yapped, staring at him.

'I know, but what can you do? If we must eat value digestives, so be it. I agreed to play by her rules this week.'

Murray glanced down at his phone. He was already five minutes late. Not that Susie Lovell was his boss. He was her boss, in fact. But he was going to be doing things the Lovell way this week, if only to prove a point, which was that he could compromise when necessary. And it was necessary. Indeed, it was vital to get her onside with this damn Christmas Market. He couldn't risk her launching an emergency complaint about planning permission, for instance, which wouldn't get anywhere but could slow things up and derail the laborious process of installing dozens of gigantic Swiss-chalet-style Christmas stalls on the site over the next few weeks.

'Well, just so long as we're clear that you're to behave yourself in there,' he reiterated, climbing out of the car and summoning Betty with a jerk of his head. 'Come on then, Little Miss Butter Wouldn't Melt. Unless you plan to sit in this car all day?

Which I would be happy for you to do, except for the inevitable mess, because I'm going to be here for hours, trust me.'

Having briefly considered that point and come to a decision, Betty bounced out in his wake. Dramatically, she shook herself all over on touching frosty ground with her delicate paws, ending this performance with an ear-splitting yelp.

'Yes, I know it's cold. Try walking faster, it'll keep you warm. Now, are you going to give me trouble in there?' he demanded, and produced her lead, holding it aloft. 'Because this can get clipped to your collar at any point, Missy.'

Instantly, Betty sat back on her haunches to look up at him in mild reproof, paws together at the front, appearing the model of canine propriety.

The air was chill and wintry that morning, so he'd taken the precaution of fastening a cosy red tartan coat about her midsection. Betty was still in her prime, being only six years old, but he still didn't like the idea of exposing her underbelly to the elements at this time of year. He'd seen warning articles on the Internet about some dogs that had caught a cold while out walking and never recovered, and this had made him uneasy.

Maybe he was overly fussy about his dog's welfare. Or rather, Genevieve's dog's welfare. But he couldn't bear the thought of Betty getting sick, especially through some neglect on his part.

'I take it we're both on the same page here?' Betty turned in a tight circle, wagged her tail, and sat down again, watching him expectantly as though in anticipation of a treat. 'And no, I don't have a bone to give you. Not yet, anyway. Maybe later.' He paused, adding with emphasis, 'But *only if* you behave.'

He coiled up her lead and tucked it into his jacket pocket, brooding on the past. It had been long enough now, surely, since Genevieve had left, for her dog to be considered *his*. And she had simply abandoned Betty. Nobody who abandons an animal like that and walks away without a single backwards glance deserved a second chance at ownership. Not in his book.

Murray paused in the shop doorway, unsure what to expect. He'd seen the shop interior before, of course. Seeing over the premises had been a necessary part of his negotiations with Susie's father when buying out the business. Lovell had insisted that he keep the transaction secret though, and Murray could see why. Susie was so vehemently proprietorial about this one-time family business, she must've exploded when she discovered her father had sold it to him, lock, stock and barrel. Oh, to have been a fly on the wall that day…

Not that he took pleasure in disappointing anyone's dreams. But he was developing a rich appreciation for her fiery temper, and guessed it must have been one hell of a firework display the day she found out. He himself would never have considered buying such a small, out-of-town business, if it hadn't been that he needed the land opposite as a prime site for the Christmas Market.

Not that he'd wanted to turn a profit. That would have been unethical, and also potentially led him into difficult legal waters. But by selling that spare plot of land to the council for a peppercorn figure, he'd been able to realise his vision of rejuvenating the town without having anyone accuse him of trying to make money out of the situation. He didn't like having lost money on the transaction, it was true. But he was hopeful that, over time, the tree nursery and adjacent garden centre would eventually earn back his investment.

Still, he was aware of not really having paid that much attention to the retail side of things when speaking to Lovell. He'd walked through the shop a few times, on days when Susie wasn't working there, and dutifully admired the Christmas displays, which existed all year round, along with various other items that kept locals coming by even during the summer months.

There was a small pet section, for instance, including animal feed in sacks, catering to breeders and smallholders with livestock. He thought it might be a good idea to expand that side of the business, so they could improve profits outside the Christmas season. Though that would mean either building an extension to the shop or squeezing out some of the Christmas decorations. And he knew that Susie, while ostensibly his employee now, would undoubtedly kick up a fuss over losing even one square inch of festive nonsense.

Betty, running ahead of him into the shop,

stopped dead and yapped at the sight of a four-foot mechanical Santa in red robes with white fur trim, clutching his large belly and crying, 'Ho ho ho!' Having yapped her disapproval, she strategically retreated behind Murray, peering out between his legs at the terrifying figure before aiming a few more piercing barks in that direction.

Susie, finishing with a customer at the till, came striding over. 'You're late.'

Betty yapped at her too but subsided at Murray's quelling stare.

'I'm sorry. Hopefully, it won't happen again. Thing is, I wasn't sure what to wear.' Murray indicated his dark jumper and jeans, shrugging out of his black jacket. 'You didn't mention a dress code.'

'Dress code? It's not a nightclub.' She indicated her own white tee-shirt with Lovell's Christmas Tree Shop written in bold red across it, accompanied by a graphic of a green tree. 'This tee-shirt is our indoors uniform. Though I also wear a fleece for outdoors work in the winter.' She glanced at his jeans. 'With black trousers, so those will do for now. But I'll need to sort you out with a shop tee-shirt. What size do you need?'

'Medium,' he said, then added defensively, 'Or maybe large, I guess.'

It felt awkward, discussing his clothes size with a woman. In general, although tall and well-built, he prided himself on being neither underweight nor overweight, but just right. The Goldilocks zone of physical fitness. He surfed to stay active and bronzed during the summer, and occasionally ran along the cliffs in the early mornings too.

But it was also true that during the winter months he rarely made it into the local gym, where he liked to join a few boxing and tai chi classes, as well as lifting weights. But he was hardly a keen gym-goer, and he knew that once the year slid into winter, he was more comfortable covering up with a loose shirt or jacket than going about in a tee-shirt.

'Let's see what we've got in the staff room, shall we?' She led him across the shop. There didn't seem to be anyone else in the shop, though he noted they had no security cameras, even if there had been. It was an honour system, in other words. He remembered Lovell saying they occasionally had shoplifters, but it was a rare occurrence. Maybe some fake cameras would deter would-be shoplifters. He made a mental note to look into it, gazing about the place with interest.

In the staff room, Susie jerked open a locker with shelves of clothing inside and began briskly checking labels.

Murray studied her thoughtfully. He wasn't into tomboys but had to admit that her rear view was rather enticing. Her tee-shirt was tucked into tight-fitting trousers that clung to a nicely rounded bum and toned legs. When she turned towards him, his gaze lingered momentarily on the pert lift of her breasts, and then rose speedily to her face when she cleared her throat.

'My face is up here,' she said coldly.

'Sorry, I was admiring the tee-shirt design,' he lied, remembering how badly she'd reacted to him on the Ferris wheel. There could be no messing about with Miss Lovell. 'So I'll be wearing one like that, I take it?'

She tossed two shop tee-shirts at him which he fumbled to catch, taken aback by her aggressive glare.

'Toilets are over there. You can try them on in the gents, see which fits best. No medium or large, I'm afraid. Those are the nearest I could find to your size.' Her gaze dropped to Betty, who was still hiding behind his legs. 'For the sake of hygiene rules, you'll need to leave your dog behind. Only guide dogs are allowed in the loo.' She saw his expression and added testily, 'She'll be fine here in the office. I'll close the door so she can't run about the store.'

Murray frowned. He could understand the point about hygiene. But he was uneasy about shutting Betty into a room on her own, especially in such an unfamiliar place. Betty wouldn't like it either and would soon communicate this in a noisy fashion. 'I'm not sure she'd like that,' he said diplomatically. 'But I can ask her to sit on the chair there, and leave the door ajar, so she doesn't feel shut in. That might help.'

Susie looked aggrieved. 'Your dog is trained, I take it?'

'Oh yes, but she has a mind of her own,' he said, adding in a mutter, 'Like most females.'

'Your ability to offend is just effortless, isn't it?' Without waiting for an answer, Susie patted a leather chair and said encouragingly to the dog, 'Come and sit here. Look at this nice comfortable chair... Wouldn't you like to curl up and go to sleep for a while? Come on, there's a good doggy.'

Betty raised her top lip, displaying two rows of sharp teeth, and growled at her.

'What did we discuss in the car, Betty? *Best* behaviour today, please.' Murray bent and scooped her up, placing the little dog on the chair where she glowered at him accusingly. 'Stay,' he instructed her in his firmest no-nonsense voice, while Susie backed out of the room. 'I'll come back and check on you soon, I promise.'

Leaving the door ajar, he strode off towards the toilets, ignoring her panicked barks. Betty would soon settle down. Or at least he hoped so.

Flustered, he dragged off his clothes and threw them in a heap on the floor, then pulled on the larger of the two tee-shirts. It turned out to be huge, a voluminous tent that ended just above the knee. The label said 3XL.

'Good grief.' Escaping from its many draped folds, he tried the other one, and had trouble squeezing into it. He craned to see the label, which was XS. '*Extra small*? Is she kidding? This must be for, like, twelve-year-olds.'

Having jerked it down as far as it would go, Murray examined himself in the small mirror over the sinks. The tee-shirt rose above his jeans waistband, revealing a strip of still faintly bronzed abdomen from summer beach-going, and stretched tightly about his chest and biceps, like he was about to bust out of his clothes...

'You okay in there?' Susie knocked on the door to the gents loo, and then creaked it open a couple of inches before he could reply. Her jaw dropped on seeing him, then she bit her lip. 'Oh... That's a bit tight, isn't it? Perhaps you should try the other one.'

'I already did.' He held the 3XL up against himself. 'It's more like a cocktail dress. If you have any heels, it might work.'

'Oh dear.' A buzzer went behind her and she pulled a face. 'Damn... Someone's at the till. You'll have to wear that smaller one for today. I'll order a medium but I doubt it will arrive this week. Maybe you could wear a shop fleece instead. They're for outdoor work, as it gets quite warm in the shop. But if you feel embarrassed...' She was eyeing the fabric as it strained across his chest.

'I'll manage for today.' Bundling up his clothes, he followed her out. Putting his things in the staff room, he stopped to pet Betty for a moment, who was still on high alert but hadn't moved from her chair, thankfully, and then joined Susie at the till. 'What can I do?'

She turned from the customer, a young woman who had clearly recognised him and was gawping, and said, 'Miss Haynes would like help choosing a new tree from our range of artificials. Could you hold the fort while I talk her through the options?'

'I'm not sure how to use this till,' he said, studying the screen.

'Don't worry, I'll show you how to log on and scan items as soon as I'm done with Miss Haynes.' Susie gave him what he felt was a patronizing smile. He was surprised she didn't pat him on the head while she was at it. 'Just smile at any customers, try to be helpful, and press this buzzer if someone needs to be served. I'll come straight back.'

She walked away with Miss Haynes, whom he distinctively heard say, 'Is that the mayor? Nice bit of eye candy, I must say, though his tee-shirt's a bit on the small side... Will you have him playing Santa in the shop grotto this year?'

Over my dead body, Murray thought, glaring at their backs.

Eye candy?

He'd never been treated as a sex object before, and it wasn't as amusing as he'd thought.

When Susie got back and had served Miss Haynes, she tasked him with carrying the ten-foot artificial tree, complete with pre-strung lights and baubles, out to the young woman's car.

'Oh, you don't need to,' tittered Miss Haynes, batting mascara-thick lashes at him, a twenty-something brunette with an impressive cleavage. 'You're the mayor, aren't you?'

'That's right,' he admitted, wondering how many more of Susie's customers were likely to recognize her new handyman. 'But today I'm working here. So I'm happy to help.'

'Too kind,' Miss Haynes purred, preceding him to her car in red heels. She bent to open the tailgate for him. 'Just slip it in here, would you? I do hope it'll fit...'

'Me too,' he muttered.

Having struggled for some minutes to squeeze the large boxed-up tree into the back of Miss Haynes' SUV, manfully ignoring her pursed lips and avid study of his torso in the miniscule tee-shirt, Murray returned to the shop, feeling almost soiled by the encounter. He was also freezing...

'Right, let's show you how the till works.' Susie spent the next half-hour teaching him how to scan items into the machine, take payment, and work the loyalty card system, before saying briskly, 'Ah, Tom has arrived. That means I can take you outside to the tree nursery while he works the till.'

Tom raised a laconic hand on his way to the staff room, already unwrapping his scarf.

'Will we be outside for long?' Murray frowned, gazing out of the window at cold skies, and then dragged down the tee-shirt, which had somehow risen again to expose his midriff. 'Shall I grab my jacket?'

'You won't need it.'

'But won't we get cold in just this, erm, get-up?' Murray saw her quick glance and felt embarrassed. Wow, he must sound like a complete wimp. 'I mean, you've got bare arms too... I was just out there, and it's getting pretty nippy.'

'There are fleece jackets at the back door. We'll grab one each as we go out.' She paused. 'What's the matter?'

'Nothing.' Murray thrust his hands into his pockets. 'That is, I assumed it would only be shop work today.'

'Didn't we also discuss weeding?'

Damn, yes, now he remembered... 'Erm, did we?'

'Mr Mayor, I asked you to do this because I want you to learn more about what we *do* here. Not just what we sell.' Susie faced him squarely, hands on hips. There was a glint in her eyes. 'You and Christmas are like strangers. I intend to see you two get better acquainted.'

She was loving this, he thought grimly. Really rubbing it in that she knew more than him in this situation. 'And how am you going to achieve that by making me work outside?'

'I'm not *making* you do anything,' she pointed out silkily. 'You came here of your own free will and as part of our deal, remember? You work here, I don't blog about the council. But those are Christmas trees out in the nursery lot, and a Christmas tree is the very essence of the season. By getting to know the fir tree, you may come to understand the spirit of Christmas.'

'Then you'd better lead on, O Ghost of Christmas Present,' he muttered, and saw a flash of irritation in her face. Oops. 'I'm sorry... That was not only uncalled-for, but facetious.' He gave her a grave look, the one he reserved for difficult council meetings when nobody was playing ball. 'Of course I want to see your fir trees, Miss Lovell.'

She narrowed her eyes but nodded. 'Let's go, then,'

was all she said, instructing Tom to stay by the tills until their return. 'Tom, this is Murray. Murray, this is Tom. We'll be out in the nursery,' she told him briskly, 'introducing Murray to the fir trees.'

When she marched off, the young man grinned at him behind her back, giving him a thumbs-up. 'She made me meet the trees too, my first day here,' he whispered. 'It doesn't take long. Just tell her they look *amazing*, and she'll let you come back inside.' His gaze dropped to Murray's tee-shirt. 'Um, though you might need a bigger size tee-shirt, bro. Just sayin'...'

Speechless, Murray hurried after Susie, wondering if she actually had a screw loose and wasn't just winding him up with the whole 'meet the fir trees' thing. But when she took a fleece jacket off the pegs by the back door into the nursery lot, he abruptly chose not to. He'd already presented a weak figure earlier when discussing the weather, and this was his chance to rectify the matter.

'I'll be fine,' he said, thrusting his shoulders back and walking out into the chill air as though it was a balmy summer's day.

He wasn't entirely pretending not to notice the cold. After sitting behind a desk all day, fielding complex mayoral calls and emails, and chairing VIP meetings, he was finding this whole experience refreshing, and the wind chill factor outside was nothing if not bracing. Most years, he took a dip in the freezing sea on Boxing Day morning, along with hundreds of other enthusiastic Cornish sea bathers, and was perfectly able to bear low and even sub-zero temperatures when necessary. Yes, even in skimpy swim shorts, or the teeniest of tiny tees. Though it was true he preferred the comfort of a wetsuit.

But if Susie Lovell thought that showing him baby fir trees was going to make him abandon his Scrooge approach and embrace the wondrousness of Christmas, she was very much mistaken. To his mind, Christmas was about making money, and nothing would ever shake that opinion.

Good God, it was a cold wind though. His nipples were sticking out like bloody bullets. Hurriedly, Murray folded protective arms across his chest and hoped she hadn't noticed...

CHAPTER EIGHT

'Well, this is where we grow the trees. What do you think?' Susie breathed in the scent of the branches, closing her eyes. It was always such a magical moment, coming out of the stuffy confines of the shop into the nursery enclosure and scenting *Christmas* on the air. Not just that, but to feel Christmas scratching at the back of her throat, drawn down into her lungs, circulating in her bloodstream... A moment of perfect happiness that made all the daily work crapola somehow bearable, even worth it.

Did it make Murray Carew's crapola easier to bear though? Yes, just about, she decided, after a moment's uncertainty. And that was saying something, because the man was chockful of it.

'What do I think of *what*?' He was right behind her, his voice loud, deep, male, intrusive. All the things that didn't fit here in her magical place.

She kept her eyes firmly closed, not yet ready to face the reality of him in her fir tree nursery. It had been raining all day yesterday, wet permeating the treetops and slowly filtering down until the scent of Christmas was even more pronounced than usual, like festive super-concentrate dripping from lush, bouncy green branches...

'Everything,' she muttered.

He took a few steps past her, the warmth of his body unmistakable, heavy feet cracking over tiny twigs and fir cones that splintered with every step.

Her eyes flew open.

'Careful!'

The mayor stopped dead, one large green welly-clad foot in the air. 'What is it?' With exaggerated caution, he peered down past his raised foot. 'Am I about to tread on a land mine? A baby squirrel? A lost tenner?'

'You broke this.' She bent to collect the pieces of a splintered fir cone, hugging them to her chest. 'And that.' She nodded, disconsolate, to an old greening twig that had been nestled in a bed of brown fir needles, and now lay in two pieces, sap showing where it had snapped under his foot.

He blinked, studying the broken twig. 'I'm sorry, were you planning to give that a dignified funeral?'

'Ha ha, so very droll.' She placed the fir cone splinters at the base of the nearest tree, and stood back, sighing. 'This is a precious place to me. Do you know what they say about being in nature? Take nothing... and leave only footprints.'

He still had one foot in the air. 'So I can leave footprints, then? Because I was beginning to worry I might be required to levitate back to the shop.'

She met his gaze silently.

Carefully, he lowered his foot to the ground,

with a distinct crunching of pine needles. 'Sorry,' he whispered to her. Then bent towards the pine needles and repeated, 'Sorry,' also in a whisper.

'Clown,' she muttered, then pulled a face. Insulting him had been unprofessional. 'Sorry. I didn't mean that.'

Murray stuck his hands in the back pockets of his jeans, swinging to face her, and the XS tee-shirt rose even higher on his midriff. She tried not to stare…

'Apology accepted,' he said lightly. 'Though I'm sure I deserved it. And I'm sorry too.' He took a deep breath, his chest swelling in the miniscule tee-shirt. 'This is clearly a very important place for you, Miss Lovell, and I disrespected that. Let's start again, shall we? Show me whatever you want, and I shall listen without comment.'

She did not remotely believe that, but nodded. 'Thank you.' Her gaze returned to his torso, every muscle in his chest and shoulders starkly outlined by the thin-stretched white fabric. His flat abdomen was also ripped, but not body-builder style, thank goodness. She was so bored by all that ubermasculinity. The mayor was clearly fit without being…

Wait, what on earth was she thinking? What did it matter to her how fit he was or how many muscles he had under that too-brief tee?

'This way,' she said sharply, and led him down the rough slope to where the mature trees waited in rows to be chosen by a customer and either dug up with their rootball to be replanted at season's end or cut down as a single-use tree.

She always tried to persuade customers to take the tree with a rootball, with instructions on how to tend it through to Twelfth Night, for the best possible chance of a replant succeeding. But she also understood why some people preferred the tree cut down and placed in a metal stand for ease and stability. Not everyone had a garden large enough to replant a six or eight-foot tree, especially every year...

Amongst the mature trees, the smell of Christmas was so pure, it was almost overwhelming, their branches thick and vibrant, each spur of needles curled with a dark attractive green that made her think of tinsel and baubles and carol singers.

'Isn't this gorgeous? I come here to think sometimes, or just to wander about in the fresh air, thinking about... Oh, everything Christmassy.' She turned to smile at him, a little shy of discussing something so personal with the mayor, of all people. But she wanted Murray to embrace the spirit of Christmas, and there was no way to get him there without becoming at least a little emotional. 'I think about family in particular, all my past Christmases growing up with my mum and dad. How it feels to give and receive presents, especially that cosy feeling of waking up early on Christmas morning and opening your stocking from Santa, then looking ahead to a wonderful day...'

'From *Santa*?' His eyebrows had shot up.

'No need to look at me like that,' she breathed.

'I *know* Santa's not real. When you're a kid, you believe one hundred percent in that man squeezing down the chimney in his jolly red suit,' she agreed, struggling to keep smiling in the face of his Scrooge-like attitudes, 'but as you get older, you realise that Santa is just another word for someone who loves you.'

'Sounds damn creepy to me.'

Susie ground her teeth. 'You know what I mean. Your mum or dad, tiptoeing into your room with a stocking full of goodies for you to find when you wake up... What could be more loving and special than that?'

He frowned. 'Sounds great, but what if you're an orphan, and in care, and your "stocking" is just a bar of chocolate, or nothing at all? What if the kid in the bed next to yours steals your Christmas present and punches you in the head for good measure?' When she opened her mouth to protest that these were very unlikely scenarios, he hurried on, 'Or say you're divorced and your wife has taken the kids away, and you won't even get to *see* them on Christmas Day, let alone give them a stocking the night before? How special do you think that would feel?'

'Obviously, that wouldn't be very nice,' she admitted, resisting the urge to point out that the glass didn't always have to be half empty. 'But even if things did go badly wrong at Christmas, there's always nature to make you feel better.'

'Nature?'

'*And, for all this, nature is never spent; There lives the dearest freshness deep down things*,' she said lovingly, quoting one of her favourite nature poets, Gerard Manley Hopkins.

He stared at her.

'Now, let me talk you through tree care,' she went on, feeling embarrassed and wishing she'd never started on about how beautiful she found this place. Nobody really understood her enthusiasm for the trees, and why she had ever thought the mayor might was beyond her. Murray Carew was probably the last man on earth to appreciate the *dearest freshness deep down things...* 'Not that you'll be expected to do much outside work this week. But I'd like you to get a feel for how we create our own little corner of Christmas here at the shop. Okay?'

He nodded, but she caught him shivering, and spotted tell-tale goose pimples on his arms. Susie stopped, frowning. 'Perhaps we should take this discussion indoors. I do wish you'd worn a fleece like I told you,' she told him disapprovingly. 'You must be freezing in just that tiny tee-shirt.'

'Honestly, I'm fine,' he began to say, but was interrupted by a cacophony of barking, followed by a man shouting behind them.

They both turned to see Murray's little dog skidding across the nursery level above them and disappearing into the outdoor ornamentals area, where stone statues and benches were housed, along with examples of Christmas outdoor decoration – life-size angels, teams of flashing reindeers, chimney-climbing Santas, and outdoor fairy lights.

His dog was being pursued by a large, snarling, grey-black bulldog, followed by a short, balding and bearded man in a plaid shirt and jeans, who was shouting, 'Dave! Get back here, Dave!'

Susie stared after the trio, bemused. Who on earth was Dave, she wondered? Surely not the bulldog?

Murray swore under his breath. 'Excuse me,' he muttered, and dashed up the slope in pursuit of the two dogs and the bearded man.

Sprinting after him up the damp, muddy slope, Susie found Tom loitering in the back door of the shop, looking distraught. 'What on earth happened?' she demanded, breathless.

'That dog in the staffroom kept whining and barking so I took pity and brought the poor little thing out to sit with me. Does it belong to Murray? Anyway, a customer brought a bulldog into the store, and the little dog went ballistic. It chased after the other dog, knocked over a pot stand, and... I couldn't catch it, sorry.'

'It's a she, and she's called Betty.' Susie stared. 'Wait... Murray's dog chased *after the bulldog*? You're sure it wasn't the other way around?' When Tom nodded gloomily, she gestured him back indoors. 'Okay... You tidy up the damage. I'll sort the dogs out.'

The sound of barking and snarling led her to the back of the ornamental garden, where she found Murray's dog cowering behind Santa's sleigh, while the bulldog's owner tried manfully to drag his furious dog away by its thick studded collar. 'Bad boy, Dave! Leave the Shih Tzu alone. I know the little rat looks like lunch, but it's not yours.'

Murray, struggling to catch Betty, threw over his shoulder, 'She's not lunch. Or a little rat. And she's not a Shih Tzu either. Common mistake. She's mixed breed.'

'Well, whatever she is, pal, you should keep better control over her.'

'Excuse me? You're blaming *my* dog for this?'

The customer threw Murray a dirty look, nodding to his miniscule tee-shirt. 'You work here, don't you? If you're going to keep a dog on the premises, you ought to tie her up. There's a sign at the store entrance… Well-behaved dogs welcome. Which kind of suggests that badly-behaved dogs are not welcome.' He shook his head, dragging his dog away with difficulty, the animal having sunk to his haunches and dug his heels in, still growling at Betty in a blood-curdling way. 'And, by the way, that tee-shirt is far too small for you. It looks disgraceful. A man your age too…' He stopped, frowning at Murray through abruptly narrowed eyes. 'Wait, I know you, don't I?'

'Huh? Erm, I doubt it.' Murray feigned confusion.

'I've got it… You're the mayor, aren't you? I've seen your picture in the paper. And you were at the funfair this last weekend.' The bulldog snarled at him, and the man loosened his grip. 'Hey… What the hell, Dave?'

The bulldog jerked free of his hold and bolted in pursuit of Betty, baying like a hunting hound...

Murray, who had been attempting to coax Betty out from behind Santa's sleigh, sighed as the tiny dog saw her enemy advancing once again and fled her hiding place, yapping hysterically.

'Perhaps you should have picked her up,' Susie said helpfully.

'What did it look like I was trying to do?' Clearly annoyed by her constructive criticism, Murray dashed after his dog, made an ill-advised grab for Betty as she splashed through an ornamental pond, missed her and his footing, and ended up on his hands and knees in the water. 'For God's sake...!'

The bearded man had more luck, grabbing his dog and somehow carrying him away, going very red in the face at the effort, like someone struggling with a large case at an airport. In passing, he threw some caustic remark at Murray which she didn't catch, most probably an insult, and disappeared back inside the store.

As Murray picked himself up out of the water, his clothes dripping wet, his look thunderous, Betty came trotting back towards him. The tiny dog yapped and danced about him, while he glared down at her in silence.

'Oh dear.' Susie bit her lip, trying hard not to laugh, though it really wasn't that funny. Pots had apparently been broken in the store, that customer would never come back, and her peaceful Monday morning had been horribly disrupted. 'Perhaps you're right and we should concentrate on exploring the indoor Christmas experience instead.'

'I'm not bothered by getting my hands dirty,' he protested, flicking wet hair out of his eyes. 'As you can see.'

'The Christmas magic happens indoors as well as out here,' she assured him, feeling guilty. Didn't she have a duty of care towards him or something? Though he was ostensibly *her* boss, so maybe not. And at least this little incident had proved her point that he was too much of a suit for Christmas stuff, that he wasn't a natural at things that happened outside offices and meetings. 'Perhaps you should start preparing our grotto for the kids instead.'

'Grotto?' His eyes had narrowed on her face.

'Santa's visit to the Christmas Tree Shop is very popular in the run-up to Christmas. It's a big job, getting that space organized.'

Still, there was no denying that the mayor did look rather cute with a mud streak on his face, his sodden white tee-shirt sadly transparent and clinging to his broad chest, outlining what were unmistakably erect nipples…

'Anyway, I'd better, um, find you a towel asap,' she mumbled, tearing her gaze away from that impressive male torso. 'And the 3XL tee-shirt too. I have a feeling you're going to need it.'

CHAPTER NINE

Murray was a busy man and still couldn't believe that he'd agreed to take time out from his job and mayoral responsibilities to work in the Christmas Tree Shop. Okay, it was only for a week... But it was day two and he was already ready to quit. Not only had he made a complete fool of himself by falling into a pool and wandering about the place dripping wet, while struggling to control a hysterical dog who had pointblank refused to be leashed, leaping up and down like a flea at his feet instead, but he had overslept that morning and turned up late for work, earning himself a stern look from *his own employee*.

He rolled his eyes, remembering her glance at the wall clock as he hurried in, throwing off his jacket to reveal the 3XL tee-shirt she'd insisted he'd have to wear until the Medium she'd apparently ordered online finally arrived. By which time he would almost certainly have finished his stint at the shop and be back in his mayoral office.

Oh yes, Susie was really enjoying herself, playing his 'boss' that week, enjoying what she no doubt considered his ignorance and buffoonery.

He, on the other hand, was not enjoying himself

one little bit. But he'd never given up on anything in his life, and he had agreed to do this, to be 'educated' about Christmas, so he was going to stay the course, come what may.

The alternative was walking out and instantly prompting another blistering blog post from Susie Lovell, opinionated spinster of this parish...

So here he was.

Working as a Christmas minion at a business he had bought and paid for.

Oh, such rich irony...

Fuming at himself, he tweaked a few sticky tufts of white cottonwool that he'd been carefully glueing to the makeshift grotto at the back of the Christmas shop, adjusting their position. 'It needs to look like snow,' Susie had instructed him, handing over what looked like a year's supply of cottonwool in a large sack. 'That stuff goes on the external walls, and you'll need to apply blue and silver glitter glue to the internal walls, so they sparkle.' She beamed. 'The kids love that.'

'Yes, boss,' he'd said, bowing his head in quiet deference, but she hadn't seemed to notice his mockery, merely nodding and striding away.

Susie Lovell did a great deal of striding, he had observed. She strode here, there, and everywhere, with a quasi-military air. He had to admit though, striding about the place suited Susie's temperament. She was a decisive person, impatient and disinclined to listen. She could never do what he did as mayor, a job which involved many hours talking to people, listening patiently to their comments and complaints, chewing the fat with townsfolk, and often chewing a good steak at the same time, sitting in a posh restaurant with his council colleagues or sometimes the local Member of Parliament.

Indeed, people had suggested he ought to run for parliament himself one day. And maybe he would. Though he wasn't sure how many steaks he could chew through without keeling over from a heart attack. But maybe he could become a vegan MP. Or pretend to be, at least, simply to get out of all the steak dinners that public office seemed to involve consuming. MPs were always telling lies, weren't they? Nobody would bat an eyelid if he reinvented himself as a vegan whenever it came to an official lunch meeting.

He was just dragging stuck-on cottonwool from his fingertips and considering the potential fall-out if he posed as a vegan and then got photographed cramming down a hot-dog when his thoughts were rudely interrupted.

'These are to go in the grotto,' Tom said flatly, dropping a stack of cardboard next to him. His co-worker produced a bag of coloured papers from under his arm and handed that over too. 'Once you've made up the boxes in different sizes, you'll need to cover them with wrapping paper. Stick on some ribbons and bows to finish, and then pile them up around the grotto.'

Murray was baffled. 'What the hell are you talking about?'

'They're meant to be Christmas presents,' Tom explained impatiently.

'You're kidding?'

Tom ignored his astonishment. 'You make the fake parcels, pile them up around the grotto interior, and a few outside too, and then Susie is happy. I had to do it last year. Now it's your turn.'

Murray glared at the young man, who couldn't be much more than twenty, judging by his spots and barely-there stubble. 'Do you know who I am?'

'Yes,' Tom threw back at him, shooting Murray a scathing look. 'You're the man who's making the Christmas presents this year instead of me. Good luck.' And with that, he turned and strode away, doing a damn good impersonation of Susie Lovell herself.

Murray was torn between the urge to run after the lad and beat him to death with his bulging sack of cottonwool, and a strong desire to jump into his car and drive away. He'd managed to find a volunteer who was looking after Betty today, so there would be no fear of being mobbed by an irate dog as soon as he got behind the steering wheel. But he had promised Susie that he would do this, in return for blog silence, and even though in his imagination this job had been all benign smiles and shaking customer's hands, occasionally also carrying a bumper box of Christmas tree baubles out to the car for some little old lady, and it had turned out to be a series of small indignities aimed at crushing his spirit instead, he was determined to see it through nonetheless.

That was what he kept telling himself as he dropped wearily to his knees and began making cardboard boxes. Or rather, flatpack Christmas parcels with absolutely nothing inside. He bared his teeth. 'What more can they do to me?'

Murray was so absorbed in the abject misery of sticking flaps together, he failed to notice the shadow falling across his workspace.

'Problem? Tom told me you weren't happy with the idea of making fake Christmas presents.'

It was Susie.

She stood over him, arms folded, lips pursed tight.

One day the wind would change, he thought savagely, and she'd be stuck like that forever.

'Problem?' he echoed, and gazed round at her, flatpack cardboard cradled lovingly in his arms. Long habit dragged a smile of pretence to his lips. 'No problem. Loving every minute, in fact. And how are you this fine day, Miss Lovell?'

Her lips tightened until they almost disappeared, her eyebrows rose into her hairline, and then she stalked away. Or perhaps strode. It was getting hard to tell the difference between a stalk and a stride when it came to Susie...

'And a very Merry Christmas to you too,' he muttered, and bent back to work. But he was smiling for real now. She had been spoiling for a fight and he'd refused to indulge her.

He'd completed three fake Christmas presents, wrapping them in shiny gold paper with a silver bow each, when his mobile phone buzzed in his back pocket.

He dug it out and frowned at the screen before answering. 'Hi, Gus, what's up?'

Gus was his liaison for the Christmas Market stallholders.

'Hey, Murray, how are you doing?' Guy asked in his cheery way, and then hurried on without waiting for a reply. 'Look, I've got some free time this afternoon and wondered if you could show me round the location for the Christmas Market? I've had stallholders asking about the size and flatness – or otherwise – of the site, and also ease of access. It's not enough to quote from your pitch documents, I really need to walk the site for myself.'

'You want to look at the site today? You're in town?' Murray straightened, surprised. Gus lived near Bristol, several hours' drive away.

'I'm down in Cornwall for a wedding anniversary dinner. Friends of ours from way back. Thought I'd swing by Penrock Downs while I'm here and get a feel for where the market will be held.'

Having agreed to meet Gus on the site within fifteen minutes, Murray rang off, abandoned his fake Christmas parcels and headed for the staffroom. He could walk to the site in three minutes, so didn't need his car keys. But he would need to conceal the embarrassing 3XL work tee-shirt under his jacket. Not that Gus was a stickler for correct mayoral attire, but he might not understand why Murray was wearing something so egregiously outsized it might pass for a dress...

'And where exactly do you think you're going?' Susie demanded, stepping out to block his path.

Brought up short, Murray realised he had completely forgotten where he was and what he was supposed to be doing. 'I won't be long,' he told her. 'I'm meeting a man over at Twelve Tree Acres who's only in town for the afternoon. You don't mind, do you?'

'Actually, I do. I gave you a job and it's not completed yet.'

Murray studied her, trying to gather a few calming thoughts. There was a meditation app he'd been using to try and maintain a level mood. Now, how did that mantra go? Something about yoga and gurus. But he couldn't focus, facing down Susie Lovell's smoking glare…

'You know that I actually own this place, yes? That I'm your boss? That it's not the other way round, for instance?'

A hint of pink coloured her cheeks. 'We agreed that, for this week, I would call the shots.'

He blinked. 'Did we? I don't recall that.'

'In exchange for me not blogging about the Christmas Market?'

'I remember agreeing to work here to avoid you getting irate online, yes… But not to you being my boss. Because *I'm* the boss here. You know that, right?'

He could have sworn he heard her teeth grinding together. But she did an admirable job of not actually baring them at him in a growl. All the same, he was reminded of Betty in one of her less agreeable moods.

'Ye-es,' she agreed reluctantly, folding her arms and glaring at him. 'The thing is, I really need to get Santa's grotto finished by Friday. We have pre-bookings in place.'

'And the grotto will be finished well before then, trust me. Hand on heart, see?' He gave Susie a gracious smile, the one which never failed to melt even the sternest heart. 'But right now, I need to be the mayor again, just for an hour or two. I really need to meet this guy. He lives several hours' drive from Cornwall, and this might be his only chance to get boots on the ground, as it were. To get a proper view of the territory.'

'You're running a Christmas Market,' she pointed out coolly. 'Not invading Afghanistan.'

'Some days I'm not sure about that,' he muttered. Then tried again with his most gracious smile. The one he used on incalcitrant parking wardens. 'Look, why not come with us? You wanted me to see your Christmas store. Now come with me and see what I've envisaged for our town's Christmas Market. I'm sure Gus won't mind you tagging along.' He glanced about the nearly empty shop floor; the place had been devoid of customers most of the day. 'If you can be spared, that is,' he couldn't resist adding, not hiding his mischievous grin in time.

'Yes, it's been quiet today,' she agreed, her eyes flashing. 'But things only really hot up once the grotto's in full swing. Come Friday, you'll see how busy we are.'

He had assumed that she would refuse the invitation. He would never have issued it otherwise. Let his enemy see what he was doing and how, quite literally, the land lay? Not a chance. But since she hated the Christmas Market and everything it stood for, it seemed a safe enough bait to throw out there...

To his surprise, Susie said, 'Okay,' and called Tom over, asking him to mind the store while she was out. 'You're right, anyway,' she went on, following him into the staff room for her own jacket. 'It's not like we're inundated with customers right now. We're not yet into the big Christmas rush when everyone's dropping by to order a tree or buy fresh decorations.' Her grin was positively malevolent. 'We still have a few days before things go crazy around here. Then you'll see what Christmas means to the people of Penrock Downs.'

Murray dug his hands into his pockets and hoped fervently that he would be back behind his desk by the time the big Christmas tree feeding frenzy began.

They walked across the road a short distance until they reached Twelve Tree Acres, where the Christmas Market would be sited, if everything went according to plan. Gus was already waiting for them, parked up by the side of the road. He got out of his sleek company car, waving cheerily enough, but his gaze swung curiously to Susie.

Warily, Murray introduced his tormentor without

going into details about their current boss-employee relationship. He was worried it might goad her into saying something scathing about the Christmas Market, which would put Gus off working on logistics for them.

To his relief, she merely smiled and shook the man's hand, saying politely, 'Very pleased to meet you. Fortunate that you *happened* to be in town today.'

Clearly, Susie didn't believe his story and was fishing. His lip curled, though he said nothing. Did she really think he'd arranged this meet-up just so he could get off work early?

If so, she must've been disappointed when Gus agreed without any hint of subterfuge, 'Yes, two birds with one stone. I'm glad to have been able to make it in person. Though,' he added, turning swiftly back to Murray, 'I'll be coming back to Penrock Downs to oversee everything once the site's open to stallholders. Those who want to set up early, you know? We'll need infrastructure in place by then.' He winked at Susie, who was looking mystified. 'Portaloos and so on. I won't leave the council in the lurch, don't worry.'

'Glad to hear it.' Murray clapped him on the back. 'Want to walk over the site with me?' He hesitated, glancing at Susie. 'I expect you'll have plenty of things you need to do back at the shop. Don't let me hold you up.'

She turned on her own sweetest smile for him, white teeth showing. It was like a lighthouse beacon swinging around. He stared, taken aback and amused at the same time. Was that what *he* looked like when he was trying to be persuasive?

'Oh, I'm sure Tom can hold the fort for half an hour. Don't mind me. I'm happy to see over the site with you both.'

'Well,' Murray began, but she cut him off.

'I do know this field intimately, after all. Every corner, every dip and hollow.' She swung that formidable lighthouse beam towards Gus, no doubt warning him not to crash on her rocks. 'This was my dad's land. I grew up playing here. We kept a miniature Shetland in this field when I was little, in fact.'

'Wow,' Gus said, grinning.

'His name was Mr Fantastic. He looked so cute, but he could be a handful. He used to nip me on the bottom if I turned my back on him.'

'I can understand the urge,' Murray muttered.

She stiffened but didn't respond. 'I know everything about this land,' she told Gus. 'So feel free to ask whatever you like.'

Murray narrowed his eyes on her face, instantly suspicious. He was damn sure she wasn't offering to help because she was suddenly onboard with this idea of a Christmas Market. She just wanted the chance to stick a spoke in his wheel, maybe make Gus think twice about working for the council on this project. He would have to keep an eye on her.

'Thanks. I guess you're the owner of the Christmas tree shop, then?' Gus asked her, nodding towards the buildings on the other side of the road.

'Manager,' Murray corrected him swiftly. He intercepted a flash in Susie's eyes and cleared his throat. 'She's the manager and I'm the owner. I bought the shop and land from her father earlier this year, including these fields.'

Gus frowned. 'I see.' He rubbed his chin. 'Forgive me for being blunt, but won't that be seen as a conflict of interest, the market taking place on land that you own?'

'I've just sold Twelve Tree Acres to the council at a special not-for-profit price. So it's no longer mine. We've consulted lawyers and it's all above board. Plus, I've been granted permission to talk to you on the council's behalf, as our clerk will confirm. We're all very keen to see this Christmas Market happen. Please be assured, there's no conflict of interest.'

'In that case, I'm happy. Please... lead on.'

Without delay, Murray led them across the frosty field, his wellies squelching as he ran through the arrangements they'd put in place so far, talking fast without pausing to prevent Susie from getting a word in edgeways. He saw her mouth open occasionally, as though to interject or protest, and hurried on, speaking loudly.

When they reached the centre of the field, he stopped and described an arc with his arm. 'Stalls will go there, there and there, roughly in a semi-circle around us. The clerk will email you the exact numbers we can accommodate, and the spacing legally required for free flow of customers. We've already accepted a number of applications from stallholders who meet our eligibility criteria. And essential infrastructure – loos and so forth – will be sited near the entrance, and also at the top of the field.'

'Customer parking?' Gus asked, turning on his heel to peer up and down the bare green land as though already imagining the Christmas stalls in place.

'Parking will be on the adjacent land just over there, with a constructed walkway between the two sites. We estimate we'll have space for maybe six hundred cars up there.'

'Six hundred?' Susie looked aghast. 'I had no idea it would be so many.' Her eyes widened. 'God, the ground will be a quagmire by Christmas.'

'Six hundred is only an estimate for peak times. For the Christmas Eve pageant, for instance, when we hope to have festive-themed floats circulating before heading down into the town. But there's room for an overflow area if things get desperate. Plus, we'll have matting down throughout the field to protect the busiest areas from getting too muddy.' He shot Gus an assessing look. 'You're the expert on event management. What do you think?'

'Looks tight for six hundred.' Gus shrugged. 'Sorry. I've already studied the specs your clerk sent over. This field seems to tally with what you told me, the numbers involved. But I think you'll be unlikely to park more than five hundred in that adjacent field. Added to which, you'll need attendants to make sure drivers keep to disciplined rows, or it will only accommodate three hundred at best.'

'We have paid help already sorted for peak times,' Murray reassured him. 'Parking attendants experienced at handling large-scale events.'

'Then perhaps with careful management... Will the parking be free?'

'Free for three hours. We want to encourage people to eat as well as shop. There'll be food stalls and eating areas here in the centre, and a few around the periphery. We anticipate most people will be here primarily for shopping though. Christmas gifts, decorations, lights, everything to do with the festive season. So it'll be street food, purely eat on-the-hoof catering stalls. Christmas themed too, where possible. Toffee apples, stollen, turkey and stuffing paninis.'

'Sounds great.' Gus glanced round at their silent companion. 'What do you think, Miss Lovell?'

Susie hunched her shoulders as she looked around, her hands dug deep into her jacket pocket. She looked a little forlorn. 'I keep remembering how I used to play here as a child,' she murmured, a faraway look her eyes. 'It was so wild and natural back then, birds and bunnies hopping about everywhere. Sometimes I'd see a fox too, and have to run home to tell my mother, because we kept chickens back in those days. Now this monstrosity...' She shook her head, turning to Murray with an accusing look. 'I hate the way everything is so *commercialised* these days. I mean, I want Penrock Downs to thrive as a town as much as anyone else. But do we have to sell people *Christmas* to do it? It's a sacred time, a time of love and giving. It's not just about bloody turkey paninis –'

With a gasp, Susie stopped abruptly and stalked away across the field, heading towards the road and the Christmas Tree Shop opposite.

Gus stared after her. 'Oh dear. Was it something I said?'

'No, don't worry, it's me who's to blame.' Murray's mouth twisted. 'To her, I'm the Anti-Santa.'

'Sorry?'

'I'm like the fox in the henhouse. I came along and bought the business Susie thought would be hers one day.' Watching her cross the road, he shivered in the chill November wind and hunched his shoulders. 'And she's never going to let me forget it.'

CHAPTER TEN

In Susie's dream, she was having an argument with the mayor, and thumping her fist repeatedly on the table to emphasise each point. 'Christmas is not about money,' she was almost shouting in his face, in a not terribly festive manner. 'It's about love. It's about giving and the pleasure of seeing someone's face light up as they open your present. It's about family, everyone gathering to share stories about the past year and have a great time.' And as she spoke, she could see him throwing back his head to laugh at her, mocking every word she said, while her thumping on the table became angrier and more insistent.

'What the hell...?'

Waking with a start, Susie rolled over to flick on the bedside lamp. Someone really was thumping repeatedly, possibly with their fists, but not on a table and not during a conversation with Murray Carew. Someone, in fact, was banging on her front door.

'Hang on,' she yelled, still groggy with sleep. 'I'm coming... Just a minute!'

Confused, she stumbled downstairs in the dark,

belting a fluffy dressing gown over her pyjama top and shorts. Putting on the porch light and flinging open the front door, she was confronted by the sight of her best friend, tears streaming down her cheeks, a tissue in one hand, the other raised to thump on the door once more.

'Tansy? Whatever's the matter?' Susie demanded, stepping back to let her friend come into the house. 'You look awful. And, erm, a bit soggy.' Tansy was looking damp and bedraggled, while her wellies were caked in mud. 'Do you need a change of clothes? Better come in and have a nice hot drink.' Glancing at the clock on the wall, she realised it was barely half past six in the morning. 'Wow... It's earlier than I thought.'

'I'm sorry, I'm so sorry!' Tansy sobbed on her way through to the kitchen. She threw herself onto a chair at the kitchen table and dabbed at red-rimmed eyes. 'But I had nowhere else to go. You see, I've been made homeless!'

Filling the kettle in a befuddled manner, Susie jerked her head round to stare. 'What? What on earth do you mean?'

For the past five years, since the bank had repossessed her flat, her friend had been living in an ancient caravan beside the river, in a peaceful, idyllic site surrounded by bulrushes and shaded by low trees. She'd been camped there for several years, living alone apart from her cats, and racketing about in her hippyish VW van.

The ownership of the land had been in dispute

for years, so nobody had bothered her thus far. Somehow, she had just assumed that Tansy would never be moved on. But perhaps the worst had finally happened.

'Have you been evicted?' she asked, frowning.

'No, it's the river... It rose overnight, and practically the whole field is under water. The caravan is uninhabitable, and my poor VW van isn't much better... I parked it a little way from the river last night, thankfully, but the engine was still flooded and there's no chance of it starting again until it's dried out.'

'Oh no, you poor thing.'

'It's all that rain we had a day or so back. Last night, it was swirling about the caravan steps, and I really thought it would go down overnight. But then it rained again, quite heavily, about three in the morning. Didn't you hear it?'

'Sorry, no.' Susie had gone out like a light the night before after an exhausting few days at work, coping with Murray Carew's brooding presence everywhere she turned and the gnawing realization that her dad's former land would soon be swamped with ugly vans and hotdog stalls and Christmas tradespeople. She fetched cups and rummaged for teabags in the bottom of the caddy. 'It sounds like a nightmare though.' Then she gasped as a realization struck her. 'But what about your cats? Are they safe?'

'Yes, thank goodness. Though they were so wet and frightened, poor little things.' Tansy looked stricken. 'As soon as I realised water was creeping into the caravan itself, I put them up on the top bunk above the driver's cabin and slept there with them myself. But it was so scary. Then the generator cut out, and I had no heat or light. Me and the cats had to cuddle together to stay warm.'

'How awful.'

'I managed to make an emergency call and got rescued about two hours ago. The local cat shelter has taken the cats until I've found somewhere else for them to stay while the caravan dries out, but they were so miserable and stressed... I can't bear to think of them stuck in that shelter, even for a few days. The director quit in the summer, and it's being run by a couple of young volunteers... They mean well but they don't have much experience with rescue animals.'

'At least the cats will be dry there.'

'But not happy.' Tansy blew her nose unhappily. 'You know me, I wouldn't mind sleeping on the streets if I had to. I've done it before. But my darling cats... I need to get them back with me as soon as possible, and that means having somewhere to live.'

'You can't go back into the caravan after a day or two?'

Tansy shook her head. 'It was fully flooded by the time the fire service got to us.' Her face crumpled under a fresh wave of tears. 'They towed it back from the river a hundred feet or so, and most of the water drained out pretty quickly. But everything was soaked with mud and river weed. Upholstery, flooring, the electrics... They say it's not fit for anyone to live in. And it could take weeks to dry out. Maybe months. I rang the insurance company, and they said I might not be covered, because I was stupid enough to park it on a flood plain, so it's all my fault. Oh, what am I going to do?' she wailed.

'Okay, that is a serious problem, you're right.' Susie crouched beside her and patted her hand. 'But not one we can't solve. First off, you can move in here with me.'

'What?' Tansy looked amazed.

'Now Dad's gone, there's a spare room. I was thinking of using it as an office but you're welcome to stay there for as long as you need.'

'Oh Susie, you're a lifesaver!' Tansy leapt up and kissed her on the cheek. 'But what about the cats?' she asked, a little more hesitantly.

Susie bit her lip. She wasn't hugely keen on cats. She was a little allergic to them. But she also knew Tansy wouldn't be able to cope without her feline friends. Though 'fiends' was probably a better description for them, she thought uncomfortably. They were all problematic rescue cats that nobody else had wanted, and some of them were positively feral. At least one wasn't housetrained, by Tansy's own admission.

'Of course you must bring them too,' she agreed, but reluctantly. On top of her allergy, she was suspicious the cats had fleas. But she didn't like to say that in case she offended her friend. 'Although I'd prefer if you could stop them roaming about upstairs. And that angry little tortoiseshell -'

'Timmy.'

'Yes, Timmy. I'm afraid he may need to be kept outside. There's a lean-to by the Christmas tree lot. It's used for logs right now. But you could put a blanket down for him under the sheltered area.'

'Sure, sure... Timmy won't mind roughing it for a while.'

Susie laughed as Tansy did a little jig. 'So that's all sorted then,' she said, relieved to have made her friend so happy. 'I'm assuming you haven't had breakfast yet?'

Tansy shook her head, sitting down again. 'Since my van was also flooded and wouldn't start, I got the nice bloke from the fire service to drop me off here straightaway. I couldn't think of anyone else to turn to.' She gave Susie a huge smile. 'I knew you'd come through!'

Suppressing a sigh, Susie smiled back at her. 'What are friends for? Now, how about I find you some spare togs so you don't have to sit there dripping on the kitchen floor? And then maybe some breakfast?'

'You, Susie Lovell, are a star,' Tansy exclaimed, and began stripping off, right there in the kitchen. 'My thighs have been chafing something rotten in these wet jeans. And the smell! River mud...Ugh!'

Susie carefully averted her eyes. 'Here, take my dressing gown,' she said, unbelting it, 'while I go and find you something dry to wear.' And she hurried away in her PJs.

It was only when she was getting dressed for work

at half past seven that she remembered today was Friday, the last day that Murray Carew would be working at the shop. It was also the first day of the Santa grotto, and they had a full roster of young kids wanting to talk presents with the big guy.

Weirdly, she felt regretful that Murray would no longer be at the store after today. And yet hugely relieved too. Her fault, entirely, for arranging his internship, but he had caused her more than a few headaches this week, at least one per day, and she wasn't sure that her mission to teach him the true meaning of Christmas had even been successful.

It was hard to beat the drum for a non-commercialised festive season when she was in the business of selling Christmas too, as he'd pointed out.

She already had her coat on and was pulling on her work wellies in the hallway, when her phone rang shrilly. Taken aback, since it was still incredibly early, she answered it in a hushed voice. Tansy had already gone up to bed, and she didn't want to disturb her friend. She'd looked so exhausted after her dreadful night, poor thing.

The screen display told her it was Pete calling, who'd played Santa at the shop for the past few years. He made a good Santa, being both portly and silver-haired, and was fun to have around. No doubt he was calling to check what time she needed him in store.

'Hi, Pete, great to hear from you. All set for today?'

'Hi, Susie.' Pete sounded croaky and miserable.

'Bad news, I'm afraid. I've got Covid. Third time for me. I can't believe it.' A noisy bout of coughing followed this horrific news. When he'd recovered, he rasped, 'Obviously, I can't be Santa for you this year. I'm so sorry.'

'How awful for you. Covid's the pits.' One boot on her feet, the other still in her hand, Susie stared at herself in the hall mirror. What on earth was she going to do now? 'I hope you're not feeling too bad. Is there anything I can do to help?'

'I'm no worse than last time, and my wife's looking after me pretty well, thanks. She's bringing me chicken soup, ice cream, the works... But look, my brother might be able to step in for me as Santa.'

Relief flooded her. 'Oh, that's brilliant, thank you!'

'Don't celebrate too soon,' Pete warned her. 'He's already booked up to do a catering course in Truro. But he'll finish out the season for you in a fortnight or so. And we're pretty much the same size, so he can use my outfit, fake beard and all.'

'I'm grateful for that. But I suppose I'll have to get somebody else to cover until then.' She chewed on her lip, frowning over the dilemma. 'Thing is, we've got appointments booked in from this morning. Ten o'clock start through to four-thirty.'

'I'm terribly sorry. I know it's a massive inconvenience, and the last thing I like doing is disappointing the kiddies. But maybe Tom can do it?'

Tom?' She struggled to imagine Tom, who was too shy to speak to most customers, somehow managing to play Santa and talk cheerfully to small children about their Christmas wish-list for six or seven hours a day. 'I'm not sure that would work.' She hesitated. 'But maybe I could do it, instead. I'm sure Dad left a Santa outfit somewhere around the house.'

Pete started to laugh but ended up coughing. 'If you do, please make sure someone take some photos. *You*, dressed as *Santa*? This I must see. Look, I'm really sorry about this. I hope you don't lose business over it.'

'You look after yourself, please, don't worry about us. Text me your brother's number and I'll be in touch with him as soon as I can.' Wishing him a speedy recovery, she rung off.

She was still holding the boot in the air a minute later, staring into space.

Then she dialled another number.

Murray answered, sounding weary. 'Susie? What is it? I'm not due in for another half hour at least.'

'I'm sorry to disturb you,' she began, but he interrupted her.

'Oh God, what is it?' He groaned, breathing heavily as though sitting up with an effort. Had she disturbed him getting out of bed? Or doing his morning exercises, perhaps? She dreaded to imagine what else he might be doing to merit that kind of groan… 'You never usually speak to me nicely, so this must be something bad.'

Stung, she said sharply, 'That's not very –'

'Nice? Well, I'm not at work yet, so this is still my time, and I'm busy. What do you want?'

Susie ground her teeth. 'Forget it.'

'No, you rang me, you woke me up, so you might as well spit it out. What do you want?'

'I woke you up? But you're meant to be in store by eight-thirty.'

'I'm a fast dresser.'

In disbelief, she ogled the phone as though she could see him on the other end. 'Okay, but what about washing? Were you even *planning* to take a shower?'

'Excuse me? Are you once again telling me I smell?' His voice was silky. 'Let me remind you, Miss Lovell, in case you've forgotten, that after tomorrow, the boot will be firmly back on the other foot. You know… Me boss, you employee.'

'Like you Tarzan, me Jane?' The silence that followed this quip made her hastily backtrack. He was, in fact, her boss, and much as she felt he had sold his soul in exchange for a handful of Christmas bonuses, she still loved watching her trees grow and didn't want to be fired. 'Look, sorry to be short with you, but I've got a bit of a disaster on my hands here.'

'Did my shop burn down?'

'No,' she admitted, baring her teeth at the phone in a furious grimace, 'but Santa got stuck up the chimney.' More silence greeted this, so she explained briefly, 'The grotto opens today, only the guy due to play Santa has come down with Covid, and although he's suggested a replacement, we can't get him yet.' She hesitated. 'I don't suppose there's any chance that you might –'

'Not a chance in hell.'

She exhaled, aware of unreasonable frustration at this refusal and trying to suppress it. He was her boss. He was only working in the store as part of his deal with her over that bad publicity. And today was his last day. He certainly hadn't signed up to play Santa.

And maybe she was still feeling a tad guilty over the way she'd been so rude to him and Gus out in Twelve Tree Acres. She had genuinely intended only to watch and listen. Instead, she had flared up like a sulky teenager, blurting out some dogma about Christmas being sacrosanct and here he was, commercialising it... As if she didn't do exactly the same when she sold people tinsel for their trees or carefully handcrafted table decorations made of holly and ivy and silver-painted logs.

She hated feeling like a hypocrite. The key difference between them was one of scale, of course. He wanted to support the town's economy. She just wanted to support herself. But she couldn't deny their positions on Christmas and money-making had more than a little in common.

'Fair enough,' she said reluctantly.

'I don't like Santa.'

This admission threw her. She really shouldn't ask, she told herself. None of her business, she thought firmly. Then asked, 'You don't like Santa? Who doesn't like Santa?'

'Me.'

'But why, exactly?'

There was a short silence, then he muttered, 'That's my business.'

Wow, okay…

'Well, I need to go dig out a Santa outfit,' she announced, trying not to sound snippy, 'since I can't get anyone else to man the grotto today. And the shop's meant to be open in about ten minutes, so if I don't want to be late opening up, I'll have to dash.'

'Me too, very busy,' he sniped back at her. 'Also, I should warn you, since I don't relish being compared to a half-naked tree-dweller in furs, that I may be slightly late myself this morning, due to my apparent need for a long hot shower.'

And with this, he hung up.

She stared at the dead phone in bemusement, not quite following. *A half-naked tree-dweller in…*

'Tarzan!' she exclaimed, and groaned.

Kicking off her one boot and shrugging out of her coat, Susie ran upstairs and began hunting through the landing cupboard, moving pillowcases and tablecloths about, desperate to locate the Santa costume she'd last seen tucked in a corner there.

Finally spotting a gleam of silvery white, she drew out the folded bundle of beard and bright red outfit, shook off a spider, and groaned at the sheer size of the trousers. She would need some serious padding to carry this off…

Yet what other choice did she have?

Tom couldn't do it, and Murray had refused pointblank to help. Which only left her. She couldn't cancel a week's worth of grotto appointments, disappointing all those little children and their parents, just because she was a woman and not even remotely old or fat, though she did have a little more padding about her hips and thighs than in her uni days.

It was nearly Christmas, and Santa's grotto was a time-honoured tradition in the Christmas Tree store at this time of year. Her dad had played Santa at first, and she still remembered how much fun it had been as a kid to see the sparkling grotto surrounded by intriguing parcels and a team of flashing reindeer, and know it was her own dad under that big bushy white beard...

Making even one little kid unhappy by not providing them with the jolly bearded Santa they were looking forward to meeting today was simply out of the question.

CHAPTER ELEVEN

Murray lifted his beard up to his nose to scratch his chin. Bloody hell, the fake hair was itchy. And by rights he shouldn't even be wearing it. But as soon as he'd hung up on Susie that morning, a wave of guilt had assailed him. He was not a sentimental person. He was not easily manipulated. Yet as soon as she'd started going on about disappointed kids turning up at the grotto and finding it empty, no Santa in sight, an image of a small child with tears welling up in their eyes had haunted him, and he had clutched his hair and groaned.

There was nothing for it.

The council kept a Santa outfit in the offices of the clerk, a five-minute diversion off his route on the way to the Christmas Tree Shop.

Without even meaning to, Murray found himself steering towards the town hall, and ran in to collect the damn Santa outfit, pulling it on over his outdoor clothes in the men's toilets, and staring at himself in disbelief before stamping back out to the car.

'What on earth?' the clerk had demanded, getting out of her car, jaw dropping as she took in his jolly red outfit and fake beard. 'Mr Mayor, you... you're... '

'Yes, I'm Santa,' Murray threw back at her, jumping into his vehicle. 'And if I see anyone talking about this on the WhatsApp group, Cynthia, I'll know who told them.'

With that, he backed out of the car park and drove away, leaving the clerk gawping after him.

It was his last day at the Christmas shop, and he ought to have been giddy with joy at the prospect of hanging up his work wellies for good. Instead, he was apprehensive enough about Susie's reaction to his outfit to lurk hesitantly on the threshold of the shop, peering up and down the aisles of tinsel and baubles.

To his relief, there was no sign of her on the shop floor.

Murray checked his watch. He was seriously late due to his little diversion to the town hall, not to mention having stopped to wrestle into his Santa outfit, and it was now gone nine o'clock. He could see Tom through the nursery window, doing something outside with the Christmas trees, probably singing to them or something equally crazy. But there was no evidence that Susie was even on the premises.

Maybe she was still busy on the phone, trying to organise an alternative Santa for this week. Well, he would just have to surprise her, wouldn't he?

Struggling with his large, rubberised paunch, which kept attempting to escape the belt section and slip partially down one leg, he made his way awkwardly to the back of the store where Santa's grotto had been set up, almost entirely by him.

It now boasted a sign that read: NORTH POLE, SANTA'S GROTTO, THIS WAY, alongside a thick black arrow pointing through the low doorway, the sign illuminated by strings of Christmas lights flickering on and off in an annoying way.

Ducking his head to enter the glittering, light-strung interior, he was brought up short by the sight of another Santa, already in situ, bending over a fake parcel as though intending to open it.

'Oi,' Murray exclaimed, sucking in a breath of pure exasperation, 'what do you think you're doing, mate? And how the hell did Susie manage to get a replacement Santa out here so quickly?'

His rival straightened, looking round at him, clearly shocked.

'Unless you're the guy who's got Covid,' Murray went on, frowning, 'and you've come here to spread Christmas cheer and disease to the good people of Penrock Downs? I sincerely hope not, because otherwise I'll be ejecting you before you even get the chance to breathe a single "Ho ho ho" in my direction.'

'Murray?' Santa exclaimed, his voice a little shrill for old St Nicholas.

Bemused, Murray looked his rival up-and-down, and only then noticed that Santa was surprisingly short, with a paunch that bulged in all the wrong places, suggestive of poorly inserted padding. The other Santa's hair, peeking out from under the hat and long straggly white hair, was reminiscent of Susie Lovell's reddish mop, and the eyes were oddly familiar too, being green and narrowed in outrage.

'Susie? Good God... Are you joking? A *woman* can't be Santa.'

At this pronouncement, the other Santa placed his – or rather her – hands on their hips and glared, pursing his – or rather her – lips.

Things were becoming confused, Murray thought, shaking his head.

'Oh really?' The snarky, high-pitched voice definitely belonged to Susie Lovell. 'Is that what you think? And what the hell is going on with your belly, Mr Mayor? It's halfway down your right leg... Or are you just pleased to see me?'

Flustered, he turned away and wrestled his paunch out of his left trouser leg and back up into the mid-section. While he was looking the other way, his nemesis somehow appeared next to him, drawing herself up as though to match his height, though there was no way that would going to happen unless she stood on a box.

'Bit short for Santa, aren't you?'

Clearly determined to be a contender anyway, Susie puffed out her clearly female chest and stood on tiptoe. 'Since Santa spends most of his time sitting down,' she pointed out, 'while children come and go, asking about presents, there's no reason why *a woman* can't play Santa. I just have to say ho ho ho in a deep voice a few times, and ask them what they want for Christmas. Nobody will be any the wiser.'

'Nobody, *what*?' He threw his head back and guffawed. 'Maybe kids under two would be none the wiser. But everyone else will have serious suspicions about you within about ten seconds.' He pointed to her chest. 'For starters, Santa Claus doesn't have *those*.'

'What?' Susie glanced down at her chest, distinctly non-bushy eyebrows drawing together in a frown. 'Does it... I mean, do they stick out, then?'

He couldn't believe she didn't know the answer to that.

'Yes.'

'Oh.' She pressed them tentatively, as though trying to flatten what was clearly a protruding bosom. 'I thought nobody would notice, what with the paunch and all.'

'Trust me, they'll notice.'

'Huh.' Her lips tightened, causing the fake beard to waggle in a disconcerting way. 'Well, honestly, thank you, but you are not needed as a Santa.' Her frown deepened. 'Anyway, you told me straight out that you didn't want to be Santa. You said, *not a chance in hell*...' She imitated his voice, making him sound like he smoked twenty cigarettes a day. Was he really that brusque and gravelly? 'And then you wouldn't explain why. But it was clear that you were not A-star Santa material.'

'Excuse me?'

'I don't want those kids traumatised by finding a reluctant, miserable, disgruntled old Santa in their grotto.'

'*Old?*'

'So you can just rip that Santa suit off and man

the tills while I... I...' She stumbled, seeming lost for words.

'*Woman* the grotto?' he suggested delicately. 'And surely you don't want me to man the tills with nothing on at all?'

She flushed and swore under her breath.

His eyebrows rose.

'Why, Santa, or should I say, *Mrs* Santa? What a dreadfully rude word you just uttered... And in your own grotto too. Whatever would the parents think? I only hope such bad behaviour won't make the papers. Or your blog!'

'Why, you...'

She took another step towards him. They were standing very close and would have been face-to-face if she'd been a little taller. As it was, her unevenly packed paunch thumped into the base of his own massive padding, her thick white beard reaching his chest, his own tickling her forehead. They were like two sumo wrestlers facing off before a bout.

'Go home and change out of that,' she said flatly. 'I'm going to be Santa today.'

'I haven't done my sixth day yet.'

'You can consider your deal fulfilled. You've finished your time here.' She heaved her paunch upwards. 'I won't write about the Christmas Market in my blog, okay?'

'I'm glad to hear that, but I changed my mind on the way over here. I'm Santa now and that's final.'

'But you're only going to confuse everyone,' she

pointed out.

'What?'

'This is your last day, and tomorrow it will be a different Santa in the grotto. Maybe me. Maybe Tom. What if some of the kids today come back another time and discover there's a *different* Santa in the grotto, and then my sick Santa's brother will be standing in for him later, and those kids might come back again, and discover there's a third Santa. And that will be partially *your fault.*' She prodded him in the paunch twice to emphasise his guilt. 'Their belief in Santa is going to be severely tested. There should be one Santa and one Santa only.'

'Well, it can't be a *Mrs* Santa. That's going to confuse them even more. So it has to be me.'

'Forget it.' She thrust her beard against his chest, their punches rubbing hard against each other. 'Over my dead body. Santa's grotto is about faith and trust. Those kids believe one hundred percent in Santa. They trust us adults not to deceive them with fake Santas.'

'Yeah.' He guffawed again, his huge belly shaking against hers, his beard flapping in her face. 'And then they have a good laugh about it when they're nine.'

'See, this is precisely what I was afraid of. You can't be Santa Claus. You're mocking Christmas. You don't even understand the true meaning of the St Nicholas legend.'

'Maybe not, but I understand that Santa isn't meant to be a *woman*.'

'Bigot!' she threw at him.

She looked incensed. It was time to take the temperature down a few degrees. 'Look, the only reason I didn't say yes immediately is because… because…'

'Because what?'

Murray stared down into her eyes, struggling. He wanted to tell her the reason why, but he was unexpectedly unsure of himself. Which was ridiculous. 'I had a bad experience with a Santa in a grotto once. I was five years old and…'

She seemed to hold her breath, holding his gaze too. 'What happened?'

'I don't want to talk about it.'

'Murray…'

'I fell off his knee, all right?'

She glared, releasing that long-held breath like a balloon deflating. 'Is that *all*? You fell off his knee? Good God, I thought you meant –'

'What do you mean, is that *all*? Isn't it enough? I was humiliated in front of my friends and mother. Plus, I broke my clavicle.'

'Isn't that a musical instrument?'

'That's a clavichord,' he told her impatiently. 'I broke my *clavicle*… my collarbone. It was incredibly painful. I had to be taken to hospital. Worse still, the present Santa gave me turned out to be a Barbie doll. In the confusion, he'd given me a girl's present instead of a boy's. All the nurses at the hospital started laughing when I unwrapped it…' With dislike, he gazed about the shiny grotto walls that he himself had smeared with glitter glue. 'I've never been near a Santa grotto since. Until this week.'

Susie met his eyes, looking half suspicious. 'Mayor Carew, are you making this up?'

'I can't believe you would even ask me that.'

'Hmm.' She turned away with a frown, hands still on her hips. She made a cute Mrs Santa, he thought absently, his gaze following her bottom in the tightly belted red trousers. 'But you're over the trauma? You feel up to being Santa now, is that what you're saying?'

'I've told you, I'm up for it. Can't let these kids down.' He couldn't believe he was actually saying that. She must have infected his brain somehow…

'So, when Pete's brother turns up –'

'Tell him no thanks, you've found a replacement for the whole season.'

She stared. '*You?*' She shook her head. 'You can't play Santa for the whole month of December. You've got a Christmas Market to oversee. And a town council to chair.'

'We can job-share. You can be Mrs Santa when I can't make it. And Tom can be a Christmas Elf, if neither of us can make it. The kids will buy that. Where there's a Santa, there has to be a Mrs Santa. And Santa always has an elf or two around the place to help out, right?' Now he really couldn't believe what he was saying. Good grief.

She stroked her tangled white beard. 'I suppose so.'

'This will work, Susie.' He checked his watch. 'But you need to make a decision because it's almost time for the first appointment. We can't have kids spotting two Santas in here arguing. They'll think they're seeing double.'

Susie unbuttoned her huge trousers, fishing around inside them with a distracted expression. 'I'd better whip these clothes off, then, and leave you to it. Don't forget to hand each child a goody bag before they leave.'

'Goody bag?'

She nodded. 'Over there in a pile. Tom spent all last night preparing them, poor lad, while watching telly. He's got callouses, he told me.'

'I doubt those are from the goody bags,' Murray muttered.

'They're in two age ranges, clearly labelled. Pink for girls, blue for boys, and yellow or green for undecideds.' She dragged a lumpy fringed cushion out of her trousers. 'Oh, thank God, that's better... I swear that fringe has given me a rash.'

She yanked up her trousers, which were now in danger of falling down. Murray found himself rather wishing they would.

'Hey, maybe you were an undecided,' she added, 'and that's why Santa gave you a Barbie doll.'

'Be careful, Miss Lovell,' he warned her, wagging a finger. 'Be very, very careful.'

'Yes, Santa,' she said with surprising meekness, and scurried away to remove her clothes.

Murray stood at the doorway to the grotto and watched her slip into the staffroom to change. Had he really just volunteered his services as Santa for the next few weeks?

He must have lost his mind.

'Hello, I'm Jessica. Are you Santa?' A girl of about five or six was hopping impatiently up and down beside the grotto sign, her bored-looking father scrolling on his phone beside her. His first appointment, he guessed.

'Yes, I'm Santa,' he agreed, forcing himself to clutch his large belly and sound suitably festive. 'Ho ho ho.'

'Then who was that?' she demanded, pointing in the direction Susie had taken.

'That was, erm... That was my *Mrs* Santa.'

'But she had a beard.'

'Yes, well, we don't like to talk about that.' Murray took the pre-paid ticket the girl's father was holding out to him. 'So, Jessica, what are you hoping to get for Christmas this year?'

CHAPTER TWELVE

A few days after the double Santa incident, Tansy's cats arrived in three large wire crates, conveyed to the house by a posh young volunteer called Petunia, who parked in front of the house in the large cat sanctuary van. Tansy ran outside to greet her pets, absolutely beside herself and apparently not even aware that she was barefoot on a frosty morning. Forewarned about the cats' impending arrival, Susie had left Tom in charge of the store, knowing that he could always call her in an emergency, and had hurried over to the house to help.

Luckily, the house was only on the other side of the Christmas Tree Shop car park, so it wasn't far to go...

'Oh, my darlings, my poor darlings,' Tansy was chanting, delirious with joy, as she stuck her fingers through the wires to reach her imprisoned cats. In return, the cats made chirruping noises, rubbing themselves against her fingertips. At least, two or three of them did. The other cats seemed as bad-tempered as ever, perhaps more so. 'Yes, I know... But you're back with me now. You'll be safe here, okay?'

Susie smiled, putting her arm about Tansy's shoulders, glad to see her friend so happy again. She'd been miserable these past few days without her precious cats.

'Thanks,' she told Petunia, whose name was emblazoned on a badge pinned to her chest. 'It was very kind of you to bring them over to us. The garage says it could be some time before her VW's drivable again, and Tansy's been going stir-crazy without her wheels.'

'And what about the caravan itself? Is that going to be salvageable?' Petunia frowned, lips pursed, as Tansy struggled to select which crates to carry inside first. 'Because I can't believe all these cats were living with you in *one* caravan.'

Tansy shot her a resentful look. 'There was plenty of room. Besides, two of them were born wild and hate being indoors. I kept a sheltered area outside for them. Only three of the cats ever came into the caravan at night.'

'Besides, you can see how much they love her,' Susie pointed out, feeling protective and aggrieved for her friend. Yes, perhaps it had been a bit of a squeeze at times. But given that two of the cats were almost feral, it was likely they would have been put down without Tansy's intervention. At least with her they'd been given a second chance at life.

Tansy carried two of the three crates into the house and shut the door behind her, so she could let the cats out safely and let them get used to their new territory.

Petunia fiddled with the door of the third crate, housing two of Tansy's most unfriendly cats, who were even now hissing and crouched with their ears flat on their heads, glaring at her and Susie.

'Gosh, these two are pretty nasty, aren't they? Are they the feral cats?' Petunia banged on the crate as though hoping this would shut them up. 'Quiet, you horrid things! They've been hissing and yowling like this all the way from the shelter. I don't know how your friend can bear it. I'm sure that little black one would have my hand off if I was stupid enough to – oh no!'

Somehow, kicking the crate must have loosened the door fastening, because when one of the cats threw himself at the wires, it gave way.

To Susie's horror, the door swung open a tiny crack. Not much, but enough for him to escape. The second cat wriggled after him through the gap while Petunia faffed around them, trying to catch both cats without actually making contact. No doubt she was scared of losing her fingers.

The two cats skedaddled in different directions across the car park, one heading at a pelt for the Christmas Tree Shop entrance, the other slinking behind the dustbin area.

'Tansy!' Susie shouted back towards the house. 'Two of your cats have got loose. We need you now! Like, *right now*!'

A horrified looking Tansy burst out of the house within seconds, staring at her in dismay. 'What? Where are they?' When Petunia pointed towards the dustbins, Tansy dashed that way, and scooped up the world's meanest tabby as though it were a tiny lost kitten. 'Hush now… Where were you going, Caesar? You mustn't run away. Stop hissing, and come and join your friends inside the house.' She squeezed the cat as it tried to escape up her shoulder. 'Don't be silly now. I've got your favourite biscuits!'

'What about the other one?' Susie demanded, swinging round to look for the missing cat. But she couldn't see it anywhere. 'What if he or she gets onto the main road and is run over? That would be too awful.'

'Let me put Caesar safely inside, then I'll come back and help find him.'

Looking embarrassed, Petunia thrust the empty crate back into the van, and then threw a longing glance towards the house. 'Erm, I need the other crates back. I don't suppose you would…'

'Let's find the lost cat first, shall we?' Susie suggested in a not altogether friendly manner. If the volunteer hadn't bashed the cage so hard, those cats would never have got out.

Petunia rolled her eyes. 'Okay.' She began wandering the car park, occasionally crouching to glance under parked cars, calling feebly, 'Here, Kitty Kitty… Here, Kitty Kitty.'

Tansy soon returned to join the search, the three of them scouring the car park in search of the slitty-eyed black cat that had escaped from the crate first. His name, Tansy informed them, was Rocky. 'Because he's a fighter,' she added, her eyes misty with emotion. 'People think he's horrible, but I love him. Poor Rocky... He must be so scared.'

Petunia threw her a scornful look but said nothing. No doubt she was among those who thought Rocky was horrible. And perhaps she had good cause.

Just as they were beginning to give up hope, a bulky figure in a red suit and white beard emerged from the Christmas Tree Shop. In his arms, he held – gingerly, it had to be admitted – a small, black, spitting cat.

'Oh thank goodness, Murray's found him,' Susie muttered.

Murray came towards them, holding the cat out at arms' length. 'You lost this one?' He grinned as Tansy extricated the cat from his hands. 'He was running amok in the shop. I don't think Tom likes cats. I left him having a panic attack. He may need oxygen.'

'Aww, how could anybody not like my Rocky Wocky?' cooed Tansy, cuddling the black cat and stroking behind his flattened ears. He hissed, but not at her specifically, and Susie had the impression he was only letting off steam. 'Let's get you some nice, tasty biscuits, shall we? Who's a good puddy tat, then? Yes, such a good boy.' Tansy was still murmuring sweet nothings in her pet's flattened ears as she carried him back towards the house.

Several cats were already on the windowsill in the hallway, peering out of the window and miaowing.

Well, she couldn't hear them. But their mouths were opening and closing in a comic way. She was glad Tansy had been reunited with her precious cargo. But she wasn't looking forward to her house being invaded by so many felines at once.

'Excuse me.' Petunia hurried after Tansy to collect the cat crates so she could leave.

Susie turned back to Murray. She couldn't believe he'd stooped to catch Rocky for them. Perhaps he wasn't the ogre she'd thought he was.

'Thanks,' she said, smiling shyly. 'That's the last one, thank goodness.'

His brows rose steeply. 'Last one?'

'Of Tansy's cats. She has five.'

'Good grief.'

'Mostly rescue animals. Two of them are old, easily over fifteen, which is fairly ancient by cat standards. Tansy hates the idea of any cat being homeless though, especially cats that are unlikely ever to find a home. Of course, rules on adopting have tightened up in recent years, so she hasn't taken any new ones in for a while now. The cat sanctuary disapproves of caravan life, it seems.'

'Or of five cats in one household, perhaps,' he suggested mildly.

She considered that. 'That too, perhaps.'

He looked strangely alluring in his Santa outfit, a thought she swiftly dismissed as being on the insane side of ridiculous. It had proved impossible to dissuade her boss from playing Santa for the rest of the festive season, but she was still suspicious about his motives. It was hard not to speculate that he was there to keep an eye on her, and indeed Tansy had suggested as much on her first night in the house, when they were enjoying a bottle of fizzy wine together while watching an old romcom movie.

'You're right, he doesn't trust you,' Tansy had slurred, grabbing a handful of salted pretzels and almost knocking her glass over. 'That's why he's offered to play Santa. It's an excuse to hang around the place, see how good you are as a manager.'

'But why would he bother doing that?'

'So he can replace you with one of his cronies, of course!'

Susie had been shocked by this idea, dismissing it as drunken nonsense. But she had to admit it made better sense than any of the other wacky reasons she'd dreamed up for why he was still on the premises most days.

The Santa gig was a job share, so he wasn't there the whole time, of course. She did a stint as Mrs Santa for two hours a day, usually in the afternoon, and all Saturday morning too. She was glad of the help, and he definitely made a more convincing Santa than her. The kids always cheered when he appeared. But it was unsettling to have him permanently about the place.

Besides, she was sure he must have better things to do with his time, especially since he wasn't getting paid. Though it was *his* business, after all. Perhaps Tansy was wrong, and he just saw playing Santa as a necessary part of being the owner.

Stepping in when things went wrong. But she doubted it.

'Cats aside,' Murray murmured now, showing no sign of returning to his post at the grotto. But there had been a few gaps in the schedule that morning, she recalled, so no doubt it was his break time. 'How's your friend settling in?'

'Fine,' she said suspiciously.

'You said her caravan down by the river had been flooded out? There's been chatter about that on the council WhatsApp group. No one's sure who owns that part of the riverbank, so we don't know where to send the bill for the clean-up, or if it might be the council's responsibility anyway.'

'Tansy doesn't know either,' she admitted. 'She's been living there in her caravan for years, and nobody's ever asked her to move on or pay rent. Highly illegal, I suppose. But that's Tansy. She likes to live on the raggedy edge. Besides, people don't mind so much about that sort of thing down here. Loads of people live in vans in Cornwall.'

She worried for her friend though, in case this flood meant she'd never be allowed to park there again. She didn't think Tansy had the means to pay rent, which was why she was living in a battered old caravan in the first place. A loner, Tansy had only ever worked odd jobs, mostly during the summer or the Christmas rush, which left her free to do her own thing but also meant she often struggled to get by.

'I've asked one of the other councillors to look into

it for me. I take it your friend hasn't considered applying for housing benefit and a council property of some kind? It sounds as though she ought to qualify.'

Susie's eyes widened in horror. That was precisely the kind of intervention Tansy hated. 'No, she doesn't like being part of the system. She hates living on handouts too.'

'That's commendable, of course. But as she gets older, she may find it less fun living in a caravan, and may decide to revise her policy.' His gaze was serious. 'Should I offer your friend a job at the Christmas Tree Shop, perhaps?'

Susie blinked. 'That's very generous of you… But no.' She saw his surprise, and added quickly, 'Dad offered her a job several times and Tansy always said no. She's only ever helped us out when someone was sick, and we were absolutely desperate. To be honest, she's not cut out to hold down a nine-to-five.'

'I see.' Murray was frowning. 'In that case, I'll gladly look into the housing situation for her. There must be something the council can do, seeing that she's homeless at the moment.'

'She's not homeless. She's living with me.'

'But that's not a long-term solution,' he pointed out. 'Not with *five* cats, surely?'

Susie folded her arms, feeling mutinous. He was right. She couldn't spend the rest of her days with Tansy and her five cats. But it was hard not to worry about his motives. Murray Carew was the mayor, after all, and everyone in Penrock Downs knew how ambitious he was. He certainly wasn't renowned for his touchy-feely gestures of good will. So what would be in it for him?

'I'll tell her about your concerns,' was all she said.

Far from being taking the hint, he was still looking thoughtful. 'She clearly loves cats. Five is extreme though. Yes, I imagine she would struggle to get a tenancy with all those felines in tow... Even a council tenancy.' He folded his arms too. Was he copying her? 'And most were rescue animals, you say?'

Having finally retrieved her cat crates, Petunia gave them both a relieved wave as she drove away, heading back into town. Her white van had Penrock Downs Cat Sanctuary written in red lettering on the side, along with a charming graphic of a black cat.

'I think several of the cats would have been put down if they couldn't be found homes,' Susie admitted. 'They were feral, basically. So Tansy saved their lives. She's pretty good at saving cats. You could even say it's her talent.'

He was nodding slowly. 'The Penrock Downs Cat Sanctuary is council-run, did you know that? Unfortunately, we lost the director this summer. Well, we didn't *lose* her. She got a better offer and moved on. I think she's running a privately owned animal shelter near Truro now. Better money, more prestige. We can't offer much to a director here in Penrock Downs, unfortunately. But we are keen to keep the place running.' He scratched his chin, and the fake beard bobbed up and down in an alarming way. 'At the moment, we have two volunteers doing everything.' He nodded in the direction of the now-vanished van. 'Like that young woman.'

'Petunia,' she muttered, rolling her eyes.

'Bless you.'

'I didn't sneeze. Petunia... That's her name.'

'Right. But obviously that situation can't continue. We need a paid director to live on site and organize the work of the volunteers.'

Susie shrugged. 'Then advertise.'

'We have advertised. Several times, in fact. The only applicants we had were wholly unsuitable for the job. The money isn't good enough to attract the right people, you see. But there is single accommodation within the cat sanctuary. The building itself was bequeathed to the council for that express purpose about fifteen years ago. Most of the rooms have been converted to cat quarters. But there's a small bedroom with an ensuite. A bit cramped, but if Tansy's used to living in a caravan, that shouldn't be a problem for her.'

Abruptly, she realised what he was suggesting. Her eyes widened in amazement. '*Tansy*? You think *she* should be the new director?'

'Why not? It sounds like a match made in heaven to me. But she'll need to make a proper application to the council. And commit to a five-day, nine-to-five working week at least, which you say may not be appealing to her. But I'd advise her to reconsider that.' He paused. 'We'll have to check her references and her history, of course, and put her through a rigorous interview process. It's not a shoe-in.'

Susie was dumbfounded. 'I'll certainly talk to her about it.'

'I'll email a link to you so she can look at the job description online and fill out the job application if she's interested, listing any previous qualifications and experience. Though it sounds like she's already running a cat sanctuary of her own.' He paused. 'In your front room.'

Susie pulled a face. 'It's not ideal, I know. It's not a big house. But I couldn't bear to see her so unhappy, separated from the cats for days on end.'

He was pulling cat hairs off his red Santa outfit. 'I just hope it doesn't make *you* unhappy, Susie, having to put up with all those cats. There's such a thing as being over-generous, you know.'

'Not when it comes to Tansy,' Susie exclaimed, taken aback. 'We've been friends forever. She's like a sister to me. *Over-generous*?' She shook her head. 'Just because *you* wouldn't take in five cats...'

'True. But I'm not crazy.'

'Wow, you're so rude! Do you ever stop to think before opening your mouth?' His brows rose as she swept on, too furious now to guard her tongue. 'Though I don't know why I'm surprised by your rudeness. Ever since I met you, I've seen first-hand how everything you do is about getting ahead. Pursuing your own ideas and agendas, regardless of what other people think. Even that get-up...'

His brows rose. 'My Santa outfit?'

'At first, I thought you were volunteering to play

Santa to be kind and save the kids from being disappointed. But now it occurs to me that you're only standing in for Pete in order to... to keep an eye on me,' she blurted out, voicing her fears at last. 'Because you don't trust me to manage the shop adequately on my own.'

There. She'd said it out loud.

Murray did not reply but his face had tightened during her tirade.

Having splurged all that accusatory ire, she felt unaccountably guilty, and yet Murray wasn't denying it, was he? He wasn't saying anything, in fact. So maybe she'd hit the nail on the head.

But he was her boss now, she recalled belatedly, her temper faltering as she met his steady gaze. And he'd been so helpful where Tansy was concerned, suggesting ways the council could help her and the cats. So he couldn't be all bad, could he?

'Sorry,' she muttered. 'Now I'm being rude again. That was uncalled for.'

'Forget about it. I'll email you that link for your friend,' he said curtly, turning on his heel. 'I'd better get back to my grotto, or I'll be late pursuing my relentless ambitions as Santa.'

Staring after her boss in dismay, she groaned under her breath. Though it was more of a whimper, really.

For a moment there, talking over Tansy's problems with him and trying to find a solution, she'd felt he was almost becoming a friend. And then she'd grossly insulted him, and after his kind gesture in stepping into the role of Santa too.

She doubted he would ever forgive her for that.

Awesome job, she told herself wretchedly, watching Santa's burly red figure disappear back into the Christmas Tree Shop. She'd make Employee of the Month, for sure.

CHAPTER THIRTEEN

Murray picked up a long, muddy stick and threw it along the riverbank for his dog. 'Go get it, Betty!' he exhorted her, laughing as she chased after the flying object with gusto. 'That's my girl. You stretch your legs. I know you've been bored these past few days, cooped up indoors while I'm out enjoying myself. And I'm sorry about that. It'll be over in another three or so weeks, and then we'll be back to normal.'

He ought to have been pleased by the thought of getting Christmas behind him at last. Oddly though, he wasn't looking forward to the New Year. But no doubt that was because of the Christmas Market looming so large in his mind… They were close to the first shipment of stalls being set up in Twelve Tree Acres.

Betty trotted back towards him with the dirty stick in her mouth. It was almost as long as herself. He bent to take it from her, and she mock-growled, crouching with her paws dug deep as she fought him for the stick.

Eventually, he won it back, and threw it again. The comedy began anew, as Betty charged after her prey, this time barking exuberantly, tail wagging.

His hands in his pockets, Murray walked on a few more paces while Betty rummaged noisily in the undergrowth for the lost stick, and looked down into the river. The muddy surface still swirled brown with leaves and other debris since the recent flood. He had decided to walk beside the river that morning before work, and hadn't really interrogated himself on the reason why. But even as he'd pulled on his Wellington boots and shrugged into a raincoat, he'd been half aware, at the back of his mind, that he intended to walk down to the flooded area and see the damage for himself.

The waters had receded since the flood but left behind a sticky morass of mud. The path that ran beside the river had been laid to tarmac, so that was in pretty good condition. But the fields beyond it still showed signs of flooding, pockets of water glinting among coarse grasses here and there, the earth churned up where a JCB must have moved back-and-forth, and probably a tractor too. He could see deep gouges in the soil where they'd dragged Tansy's old caravan away from the riverbank. It sat now, forlorn, at a good distance from the waterlogged area, external walls greening, windows filthy with mud. It certainly didn't look as though it could ever be habitable again, if it had really been habitable before. He couldn't believe that anyone could live in such an awful old van. It looked as though it had been deserted for years. And he could imagine what it smelt like inside, now the river had done its worst...

People in his district shouldn't be living like this. Not when there were viable alternatives. It made him angry. Not angry with Tansy for having chosen this lifestyle. He was sure it had been forced upon her by circumstances. Or maybe it had seemed like a good idea to her once, and she hadn't noticed how far into squalor she had fallen until the flood came along to expose it.

No, he was angry with himself. For turning a blind eye to the serious housing issues in this area of Cornwall. He was guilty of ignoring the pressures on younger people in particular, but also on older renters, many of whom were unable to afford to buy property hereabouts. House prices were astronomical and beyond their reach. Even rents were too high for most people to manage without difficulty, unless in very well-paid jobs, which were rare in this part of the country.

He ought to have made such problems his priority when he accepted the mayorship of Penrock Downs. Instead, he had bowed to pressure from better-heeled citizens to improve the profile of the town and stretch out the tourist season to include Christmas as a major draw for visitors. Well, his big Christmas Market would answer their demands. But most of the stallholders selling their wares were coming from outside the area. Meanwhile though, what about local people like Tansy? They were still suffering, and what was he doing about that?

Nothing much, that's what.

Betty came tearing back with the stick in her mouth. She dropped it at his feet and panted, clearly triumphant.

'Sorry, Betty, but I can't throw it again. We have to get back.' He turned, whistling her to follow him. When she didn't, he turned to find an accusing expression on her furry little face. 'Okay. You can bring the stick with you, if you must.'

Betty did feel it was necessary. Picking up the stick, she bounded after him enthusiastically, her spoils protruding lengthily on one side, so that it struck every bramble and clump of weeds along the path.

As he reached the car, his phone buzzed, and he glanced down. It was Cynthia, the clerk of the council. 'Hey there,' he said, answering the call. 'I'll be in the office for a couple of hours this afternoon. Unless there's something specific you need now?'

He knew some of the members of the council were irritated that he was spending so much time at the Christmas Tree Shop these days. But some of them had full-time jobs and were only able to attend evening meetings, so he didn't see why it was such a big deal.

As mayor, of course, his responsibilities were rather more full-on than for other councillors. Most days he had to liaise with somebody or other about some 'urgent' issue. He'd lost count of the number of meetings he had attended since becoming mayor. It seemed that everyone wanted the mayor at their meeting, whether his input was relevant or not. But since donning a Santa suit, he had skipped numerous meetings, taking zoom calls in the car instead during his lunch break, or just dealing with issues through the WhatsApp group or via email, usually with a few pithy words. And he'd found that just as effective, frankly. So his fellow councillors could go jump off a cliff. Of which there were many fine examples in Cornwall.

'Actually, there is. You asked if there'd been any new applications yet for the directorship of the Penrock Downs Cat Sanctuary. I checked and there's been nothing new online. Were you expecting an application?'

'I had hoped for one, yes. But that's okay. I'll see if I can discover what the issue is.'

'It's not a very glamorous job, is it? And the money is, quite frankly, a bit dismal.' The clerk hesitated. 'Though it's a live-in job. And it can be hard to find accommodation in Cornwall, so that might make it more attractive. But only to a single person, given the space limitations.'

'I'll have that conversation with them. Look, I think all the stall holders are finalised for the Christmas Market. You don't know of any spaces left, do you?'

'Only the ones we've left reserved for local businesses. Not all of those have taken up the offer.' She paused. 'Including your own Christmas Tree Shop. You own the business now, don't you? You haven't sold it on yet?'

He came to a standstill, and Betty bumped into him, dropping her stick and glaring up at him, accusation back in her eyes.

'Yes, I still own the business. I don't have any immediate intention of selling.'

'I'm sorry. You gave me the impression it was just a temporary investment when you first mentioned it.'

'Did I?' Murray was confused, thinking back to before he'd met Susie Lovell. Perhaps he had intended it as a temporary investment on acquiring the business from her father. Buy the business, sell the adjacent land to the council for the Christmas Market site, and then resell as soon as he could get it off his hands for a reasonable profit. After all, what did he want with a Christmas tree nursery? He didn't even like Christmas that much. Had he forgotten that? It seemed he had, in all the chaos of playing Santa and 'ho-ho-ho-ing' around the store so none of the kids felt left out.

'Maybe I misunderstood,' the clerk said dismissively. 'By the way, you haven't forgotten the party, have you?'

Party?

He had forgotten, obviously. 'Remind me.'

'You'd forget your head if it wasn't glued on.'

'My head isn't...' He stopped, adding in a mutter, 'The beard's glued on though.'

'Beard?'

'Never mind, go on.'

'Okay, the party's not until next weekend, so no need to panic. Friday night, seven pm sharp. It's a celebration for the key sponsors and partners of the Christmas Market. Smart casual but with an emphasis on the smart.' Cynthia paused. 'You're meant to be giving a speech though.'

'Brilliant.' He ran a hand over his eyes, wincing. He had obliterated the entire event from his memory. 'Thanks for the nudge. It's at the Cherry Orchard, isn't it?'

The Cherry Orchard was one of the more exclusive hotels in Penrock Downs, where the council usually rented a large upstairs room for events that required top-notch outside catering, especially booze.

'That's right. Most of the councillors are going, and I'll be there too, mainly to greet guests. Could I have the name of your plus-one, while I'm making a list of everyone who has RSVP'd?'

'Is RSVP'd a real verb?'

'Probably not. But we still use it.'

He'd raised his arm to throw the stick for Betty one last time before they got into the car, but a sudden thought stopped him in his tracks. Betty barked at this unnecessary delay, jumping up and down in impatience, while Murray stared blankly at nothing. 'Wait... *Plus-one*?' he repeated slowly. Betty pawed at his leg, leaving a muddy mark on his jeans. 'All right, all right,' he muttered, and threw the stick.

Betty charged after it like an animal possessed, ears flying.

'That's right. Everyone was given the option of bringing a party guest. I presume you'll be coming on your own, then?' The clerk's voice was coy. 'As usual.'

He bridled at 'as usual' and glared at the swollen river flowing so rapidly beside him, as though it had personally affronted him in some way. 'Erm, let me get back to you on that. I'll give you a name by the end of the day.'

Ending the call, he scooped up Betty, who'd just retrieved her stick, and bundled the dog into his car, grimacing at her infuriated, high-pitched yaps in his ear.

So he needed a plus-one for the party next weekend. Or he'd end up looking either like he was on the prowl or, worse, so unattractive that he couldn't manage to persuade any woman to tag along with him to this party. Most of the other councillors had wives or husbands and would be bringing them. The clerk would no doubt be bringing her boyfriend. Meanwhile, the Mayor himself...

'I need a date, Betty,' he told the dog as she settled on the passenger seat, panting and smearing the upholstery with her muddy paws. 'I don't suppose you'd fit in a cocktail dress, by any chance?'

Betty sneezed violently.

'I'll take that as a no.' Murray started the car, glancing grimly at himself in the rear-view mirror. Somehow, he'd got mud on his face. Typical. 'Which leaves only one possibility.'

That morning, every time Murray poked his head out of the grotto to check how the Santa queue was doing, he would catch Susie stalking about the place with a stormy expression, and hurriedly retreat.

The mere sight of her filled him with dread. Was he really thinking of asking one of his own employees to be his plus-one?

It would be a mistake, he told himself firmly. She could only be considered as a last resort, and he was hardly there already. He must know at least a dozen other women he could ask first. Several dozen, perhaps, if he included all his wider female acquaintance in Penrock Downs. Though most of those were considerably older than him, not to mention married with kids, and probably only aware of him as Mr Mayor.

He forced himself to look at the situation logically. All right, so perhaps his pool of potential plus-ones was narrower than he'd thought when talking to Cynthia. But that didn't mean he would have no choice but to ask Susie Lovell.

Infuriatingly, every name he came up with presented a different problem. Too chatty; not chatty enough; a bit on the flaky side; hadn't forgiven him for some minor slight years ago; terrified him whenever she opened her mouth; steals food off his plate during dinner… No, actually, he'd already ruled out Betty as a potential plus-one.

It was a shock to his system to realise that, amongst his acquaintance and even his closest circle of friends, there was nobody he could reasonably ask to a party.

Except Susie Lovell.

Which was a non-starter, because she thought of him as a lightweight in a suit, a cold-hearted executive whose sole purpose in life was to turn a quick buck. Despite playing Santa for the kids, he'd been unable to shake her unfavourable impression of him as a man. And how did he know that? Because of the way she still looked at him as though he were a parasitic bug she'd just found on her favourite Nordic fir…

'Excuse me, Mister Santa,' the little boy standing before him said in an aggrieved tone, 'you asked me what I wanted for Christmas, and I told you, and you haven't said a word since.' He tipped his head to one side, eyeing Murray speculatively. He looked at least seven or eight years old, which was on the mature side for visiting a Christmas grotto. Hadn't he realised yet that Santa didn't exist? Though some kids came to that stark realisation later than others, he guessed. 'Are you like my dad? He never listens to me either. Or to my mum.'

'Steven, don't be rude to Santa or you won't get *anything* for Christmas,' his mother hissed, turning to Murray with an apologetic smile. 'Sorry.'

'No, my bad.' He gave the kid an appreciative smile. 'You know that moment in class where you drift off and realise you haven't heard a word the teacher's said for at least five minutes?'

'Yes,' the boy admitted.

'That just happened to me. But I'm back in the moment now. What did you want for Christmas, then? Go on, Steven… I promise I'll listen this time.'

'New bike.'

'Got it.' He caught a panicked look on the mother's face, along with a slight shake of the head, and added in a cautious way, 'But, erm, that might be hard to fit down a chimney.'

'We don't have any chimneys.'

'There you go, then. Maybe something smaller?'

Steven looked annoyed but thought for a moment. 'Okay, maybe a new computer?'

Again, the mother's eyes widened. Behind the boy's back she mimed what seemed to be riding a horse.

'Sorry, that's also a bit on the large side. I don't have room on the sleigh for sizeable items. I've got a lot of houses to get round in one night, you know. How about riding lessons?'

The mother's head shook frantically from side to side. More energetic miming. Jigging her hands up and down.

'Or... a skipping rope?'

Steven stared at him, aghast. 'A skipping rope? What kind of present is that?'

'Yeah, you're right, that's not it. Gardening gear then, maybe? Digging? *A spade*?' He was desperately trying to interpret the woman's wild arm gestures. 'One of those big hand-held electric sanders?'

'Let go!' the woman seemed to be mouthing at him, eyes almost bursting out of her skull. 'Let go!'

'You need to... let go,' Murray mumbled, feeling like he was going mad. What on earth was the woman talking about? 'Therapy sessions, perhaps?

Or rock-climbing...' He sat bolt-upright, sure he understood at last. 'I've got it... Outdoor activities like rock-climbing to help you combat anxiety. Sounds like the perfect gift for a kid your age.' He shook the boy's hand while the kid stared at him, open-mouthed, and then handed him a blue goody bag. 'Merry Christmas!'

'Building bricks,' a voice said from the door. 'That's what he'd like for Christmas. A building brick kit.'

'Yes, oh yes!' the mother gasped, turning to smile at Susie with pathetic gratitude. 'Steven loves making things with building bricks. Thank you.'

'I'd prefer a new bike,' Steven grumbled as he was bundled away by his mother.

Alone with Murray in the grotto, Susie shook her head in disbelief. 'Just as well I arrived when I did. That poor woman...'

'I had no idea what she was trying to say.'

'Clearly.' She began tidying up the goody bags. 'Was that your last one for today?'

'That's right.' He was going into the office that afternoon, he realised with relief, so could finally get out of his itchy Santa outfit. But he still hadn't popped the question. So to speak. 'Erm, look, I wanted to ask you something – '

'About Tansy?' Susie turned to him, looking guilty. 'I've been trying to persuade her to fill out that online application form, but she's not great with written stuff.'

'It's not written if it's online,' he pointed out.

'Tansy's not great with typing either.'

'Well, she only has to be good with cats, I suppose. Though there will be some form-filling required at the sanctuary. And red tape. She'll have to follow standard procedures and regulations, and also vet prospective cat owners.'

Susie nodded, chewing on her lip. 'I think that's what she's most anxious about. In case she gets it wrong and sends a vulnerable cat home with someone who'll be mean to him or her.' She pulled a face. 'It's a big responsibility.'

'I get that, yes. But we do offer a training course. The last director took it, I believe. It's a few days away in Truro, plus some online sessions to make sure her Human Resources and book-keeping skills are up to date.'

'That all sounds brilliant.' Susie looked relieved.

'I don't make the decision of who gets the job,' he pointed out frankly, 'that's not part of my role. And it would be a conflict of interest for me to recommend her to the hiring committee, given that you're my employee and she's your friend. But it's worth her applying, at least.' He pulled off his beard and rubbed his itchy chin with a sigh of relief. 'Tansy definitely has the empathy and cat know-how we need. If her CV shows no problems and she's open to the idea of training, she ought to be a strong candidate.'

'I'll let her know.' Susie pulled a face. 'I love having her and the cats living with me, don't get me wrong. But it can feel a bit crowded sometimes.'

He nodded, then heard himself saying, 'Look, if you fancy a break from all the incessant miaowing, there's a big council party at the Cherry Orchard coming up.' Stop, you fool, he told himself. But it seemed his mouth had different ideas to his brain. 'Would you like to go?'

She stared, clearly taken aback. 'Excuse me?'

'Well, it makes logical sense for us to go together,' he lied. 'It's a party to celebrate the launch of the Christmas Market, and you *are* involved with that, since the market's taking place on your land. *My* land, I mean. That is, what used to be your land.' He blinked, aware of her open mouth and amazed gaze, and hoped he didn't sound as though he'd lost his mind. Though he presumably had, otherwise he wouldn't be asking this infuriating woman to accompany him to a party. He would probably rather do anything else than be in her company for several hours at a boozy event, such as volunteer to have a hole drilled in his brain, for example, which might not be such a bad idea right now. 'Or rather, your dad's land. Before he, erm, sold it to me. And I then sold it on to the council.'

He was babbling. Actual babble was coming out of his mouth...

'Okay,' she agreed, and whisked herself out of the grotto.

Shocked, he was left gazing at a patch of glitter glue on the wall, exactly where her face had been, and wondering what had just happened.

Well, you asked her to a party, and she said yes, he explained to himself.

Murray sat down heavily on a fake parcel, and

collapsed to the floor as the gold-wrapped empty cardboard box crumpled under his weight.

For a moment, he lay unmoving on the floor of the grotto, clutching his itchy white beard and staring up into the eerily flashing eyes of a plastic reindeer.

He'd started the day in a fairly sensible way. Now he was apparently taking Susie Lovell, of all people, to a party where his fellow councillors and townsfolk would gawp at his plus-one and wrongly assume that they were romantically connected.

What in the name of all that was holy had he just gone and done?

CHAPTER FOURTEEN

'Ugh, I must have maggots in my brain,' Susie muttered, stirring milk into her coffee mug and gazing down into the brown swirling liquid.

Tansy, making herself buttered toast on the other side of the kitchen, looked up, horrified. 'Maggots? Eww. Do you think you should see a doctor?'

'I just mean… I did something really stupid today.'

'Like putting maggots in your ear?'

'Murray asked me to a party. And I said yes.'

Tansy froze, buttered toast halfway to her mouth. 'You did *what*?' she gasped.

'I can't believe it either,' she agreed unhappily. 'But I didn't know what else to say. The mayor totally put me on the spot. He just asked me straight out and I said… Well, I said *yes*! Then I ran away.'

'But you hate him.'

Susie picked up her coffee, considering that. 'I don't *hate* him, exactly. I think he's a clown. And probably a huge raving egotist. I mean, you have to be an egotist to put yourself forward for mayor, surely?'

'Maybe,' Tansy agreed slowly, then took a bite of her toast and continued, apparently oblivious to the fact that her words were now being drowned out by crunching. 'But Murray's not... He did suggest that I apply for that job at the... And he's really quite... Not to mention... So maybe... And even...'

'For goodness' sake, Tansy, finish your toast and then say what you want to say. Don't try to eat and talk at the same time. It's never going to work.'

Tansy, looking embarrassed, swallowed with a gulp. 'Sorry.' She picked up her plate of toast and followed Susie into the living room, throwing herself onto the sofa, only to be mobbed by miaowing cats who wanted to know if her toast was edible and, more importantly, a treat for them. 'No, naughty pussies... You can't eat toast. It's bad for you. But it's good for me.' She crammed more into her mouth, as though teaching by example. 'Mmm, so tasty... Yum yum yum,' she said between chews. 'But only for humans. Not for cats. And it's not your feeding time for another forty-five minutes. So stop bugging me and go hunt mice.'

Susie sat in the comfy armchair opposite, the one her mum had loved, and pulled her bare feet up under her. She sipped at her coffee, not as soothed as usual by its creamy taste. Though drinking coffee in the early evening wasn't such a great idea. Not if she hoped to sleep today. And lying awake for hours thinking about Murray and this stupid party was not her idea of fun...

'I can't go through with it. I mean, it's impossible, isn't it?' She looked at Tansy, who shrugged in response but might just have been shifting in her seat. 'I'll tell him no tomorrow. I'll say that I've changed my mind. Or maybe that I'd forgotten a prior engagement.' Susie chewed on her lip. 'Do you think he'll believe me?'

Tansy shook her head, still chewing.

'You think he'll be offended?'

Her friend nodded and chewed, making a 'nom nom nom' noise.

'It's some dreary council party, anyway.' Susie was justifying the rejection already, rehearsing how she'd deliver it. Would it be rude to just text him a no, thank you? Or would she have to speak to him face-to-face? She wasn't sure she could lie to him in person. He was too good at seeing through her. 'It will be deadly boring. Murray probably felt forced to ask me out of sheer politeness. I can't believe he really wants me to go with him. I've made him play Santa for weeks, for pity's sake. He must be fuming, not to mention bored out of his skull. In fact, he'll probably be grateful to me for saying no. Then he'll be able to ask someone more...' She hesitated, not sure what she meant but hunting for the right word.

'Attractive?'

'I was going to say, *interesting*,' Susie replied with a snap.

Tansy pulled a face. 'Sorry,' she said again. 'For what it's worth, I think you're both attractive *and* interesting.'

'Thank you.'

'No problem. In fact, if you were a lesbian, I'd snap you up at once.' Tansy gave her a thumbs-up gesture. 'No hesitation.'

'Eat your toast.'

Ruefully, Tansy crammed the last of her buttered toast into her mouth. As she was swallowing, a cat leapt up onto the sofa and put a paw on her arm.

'Naughty Rocky... None for you, I told you.' Tansy petted the cat, who seemed to accept this sad lack of entitlement and settled down beside her, purring contentedly. Her friend looked at her pointedly. 'So, tell him no. Seems simple enough to me if you genuinely don't want to go.'

Susie said nothing.

Tansy's gaze narrowed on her face. 'You don't want to go, do you?'

'Probably not.'

Tansy's eyes flew wide open. 'I knew it!' she exclaimed, almost accusingly. Her finger jabbed in Susie's direction. The cat, no doubt alarmed by this sudden change of mood, sat up and started self-grooming in an aggressive manner. 'I knew you fancied him. All this nonsense about how annoying Murray is, and how much you can't stand Murray, and how Murray is only there to keep an eye on you,' she went on, imitating Susie's voice, rather unfairly making her sound deranged. 'I knew it was just a ruse.'

'A ruse?' Susie glared at her over the steaming rim of her coffee mug. 'You were the one who said he was only playing Santa to keep an eye on me and the shop. That was your suggestion, not mine.'

Tansy blinked. 'Was it?'

'Yes.' Susie put her coffee mug down on the table. She was feeling distinctly off-balance. 'Anyway, yes, I do regret saying yes to this event with the mayor. But the thing is, it might be good for the shop. There will be local dignitaries and maybe celebrities there.'

'Celebrities?' Tansy looked dubious.

'Oh, you know... That TV chef who does the thing with stuffed quail and has a restaurant just off the A39. And that woman who used to be a big pop singer in the Eighties. She lives down the road at Bolner's Corner. They're always dragging her out for charity events.'

'Erm, not sure who you mean, but OK.'

'The point is, being seen with him at this party might raise the profile of the shop. And we could do with more customers. Especially with this big Christmas Market about to open and steal away my custom. We're almost at crunch time for pre-orders. I need all the sales of Christmas trees that I can get, frankly.'

'But you're not the one making a profit anymore,' Tansy pointed out. 'You get paid a salary now. To manage the shop and grow the trees. So you'll get paid the same whether or not those trees sell. *Murray*'s the one who'll get any profit from big sales.'

Susie couldn't deny that. But the principle was the same. 'Okay, you got me there. However, Murray the Meanie might close the whole business down and *sack me* if we don't make a large enough quota on trees this season. I mean, why would he keep the place running if it's not profitable?'

'I like Murray the Meanie.' Tansy grinned her appreciation, but her expression sobered when Susie didn't smile back. 'You think he bought your dad out just to shut it down?'

'I think he acts on impulse, frankly. He bought the shop to get his hands on the land at Twelve Trees. But now that's been sold to the council, he doesn't need the Christmas Tree Shop anymore. And if he liquidates the business, all the baby trees that are growing now will never be sold. He'll cut them all down. It'll be a m-m-massacre.' Tears glistened in her eyes as she thought of all her cute baby trees being cut down. Destroyed before they had even had a chance to fulfil their destiny. It was too horrible to contemplate. 'I have to make sure the shop is a success this Christmas, don't you see? Those trees' very existence could depend on how I perform as a manager. So don't tell me it's not important that I go to this party with the horrid man. I'm not going to be responsible for their m-murder.'

'Hmm. Is murder the right word, would you say?'

'*Absolutely.*'

Tansy grimaced and jumped off the sofa, followed by the cat as she headed into the kitchen. 'I'm making myself a coffee too. Want a top up?'

'No, thanks.'

Susie sat brooding, then jolted upright as Tansy shrieked and came running back into the room like a maniac. 'What is it? Is there a fire?' she demanded urgently. It was dark outside, the shop was closed for the evening, and she'd just been contemplating what they ought to eat for tea. Though she'd been too busy to shop recently, so the pickings would be decidedly slim. 'Oh, please tell me it's not a fire.'

'What? No, it's not a fire. I had an idea, that's all.'

Susie sat down again, having leapt to her feet in anticipation of an emergency. Her heart was thumping. 'Good God, Tansy... Okay. What's this idea, then?'

'You're feeling down. I'm feeling down. There's beggar all in the house to eat.'

'So?'

'So let's go out.'

Susie frowned at her, uncomprehending. 'For a takeaway, you mean?'

'Erm... I was thinking more a couple of hours in the pub, actually. Or a wine bar, if you're feeling posh. Maybe followed by a cheeky kebab from Mehdi's van.'

Susie had to admit that sounded good. 'We can't drive though. Not if we're drinking.'

'But if we hurry, we can catch the last bus into town.' Tansy checked the clock on the wall. 'Come on, no time to lose. You get something sparkly on, I'll wear my smart jacket, and we'll make a night of it. Then we'll get a taxi back. I'll pay my share once my benefit comes in, how's that?'

'No, it'll be my treat. I'm the one who's working. You're the one who's homeless at the moment.'

Feeling more cheerful, Susie grabbed her bag and ran upstairs to change her slightly premature Christmas jumper for something less homely.

Tansy was right. What she needed was a night out with a girlfriend. And getting squiffy and devouring a kebab on the way home was exactly what was needed to change her perspective on this nightmarish party with the mayor.

Three hours and six shots of vodka later, as the landlord was ringing the bell for last orders, Susie was beginning to think it had not been such a great idea to go out drinking on a weekday night. There was no way she'd be able to unlock the Christmas Tree Shop before eight o'clock in the morning as usual. But at least the store didn't open officially until half past, so there was some leeway there. Though if she overslept...

She was distinctly unsteady as she grabbed Tansy's arm and shook it, trying to get her friend's attention. 'We need to go,' she slurred in her ear.

'Hush, not now,' Tansy replied impatiently, who'd spent the past forty minutes arguing the finer points of cat care with the butcher's son, William, a sturdy twenty-something with an already receding hairline. She returned to their argument with gusto. 'No, absolutely not. You need to groom them *daily* if they're long-haired. Otherwise, you'll have them coughing up furballs left, right and centre. And don't let's even talk about fur matting issues.' She shook her head. 'Don't you know *anything* about cats?'

'Tansy, I... I'm not feeling great,' Susie admitted, leaning her head against the wall. 'The room is spinning.' Her mouth was dry too. How could it be so dry when she'd been drinking for hours? 'It's going round and round and round, like I'm a goldfish in a bowl... Except the bowl is going round while I'm just sitting here, flapping my gills.' She closed her eyes with a groan.

She didn't think much time had passed while she was saying that. Yet, by the time she reopened her eyes, the butcher's son had disappeared and Tansy was standing in front of her, jacket on, dragging her up with an effort.

'Time to go, Susie. On your feet! That's it. We should be able to grab a taxi from outside the convenience store. There's usually one waiting at the rank this time of night. Hang onto my arm, we'll walk together.'

Only there wasn't a taxi outside the convenience store. The rank was empty. The streets were empty. There were some people walking past them, laughing happily, probably drunkenly, but they didn't seem to be headed towards a vehicle.

'Perhaps we can catch the bus,' Susie suggested, staring up at the streetlight above them. It was so pretty with its alluring misty halo. Was it raining?

'There aren't any buses at this time of night. This is Cornwall in winter, remember? Past six o'clock, all the buses turn into pumpkins.'

'We could catch a pumpkin, then. If it had wheels

and a driver.'

Tansy gave a cackle of laughter. 'You are so, so, so drunk.'

'What? I am not drunk. You take that back. I'm tired, that's all...It's been a long week. A really, *really* long week. This isn't drunkenness, this is *exhaustion*.' Susie weaved away from her friend and promptly collided with a large black litter bin. 'Ow!'

'Careful.'

'I'm all right.' Susie glared down at the bin accusingly. 'Who put that there, anyway? The council, I bet.' Unsteadily, she leant on the bin, ignoring the smell. 'Murray Carew, that's who. Hey, that rhymes. *Murray Carew... That's who.*' Snorting with laughter, she turned to see Tansy wrestling a mobile phone out of her jacket pocket. 'Hey, who are you calling? Hold on, I didn't think you had a phone. Wasn't it ruined in the flood?'

'This is *your* phone,' Tansy explained patiently. 'You gave it to me earlier to look after, remember?'

'No.' Susie's eyes narrowed on her. 'Okay, so who am *I* calling?' She was making an effort to sound less tipsy and to enunciate her words clearly.

'Never you mind. Just stand there and stop colliding with bins.' Tansy arranged her against the wall like a piece of luggage. 'Now, don't move.' She turned away, muttering into the phone, 'Hello? Yes, it's Tansy. I said, it's Tansy. Tansy. Can you hear me? I said it's Tansy.' With an exclamation of irritation, she half-yelled, 'TANSY,' into the phone, then smiled. 'Yes, Susie's friend. Look, I don't suppose you're sober and have a car to hand, by any chance? Because Suze and I... We're stuck in town without a ride home, and it's starting to rain.'

Susie frowned, bemused. 'Who the hell are you talking to?'

'Hang on a min,' Tansy told her brusquely, then gave a cackle of laughter, hopping on and off the kerb like a six-year-old, the phone still clamped to her ear. 'Sorry? You're in your *what*? In your *pyjamas*? That's hilarious. No, come as you are. We won't stare, promise.'

'Tansy, who *is* that?'

Ignoring her, Tansy laughed again. 'Oh yeah, Susie's as drunk as a skunk. I dunno... She said she was drowning her sorrows or something. Okay, thanks, we'll wait by the bus stop.' Then she rang off.

Susie complained as she was bundled downhill towards the empty bus stop. 'What's going on? You said there aren't any buses at this time of night.'

'No, but there's the mayor's taxi.'

'The... *what*?'

'That was Murray on the phone. He's on his way to pick us up.'

Susie stared at her, horrified. 'No.' She groaned and hiccupped at the same time, which hurt. 'Oh no, no, no, no, no...'

'Are you going to throw up?' Tansy asked sympathetically, helping her to sit down on the sloping bus shelter seat.

'You shouldn't have called him,' Susie whispered. 'Not Murray the Meanie.'

'He was at the top of your text messages. I just hit Call.'

'We have to text each other about... Santa.'

'Aww, that's sweet. Did you tell him what you want for Christmas yet?'

'Now you're being ridiculous,' Susie told her with careful dignity before almost sliding off the seat. As she straightened up with Tansy's help, she wondered why bus seats seemed deliberately designed to be uncomfortable. Then realised the reason in the same instant. 'Rough sleepers!' she exclaimed.

'What about them?'

'Hostile architecture. These seats...' Since Tansy was merely staring at her in bemusement, Susie lapsed into silence again, thinking of Murray driving out at dead of night to fetch them. It was too horribly embarrassing for words. It was also very, very odd. 'Hang on, did you say... *pyjamas*?'

'I know, I pray he doesn't get dressed first.' Tansy chortled. 'I am literally gagging to see the mayor in his PJs.'

'Bet they're stripey.'

'No... covered in teddy bears.'

'Yes!' Susie grinned inanely at the thought. 'Teddy bears. In softest velour.'

'With matching slippers.'

They collapsed laughing, clutching each other in hysterics, their breath steaming out in clouds on the frosty air.

Susie began to slide slowly off the bus shelter seat

again... 'You can't *literally* be gagging though,' she thought out loud. 'Because that would mean –'

'Here he is!' Tansy dragged her to her feet again, waving frantically at the approaching headlights. 'Wow, that was quick. Do you think he waits by the phone just on the off-chance that damsels in distress are going to call him out in the middle of the night?'

'Yes, I do.'

The SUV stopped beside them, and the passenger side window rolled down smoothly. Behind the wheel she could see Murray. Were those really pyjamas under his raincoat? She swayed and peered, trying not to appear completely drunk.

'Need any help?' he asked in a deep, authoritative voice as Tansy bundled her haphazardly into the back seat.

'Nah, we're good.' Tansy slammed the door on her and jumped into the front beside him. 'Home, James.'

Without comment, Murray turned the car and was soon heading out of town towards the Christmas Tree Shop and Susie's cosy little home. Accompanied by an eerie binging noise. 'Seatbelt warning,' he said. 'That's you, Susie.'

Swearing under her breath, Susie dragged on her seatbelt and the binging noise stopped. She tried to sober up, but was already thinking longingly of her bed, her head banging unpleasantly. Why on earth had she knocked back so many vodkas? What an idiot she was. She rarely even drank these days, there was too much responsibility involved in managing the shop. But it was all down to the stress she'd been through lately. And then agreeing to accompany him to a party?

She bet he was regretting having asked her. Murray must think her a total lush, the kind of person who gets sloshed at a work do, slags off the boss to their face and then falls over in the car park. Oh well, too late now...

Arriving safely back at the house, Susie struggled out of the warm interior of the SUV and stopped dead, staring up into the black, starry sky with a sense of awe.

It was only a little way out of town here, yet so quiet she could have heard a pin drop. The distant echo of the sea came to her between each heartbeat. The ground was hard with frost and her breath steamed visibly. Maybe she was still tipsy, but it seemed like a magical world...

She shivered in the chill of winter, glancing at the Christmas Tree Shop on the other side of the small car park. Its large front windows were lit up with Christmas lights that glinted off red and gold tinsel looped around the frames, with fake snowflakes sprayed onto the glass. A more than life-size illuminated Santa Claus was scaling the side of the building, a bulging sack of presents on his back, with a sleigh and a cluster of flashing reindeer waiting beneath him.

Her heart filled with joy and wonder as she studied the bright lights of the shop displays, and her eyes brimmed with tears. Soon it would be Christmas, her favourite time of year, and as always, she was missing her mum...

Yet she always felt closest to her mother at this time of year too. It was a strange mixture of love and grief, nostalgia for a past she had lost and excitement for a future she couldn't even imagine. On still winter nights like this, she felt as though the skin of the world was somehow thinner, so that you could almost see through it into another time, another reality...

Murray and Tansy had been chatting as Tansy fumbled with Susie's spare door key. Now he came back and touched her arm. 'Hey, you okay?' He was unsmiling and she couldn't guess his thoughts. He studied her face. 'You don't look happy.'

'I'm happy,' she insisted at once. 'Ecstatic, in fact.' She had some trouble with the word 'ecstatic' but he didn't laugh at her.

He had spotted her shivering. 'You're getting cold out here. You should go inside, Tansy's putting the kettle on.'

'I don't need a drink... I just want to go to bed.'

Murray shrugged and stood aside, but when she stumbled, he followed and steered her gently towards the front door. 'Come on, let me help you.'

She didn't argue. Her feet didn't appear to be obeying her properly anyway.

On the threshold, there wasn't room for them both to get through. So he stopped, and she stopped too, looking up into his face.

'Thank you for the lift...' she began awkwardly, not sure how to get rid of him.

'But now you want me to go away,' he finished for her, and smiled at last. 'Hint taken. I'll see you in the grotto, Mrs Santa.'

She leant back against the door frame to steady herself, studying his face through misty vodka goggles. It was a pity Murray had to be so bloody good-looking, she thought. Because he represented everything she despised. Big business, a corporate approach, slick and professional...

And yet, he was so kind and patient towards the kids who queued for the grotto. And he had dashed out to rescue her and Tansy tonight at a moment's notice, without complaint, and seemingly without expecting anything in return. Was it possible she could have misjudged him?

'Good night,' she whispered, and managed a smile at last.

His gaze dropped to her mouth.

With a shock, she remembered how he'd tried to kiss her on the big wheel at the funfair. How could she have forgotten such an embarrassing moment? When she'd complained, he had apologised at once and never tried it again since. She'd been affronted and taken aback at the time. She had instantly pegged him as one of those arrogant men who couldn't keep their wandering hands to themselves.

But now things were different.

For a few mesmerising seconds, Susie was convinced he was about to kiss her again, and although she ought to have broken the spell by going indoors, she simply stood and waited, holding her breath, every fibre of her body twanging with sensation, her curious gaze locked on his.

Only Murray didn't kiss her.

His mouth quirked in a self-deprecating smile, and he told her, 'Don't get cold,' before walking back to his car, magnificently incongruous in his long, dark blue dressing gown and slippers. In the wintry darkness beyond the meagre pool of light from the porch, she couldn't quite tell what he was wearing on his bottom half…

'Wait!'

He looked round, surprised.

'Are you really wearing PJs under that?'

With slow deliberation, the mayor turned towards her, untied the belt of his dressing gown, and flashed her.

'Red-striped silk pyjamas,' she muttered, blinking. 'Goodness.'

CHAPTER FIFTEEN

Murray was still reliving the pyjama thing two days later in the shop grotto. What must Susie have thought, witnessing him driving about in his dressing gown and slippers like that? The epitome of uncool. But he hadn't wanted to leave her and Tansy standing in the rain a minute longer than was necessary. And then he'd done that flasher gesture...

He groaned.

She hadn't said a word about it since, of course, but he was convinced there was something new about the way she was looking at him now. Embarrassment? Disapproval?

He'd taken a day off shop work yesterday to attend to important pre-Christmas Market business while Susie played Mrs Santa in his stead. But he'd driven in that morning to do his stint in the red suit and itchy beard, wishing he knew exactly what he was doing where Susie Lovell was concerned. Because things were starting to feel boggy underfoot.

He'd started out telling himself the Santa situation was purely down to profit. He owned the business now. If there was nobody to play Santa, none of those parents with young children would visit the

Christmas Tree Shop and his profits would tumble.

But as the days had gone on, and he'd found himself enjoying the whole 'ho ho ho' routine, and seeing the kids' eyes light up with excitement whenever he walked through the store, he had realised there was something else at play here. For starters, he kept wondering what it would be like to have children of his own. To watch them unwrap their presents on Christmas morning and see *their* eyes light up with excitement. Which was entirely bizarre, because he'd never really liked children or thought much about starting a family, beyond always making sure it had no chance of happening by accident.

Thankfully, he'd been able to dismiss the outlandish idea at once, horrified by the way his thoughts were headed... He and Genevieve, his ex, had never been the kind of couple to discuss having children. And there was no one else in his life with whom he might be planning to procreate. So it was a pointless exercise anyway, imagining the future pitter-patter of tiny feet.

Yet as soon as he let himself think about never having kids, Susie Lovell would leap into his brain like a neon sign flashing on and off down a sidestreet, inviting him that way.

Go away, he told that mental image, and checked his phone to distract himself. Gone noon. Surely he must be finished by now? The grotto line was usually empty by lunchtime.

A head popped round the grotto door, and a soft

voice said coyly, 'May I come in? I promise I know what I want for Christmas, Santa dear.'

Murray had been slumped on his red Santa throne, booted feet outstretched, as he contemplated what he might eat for lunch. Now his head swung towards the door and his eyes almost burst from his head.

'Genevieve?' he exclaimed, sitting bolt upright.

His ex sauntered into the grotto, wearing tight jeans with impossibly high heels and a snug-fitting cashmere sweater that emphasised every curve in a way that he remembered only too well. She flicked back dark-blonde hair and grinned at his blank expression. 'So it's true... I genuinely couldn't believe it when I saw it on the Penrock Downs Facebook page. Murray Carew, playing Santa in a grotto? Impossible, I thought. And yet here you are. And wow, that beard...' Her eyes sparkled with mischief. 'May I sit on your knee, Santa, and tug on it?'

'What are you doing back in town?' he asked huskily, trying to rise. But she was already right in front of him, pushing him back onto the throne. 'Hey, what the hell...? Don't, it's not funny.'

He'd been hurt when Genevieve dumped him, claiming that she'd rather enter a convent then go out with him for another minute. At one stage, he would have done almost anything to get her back. So he was surprised to feel nothing but shock and embarrassment at seeing her again. Horror too, when she began to climb onto his knee, still grinning.

'Genevieve, I'm not kidding... You can't do that here. Get off me.'

But she was already on his knee, one arm coiled about his shoulders, her face close to his. She smelt of perfume, the fragrance irritating his throat. 'I've missed you, Murray. I don't know what I was thinking, leaving you. That is, I do know what I was thinking... I was having a nervous breakdown. That's obvious now.' Her smile faded, her expression turning serious. 'It was after my brother died. Do you remember?'

'Of course I do,' he said gently, not wanting to upset her. 'And I know how rough that was on you. But can we talk about it without you sitting on my knee, please?'

'*Rough*?' Genevieve gave a cracked laugh, ignoring his suggestion. 'I was completely lost for months afterwards. I kept wondering what the point of being alive was, if death was the end of everything. And that made me think about God. And for while I thought perhaps I needed to change my life, to find something more *meaningful*.' She twined a finger around his fake beard and tugged, studying him as though she no longer recognised him. Which wouldn't be so strange, given his Santa disguise. 'I should have stuck with *you*, I see that now. Not fallen in love with Jesus. You could have given me the stability I needed. And now you've even got a beard. So masculine and guru-like.' She sighed. 'I love men with beards!'

'It's synthetic. And itchy.'

Her eyes sparkled, apparently finding this amusing rather than off-putting. 'You always were the sensible one in our relationship, Murray. And I didn't appreciate how much I needed that. I pushed you away instead. And I've regretted it ever since.'

Trying not to touch her, while being very aware of her delicately perched on his knee, Murray said slowly, searching for the right words, 'Thank you, I appreciate you saying that. And maybe at one time I would have been pleased to see you walk in out of the blue like this. I even pinned your photo to the wall for months... But the thing is, Genevieve, you're not the only one who's changed since we broke up.'

She smiled at him eagerly. 'Yes, I see that. You're practically running this town now, aren't you? Mayor of Penrock Downs. Owner of this place. And you're Santa too. I love it! The new you...' She winked. 'It's kinda sexy.'

'No,' he told her flatly. 'Santa is *not* sexy. Santa is an old dude in a red suit who hands out presents to kids at Christmas. There's zero sexiness associated with him. Sorry to disappoint. So if you could just...'

Murray tried to lift her off his lap. But Genevieve refused to budge, merely tightening her arm about his shoulders, hooking onto him like one of Tansy's cats.

He decided to be blunt. 'To be clear, it's great to see you back in town, and I'm really glad you don't feel called to be a nun anymore, because I don't think that lifestyle would have suited you in the long run.

But I'm not interested in starting up with you again.'

'What?' A frown appeared in her eyes, perhaps a tiny seed of doubt at last.

'I'm sorry about the stuff you went through after your brother died. I should have been there for you more. I was having issues of my own at the time, and I failed you as a friend. I deeply regret that. But we can't go back to the way things were.'

'Why not?'

'Because I'm not that man anymore.'

'But I saw you on the Facebook page, and you looked so cute in your Santa outfit. Besides, you own this business now. It's impressive that you've made such a fantastic local investment. That's why I came all this way, to see this place, to see you again, Murray... You can't mean it, sending me away after only *five minutes*?'

'Sometimes even five minutes is too long.' He battled frustration at her refusal to leave. 'Please, get off my knee.'

'But we were great together, Murray.' Genevieve tipped her head to one side, gazing at him with a pleading look that he remembered. 'And I'm over all that religious stuff now. I'm never going to lose the plot again, I swear.'

'Look, to be honest, we were *never* that great together.' He saw the hurt in her face and added hurriedly, 'All my fault, not yours. I didn't give it a hundred percent, and I should have done. I'm genuinely sorry about that. But this thing you're doing here... Sitting on my knee? Talking about us getting back together? It can't happen.'

'Why not?'

'Because I'm not available anymore.'

'Seeing someone else, are you?'

'No, I... I'm just not interested, that's all.'

'Nonsense.' Rebellion sparked in her face, and she leant forward like a cat pouncing, kissing him on the mouth before he could squirm away.

'What on earth? Murray?'

He knew that voice. Pulling away, he saw Susie standing a few feet away, her eyes wide with shock. How long had she been in the grotto, watching them?

Embarrassed, he jumped up, dumping Genevieve to the floor.

'Well, that wasn't very nice of you,' his ex grumbled, tossing back her hair with a cross expression. Flushed, her gaze rose to Susie. 'Who's this, then?'

Susie turned and walked away without a word.

Irritated, Murray reached a hand down and helped Genevieve up off the floor. 'You okay? Not hurt? Good, then we're done here.'

Genevieve stared, bemused. 'What do you mean?' She chased after him as he left the grotto. 'Listen, I checked before I bothered coming back to Penrock Downs... I knew you weren't seeing anyone else. So what's the problem?'

'There's no problem,' he insisted. 'I'm just not in the market for a girlfriend at the moment. Like I said, I'm sorry.'

With that, he hurried after Susie, furious with himself for not getting Genevieve off his knee sooner. Now she would be imagining that the two of them were still an item. And the mere idea left a bad taste in his mouth.

Susie was at the tills, helping a customer. He hesitated, not wanting to disturb her while she was working. Genevieve approached him from behind, heels clacking on the shop flooring. He tensed, expecting another scene, but she stalked straight past him and out of the store, blonde head held high.

He felt guilty, watching her go. He could have handled that better. But Genevieve had been pretty full on, while Susie… He wasn't really sure why it was such a big deal that Susie should consider him unattached. It wasn't like he was planning to make a move on her himself.

He wanted to clear the air, he guessed. To make it plain to Susie that there was nothing between him and his ex that couldn't happen cleanly in a grotto.

Before he could sort those confused thoughts into words, his phone rang.

It was Gus.

'Hey, mate, good to hear from you again,' he said, reluctantly answering the call. 'Aren't those lorries due today?'

'They're coming into town right now,' Gus told him. 'I just heard from the lead driver. It would be great if you could join us up at the field when they start unloading. Just to make sure everything's as ordered.'

He hesitated, his gaze turning back to Susie. He didn't know why he was so bothered. After all, there was nothing between him and Susie that couldn't happen cleanly in a grotto either.

'Yeah, I'll be there in ten.' And he rang off.

As soon as the customer had trundled away with a snow globe wrapped in blue crêpe paper, Susie turned to him, her eyes flashing. 'I don't want to hear it. But if you think I'm going to stand for that kind ...' She bit back the words, visibly shaking. 'You may be my boss, Murray. But that doesn't mean I have to put up with... with *lewd* behaviour in my grotto.'

'*Lewd*? *Your* grotto? Now wait a minute –'

Her hand flew up, silencing him. 'I think you'd better hang up your Santa hat,' she snapped. 'I'll get someone to cover for me on the shop floor and do the December grotto shifts myself.'

'But nothing happened in there.'

'Oh, really? That was your ex-girlfriend, wasn't it? I remember seeing her out with you a couple of years ago, before you were mayor. I take it you're back together?'

'Not even remotely,' he bit out. 'Genevieve and I are most definitely *over*.'

'Just friends with benefits, then? She certainly looked very *friendly*, sitting on your knee, kissing you *on the mouth*. Or was she just telling you what she wanted for Christmas?'

Murray ground his teeth together. 'Not that it's any

of your business, but let's talk about this later,' he threw back at her, pocketing his phone. 'Right now, I need to get up to Twelve Tree Acres. The lorries are arriving to unload the first stalls.'

He strode past her, furious and smarting at her unprovoked attack. *Friends with benefits*? Was that really how she saw him? As someone who'd treat a sexual encounter so lightly and casually, it was just a gesture between friends? No wonder she could barely bring herself to look at him most days...

'I need to change,' he added tersely. 'While I'm out, why don't you email me the latest digital accounts? I'd like to see how our takings this year have compared to this time last year.'

She didn't say anything, her face flushed and averted.

He glanced back at her. 'Did you hear what I said, Miss Lovell?'

'Yes, boss,' she muttered, and turned to the till, stabbing at the screen with angry fingers. 'Whatever you say, boss.'

Feeling oddly off-balance by what had just happened, Murray revved out of the car park, checking his mirrors for sightings of Genevieve, and almost collided with a gigantic truck that had slowed as it passed the shop premises, possibly distracted by the cluster of flashing reindeers guarding the entrance. Swearing, he slammed on the brakes, and earned himself a long, 'BARP' on the truck's horn as the driver slalomed hastily around his SUV and back onto the correct carriageway.

It turned out to be a convoy of large trucks, the next lorry also taking swift evasive action while Murray swore again, trying to manoeuvre himself back into the car park and out of the way of oncoming traffic. This he succeeded in doing, though only after another deafening 'BARP' from the second driver.

'Damn it,' he muttered, waiting until the last lorry had passed the shop entrance. Then he pulled out more cautiously and followed in their wake.

He knew precisely where they were heading, and it was with an embarrassed grimace that he drove after them through the specially widened gates to Twelve Trees Acres and waved to Gus, who was waiting there in a raincoat and Wellington boots, tablet in hand, counting the trucks in.

Murray parked out of the way of proceedings and trudged over to his master of ceremonies. He felt distinctly off-centre and in need of some calming activity, like a long run along the beach or an evening listening to Bach, one of his secret pleasures. Not that he was likely to find time for either of those right now. Life was too hectic.

He had no idea what was wrong with him at the moment, though Genevieve appearing in his life again had not helped his mood. Nor had her bouncing on his knee.

There was a distinct chill to the air at Twelve Tree Acres, the skies turning gun-metal grey as the short day stretched into afternoon. The weather report had suggested that snow might be inbound, but nobody seemed to know when. Not that anyone in Penrock Downs ever believed such doom-and-gloom forecasts. Snow might fall in other places, but it rarely fell in North Cornwall.

However, the sea winds were frequently cold and sharp along the Cornish coast in these long winter months, and today was no exception.

He kept seeing Susie's face. The way she'd said his name so sharply. 'Murray?' What had he seen in her expression? Disappointment, mostly. She'd seen Genevieve on his knee and assumed they were up to inappropriate hanky-panky in Santa's grotto. And it was clear she hadn't believed a word of his stumbling explanation.

Not that he owed her an explanation. He was her boss, not the other way around.

Yet he still felt unaccountably guilty.

It was absurd.

'Here we go,' Gus said, shaking his hand enthusiastically. 'As you can see, all shipments have arrived on site. We laid the entire field and overflow to all-weather matting last week, and got mobile loos and catering for the workmen in place. Now for the construction itself.'

A large team of workmen had also just arrived in a minibus and were jumping out, wrapped up against the elements, for it was already starting to spit with rain. They headed towards the trucks to help the drivers unload their cargo.

Murray watched the work begin with interest. But

also a shade of anxiety. 'It's quite a tight turnaround. The market's due to open next weekend.'

'Construction should only take two to three days.'

'Seriously?' Murray was astounded.

'Maybe longer if the weather turns nasty. But yes, with this number of workers, it's usually a quick process. Then, once everything's in place, and a safety inspection has taken place, stallholders will be allowed on site to stock and decorate their cabins. That should take us up to opening day.' Gus brought up an image on his tablet screen. 'By which time, the field should look like *this*.'

Murray leant in, studying the artificially constructed image of Twelve Trees Acres as a Christmas Market. It looked like one of the big city festive markets, which made him proud. All his hard work, persuading other councillors and key sponsors to get onboard, and his grand vision was soon to be realised at last…

'It looks fantastic.'

Gus clapped him on the back. 'And it's all thanks to you, Mayor.' He grinned, seeing Murray's weary expression. 'You can relax now, honestly. The thing's almost done.'

'Huh.' Murray dug his hands into his pockets, turning to watch the first pallets being unloaded, plastic sheets whipped off to reveal a stack of Swiss chalet-style cabin walls, ready to be put together. 'There are still a million things that can go wrong between now and opening day,' he muttered. 'And probably will, knowing my luck.'

Gus frowned. 'You okay, mate?'

Was he okay?

No, he thought grimly, feeling a weight on his shoulders and a hollow ache in his chest. Yet he managed a smile.

'Never better,' he insisted. 'Had a late night, that's all,' he lied. More like a sleepless night, worrying about the Christmas Market, tossing and turning. And tonight wouldn't be much better, not with his thoughts constantly slipping back to a cross-looking Mrs Santa, watching him with chin up and folded arms, her gaze disapproving…

'Ah well,' Gus said cheerily, laughing as he misunderstood, 'it is the season for it, after all. Next time, a good hangover cure is a big dollop of peanut butter. Plenty of protein and fat. Sets you up for the day straightaway.' He paused. 'Unless you're allergic, of course?'

'No, I'm not allergic to peanuts.'

But he might just be allergic to Susie Lovell, he thought, and made a promise to himself to steer clear of her and the Christmas Tree Shop until all this business was over. Though it would be hard, given that she'd agreed to be his plus-one at the opening party.

But maybe Disapproving Susie would refuse to come now, and he would have to go alone. Which was perhaps the wisest thing all round. He was used to being alone.

CHAPTER SIXTEEN

'I got it!' Tansy shrieked, jumping up from Susie's laptop, which she'd been using to check her email, and danced around the room. 'I got it, I got it!'

Susie looked up from the paperback she'd been reading, alarmed. 'Woah, slow down... Got what, exactly? Not the shingles again, I hope?'

'I can't believe it. They want me... Ha, they *want me*!'

'Do you mean the job at the cat sanctuary?'

'I went for an interview there last week,' Tansy admitted, beaming down at her in delight. 'I didn't tell you because... Well, I was afraid it would be a bust. I didn't want to be embarrassed when I was rejected. But I got it. Goodness, I'm going to be the new director at the cat sanctuary. This is like a dream come true. And I can move in straightaway, the email said. I need to go round to the council tomorrow morning, collect the keys and sign some paperwork, and then I can move in. Just like that!'

Susie was overjoyed for her friend. She got up and

hugged her. 'And you can bring your cats too?'

'Duh!' Tansy fell about laughing. 'It's a *cat* sanctuary, Susie. Of course I can bring my cats. They come with the job description.'

Susie laughed too. She was thrilled that everything seemed to be working out for Tansy, after all the horror of being flooded out of her caravan. 'That's marvellous news. Though I guess it'll take a few taxi rides to get your stuff and all the cats to your news digs. I wish I had a car... But I never needed one when Dad was here.' She clicked her fingers. 'Oh, I could take the work van... Tom's been using it for deliveries. But I'm sure –'

Tansy interrupted her. 'Don't worry, the mayor said he'd take me there in his big swanky car. It might take a couple of trips but I'm sure everything will fit. It's not like I have much, anyway.'

'Murray?' Susie pulled a face, folding her arms.

'He's been amazing. I'm really impressed... I thought he was one of these posh idiots with a stick up his butt. But he's actually really cool. And he's so great with the cats. He dropped in yesterday with another councillor to talk to me about the job. It wasn't a done deal at that point, they just wanted to go over some last questions the committee had. But it seems like they were satisfied with what I said. So now I've got a proper job, not just another short-term gig.' Tansy collapsed onto the sofa, hugging one of her fluffy cats to her chest. 'You know what this means, Susie?

'That you need to learn to wake up when your

alarm goes off in the mornings, not keep hitting the snooze button?'

'Yeah, I better had. But what I meant was… I'm a *grown-up* now.'

'Welcome to my world.' Susie grinned, but still felt awkward over the mention of the mayor. She'd emailed Murray the monthly accounts as requested, but he hadn't come into the store since their row over what she'd seen in the grotto. Maybe she should just have walked away and left him and 'Genevieve' to it. But what if a parent or child had walked in while he was messing about? Even if he was her boss, it was still right that she'd said something. And what kind of name was Genevieve? Was she French? 'I'm glad things are working out for you, I really am. And whatever I can do to help, just say the word.'

'You can tell me what's bugging you,' Tansy said frankly.

'What do you mean?'

'Come on, Susie! You've been like a bear with a sore head the past couple of days. And I haven't seen Murray about as usual. So what happened? I take it he's not Santa anymore?'

Reluctantly, Susie told him what had happened with Murray and Genevieve in the grotto. Tansy laughed, rather than looking shocked, and then sobered up when she saw Susie's expression.

'Sorry, but it's quite funny really.'

'You think I overreacted?'

'Well, he's a really nice guy. Honestly, he is. I was wrong about Murray. I wouldn't be starting this amazing new job if it wasn't for him, so forgive me if I can't be your friend at the moment and say yes, I hate him too. Though I will say that if it makes you feel better.' Tansy peered at her, her head to one side. 'Would it make you feel better?'

Susie shook her head. 'I don't hate him either,' she muttered.

'Fab.'

'Have you ever heard of a person called Genevieve before?'

'Outside of French films, no.' Tansy shrugged. 'But it's a nice name. Maybe a bit fancy. But perhaps it suits her.'

'Oh yes, she's certainly very *fancy*,' Susie muttered, narrowing her eyes as she recalled the woman's heavy make-up and figure-hugging clothes.

'You're not jealous, are you?'

'What? No!' Susie stared at her, horrified. 'Why on earth would I be jealous? Like you said, he's my boss, not my... my... *boyfriend*.' She could barely bring herself to say the word.

'Good.' The cat leapt off her lap and Tansy jumped up too. 'Hey, why don't you help me pack my stuff? Murray said he'd bring some crates tomorrow for the cats to travel in, so we don't need to worry about them. But I want to make sure I haven't left anything lying around. It's been a blast, living with you since I got flooded out. But I admit I'm going to enjoy living on my own again.' She scooped up another passing cat and cuddled it closely. Oddly, the cat didn't seem to mind this, purring so loudly its small body was almost vibrating with pleasure. 'With these super gorgeous guys, of course. I wouldn't be without them. Me and the gang!'

'And this wouldn't be anything to do with the fact that you're too embarrassed to bring your dates back here?'

Tansy blushed. 'It is a little awkward,' she admitted. 'This latest gal, she's lovely. I can't wait to introduce you two. But I can't deny it... She's a bit of a screamer.'

'Oh my God.' Susie stuck her fingers in her ears. 'I'm going to pretend I didn't hear that.'

'Well, you didn't,' Tansy pointed out. 'Because I didn't bring her back here.'

Susie chuckled and got to her feet, trying not to show how rattled she felt that her best friend not only liked the most irritating man in the world, but thought he was a 'really nice guy'.

'Of course I'll help you pack.'

'Fantastic, thanks.' Tansy let the cat go. 'And once we're done packing,' she went on, checking under the sofa cushions and mysteriously producing a lost pen and an earring, 'I'll cook us a really tasty spag bol. We've got all the ingredients in the house, I already checked. Plus, I splashed out on a cheeky bottle of wine for the two of us. A rich Italian, with lots of body.' She winked. 'Just the way I like my ladies.'

They hugged again, and Susie wished she wasn't losing her quirky friend. The house would feel too quiet once Tansy had gone. But it would be nice to have the place to herself again. Though then there'd be too much time for her to dwell on everything that had happened since her dad left, instead of burying her feelings deep inside.

The sad truth was, she was unhappy about having rowed with Murray. She didn't even know why she'd done it. She didn't want to risk getting the sack and never being able to look after her baby trees again. Some might think her crazy, but she felt the same way about the tree nursery as Tansy did about her cats. It would be a real wrench to know someone else was taking care of them, and maybe not doing a brilliant job.

She'd overreacted, that was obvious. But seeing him jiggling that attractive blonde up and down on his knee had done something funny to her insides...

Could it be that she'd somehow developed feelings for *the mayor*?

'Please, no,' she muttered under her breath, following Tansy upstairs to help her pack. 'Anything but that.'

The awkward moment she'd feared came at precisely noon the next day, when Tansy appeared in the store to tug on her arm and whisper excitedly in her ear, 'He's here! I've put my stuff in his car and the cats are all crated up ready to leave. I think we can do it in one trip. Will you come and wave me off?'

Susie smiled at the customer she was dealing with, hurriedly took payment and put loyalty points on the lady's card, and then called Tom to take over the till.

Thankfully, he'd just come back from a local delivery. The lad seemed to be coping well with having made the jump from part-time to almost full-time, but all the same, she was finding it hard to cope with the long hours when he wasn't available, especially now she was also playing Mrs Santa in the run-up to Christmas. She had hoped it might prove possible to advertise for another part-timer, but Murray had not yet replied to her tentative email suggestion.

With Tom looking after the store, she hurried across the car park in Tansy's wake. Murray was leaning on his large black SUV, peering at his phone, but straightened as they approached. His gaze tangled with hers, and Susie felt her heart jump uncomfortably.

'I'll grab the first two crates,' Tansy said, dashing off to the house to fetch her darling cats.

Murray glanced after her uncertainly, perhaps unsure if he should help or not, yet didn't move. His head swung back towards Susie instead.

'Hello,' she muttered, looking at the frosty ground instead of his face. 'Bit nippy today, isn't it?'

Gloved and wrapped in a thick jacket, Murray looked cozily warm. But he nodded. 'There may be snow, they say. Just in time for the Christmas Market. It opens tomorrow.' He hesitated. 'Have you been up there yet? The shop has a stall reserved, you know.'

'Yes, Tom and I have been stocking it ready

for tomorrow. Did you see my email about hiring another temporary part-timer? Just until we're into New Year.' She hesitated, still not daring look into his face. She still couldn't believe how rudely she'd spoken to him last time they'd been face-to-face, and was more horribly embarrassed than she'd expected to be. 'If I'm going to be on the stall all day, I can't expect Tom to hold things together alone. He says his mum is free this month if we want to take her on just for the Christmas season.'

'Of course, and I ought to have replied at once. By all means, bring Tom's mum onboard. Just send me the details for the payroll.' He moved to help Tansy load the first two crates, the wintry air filled with yowling, mewling cries, then watched her return to the house for the last one. 'Talking of which,' he added casually, 'are you still going to the launch party with me tomorrow night?'

Susie sucked in a breath, risking a glance at him. 'I thought you'd be taking *Genevieve* instead.'

His lip curled. 'I told you, that's over.'

'It didn't look over to me,' she said under her breath, and now his lip curled so far, she worried he might start drooling like one of Tansy's cats.

'Genevieve and I are not just ancient history, we're more like pre-history. Before the *dinosaurs*.' Murray took a step towards her. 'I'm asking *you* to the party, Susie. Will you come?'

His voice had dropped, somehow husky and intimate and commanding all at once. Then he ruined the effect by clearing his throat, as though the husky thing had been unintentional, and adding, 'Besides, we're a team. I own the Christmas Tree Shop and you're my manager. It's only logical for us to go to the launch celebration together. So, shall I pick you up at six-thirty tomorrow?'

'That's the last crate,' Tansy announced while Susie was still formulating her refusal, sliding it into the space Murray had prepared for it. She stuck her fingers through the bars to stroke a crying cat behind its ears. 'Don't worry, baby. We'll be in a new home together very soon. Ten minutes' drive, I promise.'

She pulled a face as the sound of cat yowls rose piteously, all her pets crying at once. 'Oh dear, this is going to be a very noisy journey. Sorry, Murray.'

'Not to worry.' He grinned, removing his gloves, and produced a packet of ear plugs. To Susie's surprise, he inserted a plug delicately in each ear, then told them both, a shade too loudly, 'Problem solved.'

Susie hugged Tansy again, oddly bereft that her friend was leaving, even though she had often longed for peace and quiet and a cat-free house in recent days.

'I'll come and visit as soon as you've settled in. You've got that spare phone I lent you, right? Give me a call if you need *anything*,' she insisted, releasing her reluctantly. 'Anything at all, okay? I'll come over straightaway, assuming the work van's available.'

She needed to get a vehicle of her own, she thought, uncomfortably aware that the delivery van now belonged to Murray, having been part of the shop package, and that he was paying the insurance and maintenance bills, so she shouldn't really be using it outside work hours. But there was little chance of her affording one at the moment... Every spare penny went towards the upkeep of the house, though thankfully the mortgage had been paid off. Her dad still owned it, but he'd taken off without really discussing what she was supposed to do if, say, the roof started to leak. Her salary at the shop would not pay for any expensive fixes, only bodge jobs, and with council tax so high these days, she was beginning to wish she'd never agreed to take on the upkeep of their house.

Except she hadn't agreed, she thought unhappily. Dad had just taken off for a 'new life' without consulting her. It was a godsend to have a reliable roof over her head, as Tansy being flooded out had proved. But it was hard not to also resent being left with a parcel of household bills and very little income to cover them...

'Thanks for taking me in,' Tansy told her. 'You're a good pal.' She clambered in beside Murray, accompanied by a chorus of incarcerated cats all wailing at once. Their owner stuck her tongue out and waved as the SUV roared away, shouting through the open window, 'Um, by the way, Caesar left a little present on the mat. I meant to pick it up but forgot. Sorry!'

A little present?

Returning to the house, Susie found a dead vole

on the front door mat and grimaced, going inside for plastic gloves to dispose of it. It could have been worse, she thought, picking the tiny, limp body up by its tail. It could have been a smellier present...

That was when she realised she hadn't refused to go to the party with Murray. She had fully intended to decline the invitation. Instead, he had said he'd be picking her up at six-thirty tomorrow night. And if she refused now, would he still be as amenable to her hiring Tom's mum to help them out over the Christmas season?

But why should she refuse to go? Because she was still angry over his behaviour with Genevieve? That had been several days ago, and it had all been over nothing.

'Oh Good God,' she muttered, groaning.

This made no sense. Not unless the burning sensation she'd felt on seeing him with Genevieve had not been righteous indignation but *jealousy*?

Tansy had called it, she realised. And she had hotly denied it.

But was it possible she was indeed jealous?

She'd always been fiercely happy as a single person. Never had the slightest interest in dating anyone seriously. Yes, she'd been out a few times with men, but only in a fleeting one-or-two dates way. Never anything lasting. Certainly nothing that had ever caused her the slightest pang of jealousy.

It explained everything. The churning feeling inside whenever Murray turned up, her furious reaction at seeing him with Genevieve, the way she kept mentally replaying that moment when he'd turned to her and unbelted his dressing gown to show off his pyjamas...

Susie apologized to the dead vole as she tossed it into the field behind the house. Poor little thing, so cruelly deprived of life by a killer cat. Caesar, of course. Who else?

The unlucky vole had got the paws down from Caesar.

Susie drew a deep breath, wishing she didn't feel so shaky at the idea of this council party. Her and the mayor at a swanky do together...

What could go wrong, apart from everything?

He wasn't all bad, of course. He'd helped Tansy get back into work and find somewhere for herself and her cats to live. But Susie had seen the way he'd been looking at her lately and knew he was interested in a flirtation with her. But *only* a flirtation...

She needed to harden up if she didn't want Murray playing with her feelings the way Caesar had probably played with that vole before killing it. He had the ability to make her *jealous*, for goodness' sake. And she hated the thought that any man could make her feel something she didn't want to.

If she was going to survive this party intact, she needed to be the cat, and Murray the mouse. Not the other way round. Because she guessed from the way he'd dismissed his glamorous, sexy-looking ex that he wasn't interested in dating at the moment, and that a strong come-on would probably make him run a mile in the opposite direction. He was only using that husky voice and too-lingering gaze on her because she posed zero threat to the man. The mayor was having fun at her expense, basically. Flirting with the boring tree nursery girl as a form of entertainment.

'Okay, so I need to find a knockout dress,' she thought out loud, stripping off her plastic gloves and throwing them in the trash. 'Something to... to make Murray's eyes pop out of his skull.'

Only she didn't own anything even remotely eye-popping. She was strictly a jeans with everything woman.

Her late mum, on the other hand, had loved slinky, sexy outfits that moulded to her curves and felt gorgeous on the skin...

Susie hadn't thrown a single one of those evening dresses away after her death, loving to touch and admire them when she was feeling low, and remember how amazing her mother had always looked when out partying with Dad.

'I need your help, Mum,' she whispered, and took the stairs two at a time, on a mission to find the slinkiest possible suit of armour against Murray Carew.

CHAPTER SEVENTEEN

Murray turned on his heel, gazing up and down the identical rows of stalls at the Christmas Market. It was the first morning when the market was open to the public, and only about half the stallholders had taken the shutters off their stall fronts. But more would open up by the evening, as the market would be open until at least eight o'clock most nights until the last possible day of shopping, on Christmas Eve. And he guessed it would look spectacular once night had fallen, stalls decorated with flashing fairy lights around the service hatches, all their Christmas wares lit up.

'This place looks amazing,' Gus said, standing beside him and grinning with pleasure as he surveyed his handiwork. 'But what do you think, Murray? Happy with what you see?'

'I'm ecstatic,' Murray told him, and the two men shook hands.

Gus took a few photos with his phone. 'Remember that day when I first came up here? It was just a bare field. This was your vision of how it could look.'

'And you've made it happen for me. I can't thank you enough, Gus. This is tremendous work.'

'Hey, I just followed your plans. But yes, I'm pretty pleased too. And look, the car park's already starting to fill up with customers. I saw a billboard on the roadside as I drove in this morning. An advertisement for the Christmas Market. It looked fantastic. I think this market is going to be a huge success and the town should be deeply grateful to you for organising it.'

Murray grinned ruefully. 'Yeah, half are grateful, and the other half hate me for it.'

Gus looked astonished. 'On what grounds?'

'You name it... Increasing traffic at peak times, overwhelming town infrastructure, taking custom away from local shops. Oh, and don't forget, *commercialising* Christmas. To some residents of Penrock Downs, that alone makes me the devil.' He pulled a face. 'I have it on good authority.'

'Who could possibly think that kind of nonsense?' Gus shook his head. 'You've done a phenomenal job. And people love Christmas. Everyone loves lights, music, life in the middle of winter... That's what you've created here. A winter paradise. I can't believe anyone would knock you for it.'

Murray shrugged and said nothing, but he was thinking specifically of Susie Lovell. He was certain she still thought of him as a 'suit' who wanted to commercialise Christmas – and had succeeded with this market. And yet she herself had accepted a stall at the market, though under protest. 'I'm only doing this because you're the boss now,' she'd grumbled as he instructed her what to sell on the stall, apparently oblivious to the fact that she was his store manager, not his equal.

What on earth had possessed him to remind Susie about the party yesterday? He felt like groaning out loud but didn't want Gus to think he needed medical attention. He could have pretended to forget he'd invited her and simply gone to the launch event on his own. Instead, he'd offered to pick her up at six-thirty tonight.

No doubt Susie would turn up in jeans and jumper, as usual, ignoring the smart-casual dress code. But she did at least have a sense of humour, he thought. She might be wearing one of her Christmassy shop jumpers, the ones with flashing reindeers on them, with lights that actually lit up as she moved about. Or emblazoned with some cheeky Christmas message to make customers grin.

There was much he found grating in Susie Lovell, but he liked her sense of humour. And she was never full of herself, she was just... natural. The thought surprised him. Perhaps with all her droning on about trees and holly and so on, he was beginning to appreciate more natural things. And the way she was able to make him laugh. Since he'd agreed to play Santa, he hadn't laughed so much or so often in years. Or felt so good about himself.

And then Genevieve had turned up and ruined the whole thing for him.

Of course Susie had been right to voice her disapproval. Boss or not, he shouldn't have been in the grotto with a woman on his knee. And he felt bad still, knowing he ought to have removed Genevieve straightaway, not dithered in that stupid way, wary of offending her. But he felt sympathetic towards her. At one time, he'd vaguely thought the two of them might get married one day, him and Genevieve. Before the convent obsession...

She'd been suffering from a nervous breakdown, she'd insisted. Was that true? And did it change anything? All he knew was that he no longer felt the same affection for Genevieve, even if he didn't want to upset her unnecessarily either.

'Look, I'm going to walk around the stalls, get a feel for how things are going,' he told Gus, his breath steaming on the cold air. They'd still had no snow but it felt chilly enough, nonetheless. 'I'll see you at the party tonight. You are definitely going, I hope?'

'Try and stop me,' Gus said, laughing. 'Free booze is a big thing with me. I'll be heading back to Bristol tomorrow morning though. It's been an honour working with you on this project, Murray, but I have other jobs lined up.' They shook hands again. 'I'll be back when the fair closes to oversee the stalls being taken down and the field returned to the way we found it. No rest for the wicked, eh?' And with that, Gus winked and slipped away into the crowd of shoppers beginning to throng the aisles of Christmas stalls.

Wandering about the market stalls, Murray felt

more and more enchanted by what he saw. And that surprised him too. He'd expected to hate all this festive stuff. When he was a child, Christmas had been something other people enjoyed. His father, a labourer, had hated this time of year, as his pay packet had always been lighter and yet had to stretch further, so he'd made damn sure his whole family hated it too. For Jim Carew, Christmas had merely been an excuse to get drunk and have a row with his wife.

These days, Christmas only ever reminded Murray that he was alone. His parents were both gone, he was single, and Christmas was about love and family, and he didn't have any of that. So he looked on the festive season in a cynical way. Or, at least, he always had done so in the past.

Now though, nodding at stallholders and shaking people's hands as they recognised him, exchanging small talk and pausing to admire seasonal displays of candy canes and sugared apple beignets and curious hand-carved objects for sale as Christmas presents, not to mention the marvellous Cornish garden gnomes stall that was attracting so much interest, he felt a strange tingling sensation deep inside.

He wasn't given much to fanciful thoughts, but what he was feeling didn't seem to be pride at his achievements. He knew how pride and satisfaction felt over a job well done and this wasn't anything like that. So was it pleasure? Or perhaps even joy? The joy of Christmas...

At the end of the second row of local stalls, he spotted Susie dressing a thickly branched fir tree outside her stall to advertise her wares, wrapped up warmly against the bitter weather with a thick green scarf wound about her neck and a woolly hat pulled down over her red curls.

Murray smiled and almost went up to her but at the last minute beat a hasty retreat instead, slipping between the stalls into another row without encountering her.

They had parted amicably enough yesterday.

And yet he suddenly couldn't bear to speak to her, as though Susie Lovell represented something so tender and raw in himself, he couldn't touch it even for a second.

Also, something told him that a chance conversation might make her change her mind about the party tonight, and suddenly he didn't want her to change her mind. He was looking forward to walking into that room with Susie Lovell on his arm. Which was absurd, given his choices of girlfriend in the past. Looking back, he genuinely couldn't understand what he'd been thinking. Because none of them had been chosen for their personalities. He had always been attracted by a well-dressed woman with a nice figure, and that had been enough for him.

Now he couldn't think of anything worse than dating someone simply because of their looks.

Having purchased a few quirky presents for friends of his, and a hand-carved, hand-painted wooden jewellery box for a cousin whom he sometimes visited in Truro at this time of year, Murray made his way back to the car. He had looked for a special gift for his aunt Alison too, whom he loved dearly, but hadn't seen anything that he thought she would appreciate. Maybe on another visit though...

Heading home, he steered into the car park of the Christmas Tree Shop without meaning to, got out to admire the flashing reindeers, and somehow found himself in the outdoor nursery area, wandering among the growing trees...

The scent among the trees was intense. He dug his hands into his trouser pockets as he walked among the young firs, drawing in deep whiffs of rich Christmassy fragrance, instantly reminded of Christmas Days from his childhood, when his mother had always insisted on a proper tree, not an artificial one, and Murray had helped her dress it with lights and baubles, and a few strands of glittering tinsel.

Why had he never carried on that tradition of putting up a tree at Christmas when he finally got a home of his own? Too busy, too dismissive of meaningless festivity.

'Can I help you, sir?' Murray turned to find a man-sized elf in a green-and-red costume peering at him through the trees, and laughed when Tom added quickly, 'Oh, it's you. Sorry, the buzzer went off to tell me someone was in the nursery area. But I didn't realise who it was. I'll leave you to it.'

'Wait a minute.' Stupidly nervous, Murray cleared his throat. 'You're on grotto duty today, I take it?'

Tom adjusted his slipping elf hat with an embarrassed smile. 'Only while Susie's at the market. I'll be up there myself tomorrow, manning the stall, while she's being Mrs Santa down here.'

'In that case, assuming the shop's empty and you don't have any kids waiting in line for the grotto, I'd appreciate your advice.'

'I'm on a break, and my mum's looking after the shop, so it's fine.' Tom came towards him, curiosity in his thin face. They had never really got on. But the younger man did seem to be warming to him these days. Perhaps because he'd finally worked out it was best not to be rude to the boss. 'What do you want to know?'

'I need to choose a tree.'

'Sorry?' The elf-boy scratched his head; the bell on his hat jingled softly. 'You mean... You want a Christmas tree? A real one, not artificial? Because we don't stock many artificial trees. Susie doesn't like them.' He paused. 'It's for yourself, I take it?'

'That's the general idea, yes.' Seeing his confusion, Murray knew he had to come clean. 'Look, I've never put up a Christmas tree at home before, so I have no idea what I'm doing.'

'*Never?*'

'I'm not a big fan of Christmas. But since I own this place now...'

'Of course.' Tom hesitated, frowning. 'Well, it depends what you prefer. We have a good selection of fir trees as well as a variety of pine. The firs keep their needles for a long time, but some people prefer the fragrance of pine. And would you like a living tree in a pot for growing on afterwards, or a tree that's been cut down and comes with a tree stand?' He glanced past Murray at the rows of huge, bristling dark green trees. 'Also, what size tree can you accommodate? Is it for inside or outside use? Short or a six-footer? Maybe even taller? We do have some very tall specimens ready for –'

'I'd like you to choose a tree for me, Tom,' he interrupted, and grinned at the lad's surprise. 'You must be pretty expert at this by now. As for what I need, an indoor natural fir tree, six-foot tall, sounds about right. Other than that, I'm completely in your hands. I want you to sell me the best tree you can. How's that?'

Tom gave him a slow smile. 'In that case, perhaps you'd care to follow me? There are some real beauties among the firs at the moment. Let's see what we can find.'

A good hour later, he and Tom manhandled a healthy six-foot fir tree into the shop's delivery trailer, which Murray then attached to his SUV, driving home carefully and smiling whenever he glanced periodically in his mirrors. There it was... A bouncy, dark green fir being towed along by his SUV for all the world to see.

He'd chosen to have Tom saw down his chosen tree while he waited, as he doubted he would ever get around to planting it out later. Besides, he didn't have enough of a back garden to accommodate a large fir tree, post-Christmas. Poor Betty had to put up with running about a small back yard and an even smaller square of lawn. So recycling would have to be the ideal endpoint for his tree.

Tom had talked him through the care of his tree and its needles, and given him a brochure explaining his options for disposal once Christmas was over, as well as selling him a sturdy metal stand and several boxes of tinsel, fairy lights and baubles, since he didn't own a single Christmas decoration.

He collected Betty from the dog sitter, who was enthused to see him, and began to erect the Christmas tree in his living room while the dog pranced about, tail wagging hysterically.

He had to move the television and some furniture to fit the tree into his chosen space, but he didn't mind that. Once the tree was up and ready, he unpacked all the lights, tinsel and baubles, and began laboriously to dress the branches. This made Betty even more wired. She ran round and around beneath the lowest branches, yapping excitedly. Since he'd never had a Christmas tree in the house before, this was new territory to them both. She even made a spirited attempt to climb into the tree at one stage, having taken offence at one of the baubles, but he scooped her out before she could ruin his tinsel arrangements.

Finally, he reached up to place a white, flowing-haired angel on the uppermost tip of the tree, and then bent to switch on the fairy lights. By then it was late afternoon, and dusk had fallen without him noticing. But that was perfect timing, he considered, as the wintry gloom would give his Christmas tree a real chance to shine.

Sure enough, when the tree lights began to flash and shimmer among the wreathed tinsel, rounded gold and silver baubles catching the light too, they transformed the stark, monochrome of his living room into a bright, magical space.

Sinking onto the sofa with Betty on his lap, Murray gazed up at the glowing Christmas tree, and a wave of nostalgia swept over him, tears pricking at his eyes. There was a lump in his throat as he stroked Betty between the ears, murmuring, 'Merry Christmas, Betty,' and knew again that same sensation of joy that he'd felt at the Christmas Market.

However, after a few peaceful moments, sitting and admiring his handiwork from the sofa, Murray's smile faded. He had put up the tree exactly as required, and dressed it beautifully with lights and baubles and tinsel, and the room looked Christmassy now.

Yet something was... *off*.

Why?

He frowned, studying the room. Everything looked festive and beautiful, and the tree gave the room a cosier, more intimate feel than before. Like being in a Christmas grotto all of his own. So why didn't it feel perfect?

Real tree: CHECK
Tinsel: CHECK
Fairy Lights: CHECK
Baubles: CHECK

Basically, he'd brought everything home that was needed to celebrate Christmas in his own living room. Yet there was still something missing. And he had no idea what...

His phone buzzed. It was the timer he'd set.

'I need to shower and get changed,' he told the dog, who whined softly. 'Sorry, Betty. It's an evening on your own tonight. But I promise I won't be out too late.' He hesitated, then decided to shut Betty in the kitchen rather than allow her the run of the house. 'Be good,' he warned her, without much hope.

Betty barked crossly at being shut into the kitchen. But Murray refused to change his mind and let her out. He didn't want to come home to a shredded Christmas tree and a dog potentially in need of an emergency trip to the veterinary surgeon. Not that he'd put any dog-killing chocolates or candy canes on the tree. But he suspected Betty would still do her level best to devour the tinsel, given a few hours alone with an unguarded tree...

It was a little after the agreed time of six-thirty when Murray pulled up with a squeal of brakes outside Susie's house, cursing under his breath. He'd stupidly forgotten to uncouple the trailer that he'd used to transport the Christmas tree home and, hurrying out in his best suit at the correct time, had realised that he would need to remove it from the SUV if he wanted any chance of a parking space at the busy Cherry Orchard.

There was no sign of Susie about the place, so he dashed out of the car, feeling the first chill spots of rain that he suspected might become snow once temperatures plummeted, and leant on the doorbell until he heard movement inside.

The door creaked open thirty seconds later, and Susie peered out at him through a narrow crack. He blinked on seeing her, taken aback to see she'd put on make-up and earrings, which she almost never did, and had also styled her reddish mop in an elegant way that looked alien on her. Beautiful but decidedly alien.

'Sorry I'm late,' he told her, playing with his shirt cuffs as he pretended to gaze up at the heavy rainclouds, hoping to conceal how shocked he was by her appearance. 'I hope I haven't kept you waiting too long. Your chariot awaits, Miss Lovell. Though you might want to bring an umbrella.'

'Okay, hang on a tick,' she threw at him through the crack, and abruptly closed the door in his face. He took a step back and was relieved when it opened again almost immediately to reveal Susie clutching a brolly and shrouded in a large plastic mac with a hood. She'd drawn the hood down over her face, so he could no longer see her styled hair or striking make up, and he also had no idea what she was wearing underneath. Not jeans though, he guessed, noting with a fresh shock how her high heels clacked as she backed cautiously out of the house and locked the door. 'Ready?'

'Sure.'

She began to run and stumbled, perhaps not accustomed to wearing heels. He caught her elbow to steady her, but Susie shook off his hand. 'I'm fine,' she insisted.

'Sorry.' He got in beside her and started the engine. 'All good?'

'Drive, why don't you?' She threw him a flustered look. 'I thought you didn't want to be late.'

With a flick of his eyebrows, he took the hint, revved out of the car park and drove fast along the winding road into town. The car park at the Cherry Orchard was packed but he found a space eventually. As they entered the posh, upmarket hotel, music was already playing from the room upstairs as a smiling young woman offered to take their coats.

He hadn't bothered bringing a coat, trusting instead to his Cornish imperviousness to bad weather, but Susie was still wrapped in her voluminous coat, which she began to remove with much rustling and creaking as though taking down a tent.

While she was sorting herself out, Murray checked his appearance in the gilt mirror on the wall opposite. He'd shaved, of course, but perhaps not closely enough, he thought critically, running a hand over barely visible stubble. His shoulder-length hair looked damp and dishevelled from the blustery evening, and he flicked it back impatiently, then straightened his tie and turned to take Susie's arm.

His jaw dropped as he looked his plus-one up and down in astonishment. He had to clear his throat twice to find his voice. 'Erm, wow.'

She was wearing a figure-hugging blue satin dress that dipped daintily at the cleavage to reveal an intriguing expanse of pale flesh, while a deep slit ran all the way from the top of her thigh to a gold anklet, so that his gaze didn't know whether to dip into that forbidden pocket or slip mindlessly down the length of her shapely leg to the glint of gold. Her red hair had been piled on top of her head in a delectable chignon, a few strands artfully tweaked to hang about her perfectly made-up face.

Murray swallowed compulsively. Suddenly, his tie was too tight and the hotel over-warm.

'You look... amazing,' he told her, trying not to gawp.

'Thank you,' she murmured, and put a hand on his arm. Her gaze tangled briefly with his, and then they began to ascend the stairs to the first-floor venue, in perfect step with each other. The music from above had a fast Cuban vibe, and his heartbeat matched its erratic, compelling rhythm as they entered the party, especially when she added under her breath, 'You look very nice too.'

He almost asked, 'Okay, who are you and what the hell have you done with Susie Lovell?' but didn't quite dare, in case the joke fell flat.

Then everyone at the party was staring round

at them both, and it was too late to do anything but nod and smile and shake people's hands, repeating, 'Hi, how are you? Yes, the Christmas Market has been a huge success!' and wondering how on earth he was supposed to get through the evening with this goddess on his arm instead of the familiar, unthreatening, mud-streaked tree-hugger he'd expected.

CHAPTER EIGHTEEN

Hurrying home after a long day manning the stall at the Christmas Market, Susie had kicked off her muddy boots and run straight upstairs to find a dress designed to repel Murray Carew. She'd spent the better part of an hour going through her late mum's wardrobe, pulling out dresses almost at random and trying them on, and then weeping silently as she recalled her mother wearing each outfit, how happy she'd been, and how tragic her early death had been. Without Tansy there to share her grief, she'd perched on her bed with a box of tissues and let it all out instead…

Finally, drying her eyes, she'd gone back to hunting for the perfect drop-dead dress, settling in the end for a snug blue satin with a daring side slit that had been one of her mum's favourites.

Yes, as someone running a Christmas tree nursery, like Susie now, her mother hadn't enjoyed many occasions for wearing all the glam dresses she couldn't resist buying. But Dad had made a point of taking his wife out for a posh dinner at least once a month, sometimes to a party too, especially in the summer or around Christmas time, where they had always danced the night away.

Those days were long gone.

But tonight, it felt as though a little piece of her mother would be with her as Susie stepped out on this chill December evening to go partying with the mayor.

To conceal the fact that she'd been crying, Susie had plastered on make-up, taking her time to get it right, as she wasn't used to putting on much make-up at all. Then she'd taken out her studs and put in delicate filigree silver earrings Mum had left her. More tears had threatened then, and she'd gritted her teeth and sworn at herself in the mirror, not wanting to make her mascara run...

Even the heels had belonged to her mum, who'd worn them with far more poise, she was sure. But the gold anklet she was wearing was all her own, a special gift to herself on finishing uni. Not that she'd had much chance to wear it since those days...

Susie had looked at herself in the full-length bathroom mirror and not recognised the woman staring back at her. Who was that glamorous creature in the sexy blue satin, with her red hair piled high and her green eyes outlined with kohl, so like her mum when she was younger, yet subtly different too?

Thankfully, she'd heard Murray's car pull up outside the house before she had a chance to start crying again, so she'd clumped hurriedly down in her wobbly heels to open the door mere seconds after the doorbell had rung.

If looking at her reflection had been a shock, staring out at Murray Carew in his elegant suit with his longish dark hair slicked back and his eyes widening as they took in her make-up and chignon, had left her gasping for breath.

Hurriedly, she'd closed the door in his face, and rummaged for the huge, shapeless raincoat left behind by her dad. This was not simply to guard against the spitting rain but to hide what she was wearing. She'd known she would have to take the coat off eventually, of course. She couldn't go to a swanky party with the mayor wearing what was essentially an enormous plastic bag. Yet somehow she'd felt too shy to let Murray see the blue satin dress until they were in company with others.

Sure enough, on revealing her outfit at the party, the mayor had stared at her in astonishment. But his reaction left her feeling awkward...

What must he be thinking now? Perhaps that she fancied him and had worn this dress as a seduction technique. Though, of course, she *had* chosen this dress deliberately, but for the opposite reason. Because she hoped it would frighten him off, not draw him in. It was a dress that said – or whispered naughtily – *femme fatale*. And, by the look in his eyes, she had at least succeeded in making him wary. But would it be enough to repel him?

After that initial stare, Murray had spun away and

was now gladhanding everyone at the party. There didn't seem to be a single person there who didn't know precisely who he was. In fact, several of the attractive women who'd leant close to kiss his cheek as part of their greeting were probably *intimate* acquaintances.

Of course, she knew plenty of the party-goers too. But only because they'd bought Christmas trees from her in the past. Not because she was a local celebrity.

All the same, people were undoubtedly looking her way. It was unnerving and she was tempted to ask one of the circulating waiters whether she had dirt on her face or maybe an embarrassing sign pinned to her back, the way they were all staring at her.

Someone came round with a tray of drinks and Murray handed her a champagne flute, taking one for himself. 'Cheers,' he said softly, clinking his glass against hers. When she said nothing, gulping down several mouthfuls of fizzy wine, he frowned. 'You look sad. Why?'

How on earth had he known that?

Taken off guard, she blurted out, 'This dress belonged to my mum. She died...' Words failed her, and she groped for what she'd meant to say. 'I miss her, that's all.'

'I'm sorry.'

'Not your fault.'

'No, but...' He steered her into a quiet corner. 'You hungry?'

'Starving.'

'Hang on.' Disappearing briefly, he came back with a napkin full of tempting canapés. They looked like mini-poached eggs balanced on top of a dry roll-up of French toast. 'Eat.'

'Thanks.' Tummy rumbling, she crunched them down, one by one, struggling to eat in a delicate manner, but that wasn't really possible with poached egg on French toast. Soon, crumbs were everywhere... And she meant, *everywhere*.

Trying not to make it too obvious, she peered down inside the loosely draped folds of her blue satin bodice, and swore under her breath.

'Ah, allow me.' To her embarrassment, Murray produced a pristine white handkerchief square from his top pocket and swept away a fine scattering of crumbs from her dress, also flicking his duster across her cleavage. 'Want any more?'

She threw him a perturbed look, hoping he meant more canapés. 'Erm, is there anything less crumby?'

'Crummy?'

'Crumb-y.' She cleared her throat. 'Less productive of crumbs.'

'Oh, you mean *crumbly*... Less *crumbly*.'

'Whatever,' she said weakly, wishing she could just sink through the floor or maybe into the walls and never be seen again. Had the mayor really just de-crumbed her cleavage with his hanky?

He stopped another passing waiter with a tray of food and selected another handful of canapés. 'How about these, then?'

'What are they?'

They both glanced at the young waiter in the Cornish tartan waistcoat, who shrugged and moved on with his tray.

'We need to prep the staff better for these events.' Murray handed her a squidgy pink-and-green canapé. 'At a guess, I'd say this is salmon pâté wrapped in a vine leaf.' Murray sniffed the other offering, his face suspicious, then passed it over to her. 'Mint and lemon jelly on a puff pastry base. Wow, these are bizarre. Who the hell devised the menu for tonight? I hope it wasn't me. Still, at least there shouldn't be too many crumbs involved with those. Maybe the puff pastry, but...' He tapped his pocket handkerchief.

She devoured the bite-sized snacks gratefully, taking care to hold the food away from her cleavage while eating. 'I didn't have time for a snack before getting ready tonight,' she admitted. 'Today's been a bit of a disaster. The shop's incredibly busy, Tom says, and now I'm having to divide my time between the Christmas Market stall and the tree nursery and the shop too...' Belatedly, she recalled who she was talking to, and that she'd basically thrown him out on his ear, and that was why she was struggling with staff now. 'Tom's mum has been a godsend though,' she added hurriedly. 'I might take her on permanently, if you agree.'

'You're the manager. It's your call.'

'She's got experience with retail, and that helps. I barely had to teach her how to use the till or the loyalty card system. She doesn't know much about Christmas trees yet. But she's getting there.'

Murray was nodding, head bent as he listened to her above the buzz of the party, tapping his feet to the Cuban music they were playing. It was a catchy tune, she had to admit. 'I never got a chance to properly apologise, by the way.'

'For what?'

'The whole grotto thing.'

'Oh.' Heat flooded her cheeks. 'It's fine,' she mumbled. 'I was out of order. It's your shop now. Not mine. I went overboard.'

'No, you were right to call me on it. It wasn't *entirely* my fault,' he added, summoning a waiter with a passing tray of champagne, and swapping out her empty glass for a full one. 'But you were right. I should have taken action sooner. Made her get off my knee,' he went on in a low voice. 'I let the situation escalate.'

'We already went over this. It's really none of my business.'

He hesitated. 'We're not *shagging*.'

'Ugh, TMI,' she muttered, glugging more champers.

'I just wanted to make that clear. In case it wasn't before.'

Susie pulled a face and stared around the room rather than at him, wishing to goodness she hadn't worn her mum's beautiful blue satin dress tonight, her skin prickling, aware of how the shimmery fabric displayed every bump and curve. She felt exposed in its tight sheath…

Folk were twisting their hips and snapping their fingers, dancing boldly to the Cuban beat in an impromptu space they'd cleared down the centre of the long room. They were pretty decent dancers, she thought, watching them wistfully. Her feet began to tap…

Murray followed her gaze. 'If I'm forgiven, perhaps you'd care to dance?'

Horrified, Susie shook her head. 'I… I don't dance. Two left feet, I'm afraid. Of course you're forgiven… There's nothing to forgive. But I always make a complete ass of myself on the dancefloor.' This wasn't the way things were supposed to happen, she kept thinking. Murray had rejected his glamorous ex. He'd just confirmed it. *We're not shagging.* She'd assumed he'd soon beat a hasty retreat if she turned up in a sexy dress and heels like she was after his body. Instead, he was being uncomfortably attentive. 'And in these heels it might actually be dangerous.'

He held out a hand. 'I won't let you fall, I promise. Come on.'

She knocked back her second glass of champagne, set the empty flute on a table, and took his hand. There was nothing for it but to accept the invitation. Anything else would be rude, especially in front of all these townsfolk, now watching with prurient interest as their mayor led a Christmas tree grower onto the dancefloor.

How had she misjudged the situation so badly?

Perhaps he was lying, and it wasn't all over between him and Genevieve, and she'd based her outfit tonight on a false assumption that he currently found 'glam' a turn-off. Or perhaps he was in fact secretly in the market for a Genevieve replacement, and her satin dress was giving off all the wrong signals.

In either case, she might just have to beat him off with a canapé tray by the end of the evening...

She had downed that second champagne too quickly; it must have gone to her head, Susie decided. And now they were dancing far too close. His hips were bumping her hips – or near enough, her heels almost making up for the height difference tonight – and her chest kept brushing against his chest in a distinctly sexual way. But her chest was no doubt to blame, being more prominent than his, despite the massive pecs he'd presumably developed doing all that surfing over the summertime.

Before she'd left, Tansy had mischievously dug up some recent photos of the mayor on the internet, including one from a local news site, downing a bottle of beer with surfer dude mates on the beach, his wetsuit dragged off his top half and hanging from his waist so he could sunbathe, with the caption, 'Penrock Downs Mayor Votes For More Breakers!'

They had both stared, and then Tansy had begun to say something like, 'If I wasn't as gay as a rainbow pony,' so that Susie had gasped and pushed her off the breakfast bar stool before she could finish.

Now she was almost touching that bronzed chest, albeit through a crisp dark blue shirt, and couldn't help wondering if his tan had faded yet, and if it had been an all-over tan, given that he was invariably pictured wearing a wetsuit over the summer months...

'What are you thinking?' he demanded, bending so close to her ear, his breath was warm on her neck.

'I was just wondering... what *is* that smell?'

'Excuse me?'

'It's...' She breathed in, half-closing her eyes. 'Something citrussy.'

'You're saying I smell again? You're incorrigible.'

'Mmm, yes, but it's delicious.' Her eyes snapped open, realizing his face was mere inches from hers, a proximity alarm having just gone off in her loins. Damn that champagne! 'Um, sorry, did I say that out loud? I meant... Never mind. Your aftershave. It's citrus-based, that's all.'

'I believe it is.' He had an arm about her waist. 'And yours –'

'I don't wear aftershave.'

'Perfume. It's sweet, floral...' Murray sniffed her hair like it was a rose bush. 'With maybe just a hint of Christmas.'

Susie blinked. 'I smell like *Christmas*?'

'A Christmas tree, specifically.'

'Gee, thanks.'

He met her gaze, his lips twitching. 'Is that such a bad thing?'

'It's going in my diary.'

He threw back his head and laughed. The beat changed, growing slower. His other arm curled about her waist, and he lowered his head until their foreheads were brushing. She could smell mint off him now. Toothpaste, she thought. Her senses were spinning. Actually, *they* were spinning. Shuffling elegantly round and round to a slow, sensual beat that she could feel in her bones.

Someone called out, 'Great party,' and slapped Murray on the back in passing.

The mayor straightened, grinning after the interloper. 'Glad you could make it, Gus.'

'Hello again, Miss Lovell,' Gus told her, studying her dress with unconcealed interest. 'You look incredible.'

'Thank you,' she muttered in return and pulled away from Murray, embarrassed by the intimate way they'd been dancing. The other dancers had shrunk away from them, she realised, leaving them alone in the middle of the floor as though they were contagious. As though dancing too close to the mayor and his slinky new lady friend might have resulted in lustful feelings. Was that what people were thinking? That she and Murray were an item? Though she didn't need to wonder, as the amused suspicion that they were sleeping together was reflected in everyone's face around the room.

Seemingly oblivious to their fascinated stares, Murray smiled down at her. 'I need a quick word with Gus.' Was that a flicker of irritation in his eyes at the interruption, she wondered? Or relief that he'd been stopped before things got too hairy between them? 'Do you mind?'

'Absolutely not. Go for it.' She threw both men a bright smile. 'I need more champagne, anyway! Don't mind me... I'll just flag down a waiter. They're so cute in those Cornish tartan waistcoats, aren't they?' And with that, she wobbled away on her too-high heels.

Standing alone near the door, Susie smiled at a group of townsfolk who'd been staring at her fixedly and who now pretended they weren't interested at all, chatting animatedly, knocking back drinks and checking their phones. With a roll of her eyes, she gazed about for a waiter and saw someone she actually knew by name, a recent shopper at the Christmas Tree Shop. Giving up her hunt for more champagne, she began the long and laborious process of crossing the room instead, her feet already aching in the too-high heels. But before Susie could reach her, someone else slid between them.

'Not much of a dancer, are you?'

It was Genevieve, clutching a large glass of red wine, a lipstick stain on the glass... Murray's ex, and she was scantily dressed given the cold weather, in flared white trousers with a matching halter top that showed off her flat midriff.

She must be freezing, Susie thought, before the words and the light contemptuous tone had really sunk in. She blinked, taken aback, and didn't know how to respond. Genevieve's eyes were sparking with temper as she glared into Susie's face. She was smiling but showing all her teeth, a blonde barracuda with legs.

'Murray's scraping the bottom of the barrel with his dates these days,' Genevieve added, looking her up and down, brows raised as she lingered on the revealing slit in Susie's blue satin dress. 'Still, I suppose he couldn't resist such an easy lay.'

Shocked by this unexpected rudeness, Susie had to clamp down on her temper. She didn't want to cause a public scene. Instead, she tried to manoeuvre around the woman instead. 'Excuse me,' she muttered, 'I need to –'

'Hang on.' Genevieve was determined that she wouldn't escape. 'You're not going anywhere until you've heard what I came over to say.' She clutched Susie's arm with a fierce grip and leant forward. 'Don't think I don't know what's going on, you thieving bitch,' she hissed in Susie's ear. 'I saw the way you were dancing with him just now… But you're wasting your time. Murray prefers blondes. In fact, he's absolutely *mad* about me.'

'Is that so?' Susie couldn't resist, also glaring now. 'Because he told me it was all over between you.'

'Well, he would say that, wouldn't he? Men can't help themselves.' The other woman leant forward again, continuing with the ear-hissing, 'Trust me, the man is obsessed. Literally *obsessed*. He's got photos of me in his house. Pinned to the wall. Ask him if you don't believe me.' Her smile was coldly triumphant. 'I was the one who dumped *him*. Not the other way around. And he can't get over it.'

'That's not what it looked like to me when you spoke to him in the grotto.'

'That was a mis–'

'A misunderstanding? I don't think so. Murray was the one who dumped *you* that day, Genevieve. *On the floor*, as I recall.'

'He was kissing me, and I slipped,' Genevieve insisted, standing so close that their noses were practically rubbing together. 'If you hadn't walked in, we'd have been going at it like bunnies.'

Abruptly furious, Susie wrenched her arm free. 'You've got the wrong end of the stick. Murray's the last man on earth I would ever be interested in, so you don't need to warn me off him. Now, if you'll excuse me, there's someone I want to talk to and you're in my way.'

As she said this, she pushed Genevieve. Just a gentle nudge, so she could get past.

'Don't you dare shove me!' With a squawk of outrage, Genevieve pushed back, only much harder.

Already precarious on her heels, Susie felt herself overbalance, and grabbed Genevieve in alarm to steady herself.

Gravity did the rest.

Susie ended up on her back, winded by the impact, dragging Genevieve down with her. The other woman lay sprawled awkwardly across her chest, conversation dying around them as people turned to stare. A pair of angry eyes glared into hers, then the blonde shrieked like a maddened parrot and clambered back to her feet, staring down at her ruined outfit.

The red wine she'd been clutching had been dashed all down the front of Genevieve's immaculate white trouser suit, staining Susie's blue satin dress as well.

'Look what you've done!' Genevieve gasped, and then jabbed an accusing finger at Susie. 'You're going to pay for this, Susie Lovell. I'll *make* you pay, see if I don't.' And with that, she flounced towards the exit, onlookers clearing a hasty path for her.

The music kept playing, but conversation had ceased, everybody in the room gawping.

Grimly, Susie tried struggling into a sitting position without displaying too much thigh, which was clearly impossible in a dress with a slit right up to her thong.

Thankfully, a firm hand grasped her arm and lifted her back to her feet.

'You okay?' Murray looked her up and down, frowning with concern. 'I turn my back for five minutes and you're on the floor? Was that Genevieve I saw running off?'

'I don't want to talk about it.' People were still staring, and she didn't want everyone in the room knowing what their argument had been about. 'I need to go home and curl up on the sofa with a stiff drink,' she added in a mutter, head bent.

He hesitated, and she realised how impossible it was to ask him to run her home. He was the mayor. This was a council event to celebrate his grand vision of the Christmas Market. He hadn't even given his speech yet. She couldn't expect him to leave early just because she'd ended up rolling about on the floor with his ex.

'I'll call a taxi,' she said abruptly. 'You stay here and do your speech. Enjoy the evening. It's your party, after all.'

'Don't be ridiculous,' Murray told her, and shrugged out of his suit jacket. He placed it about her shoulders and pulled it together to hide the ugly red wine stain. 'I do need to give my speech first, but I'll be as quick as I can. Then I'll drive you home. You're not getting a taxi. You came with me; you'll leave with me.' But there was conflict in his face. 'I can't believe Genevieve did this. I'm really sorry. It's all my fault and I'm going make it right.'

She sat in the bar downstairs, a champagne cocktail in front of her, which she made light work of while waiting. Twenty minutes later, after Murray had given his speech and said goodbye to a few key people, he drove her home, his face like thunder. 'Look, I saw Genevieve screaming something at you and running out, but I don't know what led up to that. Was she drunk? What happened?'

Shakily, she explained, and saw his hands tighten on the wheel. 'I don't think she was drunk,' she added. 'But she was certainly angry. She thought –' Susie hesitated, too embarrassed to go on.

'Tell me.'

'She... She thought you and I were an item. She warned me off you.' Feeling awkward, she left out the bit about him being 'obsessed' and having photos of Genevieve up in his house. It was none of her business how he felt about his ex, after all. 'But the fall was accidental. These heels...'

He swore under his breath. 'Okay, but Genevieve still had no right to speak to you like that or try to block your way. She caused you to slip, and she owes you an apology for that. And for the red wine on your dress.'

'No, I'm fine.' Susie was horrified at the idea of having to speak to that woman again, even for an apology. 'The dress is old anyway. I'd rather just forget about the whole thing.'

'But it was your mother's dress,' he pointed out softly.

'Yes.' Tears pricked at her eyes.

She was still wearing his suit jacket, she realised. She'd forgotten to grab her gigantic mac from the cloakroom on the way out. She glanced at him, driving in just his shirt. Thankfully, the car interior was warm. But he must have been freezing on his way out of the hotel.

'Thank you for lending me your jacket. You need it back though.'

'Don't take it off yet,' he told her firmly. 'Wait until you're inside. Otherwise you'll get cold walking to the front door.'

'If you're sure...' Guiltily, she closed her eyes and wished she could start the evening all over again.

'You should have let me call a taxi. You're missing your party.'

'I don't care about that. Parties aren't my thing.'

Her eyes snapped open again, and she stared round at him in surprise. 'Really? I had you down as a party animal. Talking to people, shaking hands, dancing the night away.' She had intended a lighter note, but her voice was still uneven. That spat with Genevieve had left her more shaken than she'd realised.

'Not at all,' he replied coolly. 'I enjoy politics. Not parties.'

Back at the house, he insisted on walking her to the front door, for which she was grateful. The ground was slippery and blanched with frost, her wobbly heels more like roller-skates. Thankfully, she'd left the outside light on so she could see her way, and the flashing Christmas lights from the nearby shop made everything feel more festive and cheerful.

Standing under the porch light, she gave him a subdued smile. 'Thank you for seeing me home. I'm sorry again about dragging you away from the party. I was going to say thank you for a lovely evening too, but –'

'Yeah, maybe not.'

She gave a short laugh, though she felt awful about what had happened with his ex. 'I bet you regret asking me.' Having unlocked the door, she began to remove his suit jacket, but he shook his head, insisting she should wait until she was inside the house before taking it off. She didn't refuse, as the frosty air did feel several degrees below zero. 'You'd be enjoying yourself now if it wasn't for me.'

'I am enjoying myself.' He paused, a flicker of something indefinable in his eyes. 'In fact, this gives me an excuse for something I've been wanting to do again for ages. Until now, I hadn't quite found the perfect moment.'

And he bent his head and kissed her on the lips.

She ought to have been shocked. To have pushed him away and sent him packing, just like when he'd tried it on during their Ferris wheel ride. But that felt like a long, long time ago. Centuries, perhaps. Instead, in a champagne-fuelled trance, Susie linked her arms about his neck and kissed him back. Because why not? She'd told Genevieve tonight that she had no designs on Murray Carew. She'd insisted he was the last man on earth she'd ever be interested in. And yet here she was, less than an hour later, arms about his neck, sucking on his tongue like a throat lozenge...

Still, she had to admit, he was an amazing kisser. And she could still smell that citrussy scent that had driven her wild earlier. His aftershave? Unless he smelt naturally of citrus. Half man, half lemon, she thought dizzily. Though his lips were far from sharp. More sweetly addictive.

Her head fell back as his kiss deepened. His pelvis bumped hers, he pushed back the jacket she was still wearing, and one hand gently moulded her breast through the cool damp satin of her dress.

'Watch out for the wine stain,' she whispered.

Murray gave the ghost of a laugh. 'Are you worried I might get sticky fingers again? Trust me, I'm counting on it this time...'

Her cheeks flushed at the implication, and Susie moaned softly as he kissed his way down her neck almost to her plunging cleavage. Her hands clutched his hair at the nape, dragging him closer. Heat coiled low down and she gasped, rubbing one thigh restlessly against his. The satin dress fell away, exposing her leg to the chill night air, but she didn't care anymore.

With exquisite slowness, he moved aside her dress strap and kissed the tender skin there. Susie felt him shiver and didn't know if it was from the bitter weather or excitement.

'You're getting cold,' she whispered.

'Quite the opposite,' Murray assured her, and scooping her up in his arms as though she weighed nothing, which clearly she didn't, he stepped over the threshold, shut the front door with his foot, and carried her upstairs.

CHAPTER NINETEEN

Sometime in the early hours, Murray woke with an abrupt start, momentarily thrown to find himself lying in an unfamiliar bed, staring up at an unfamiliar ceiling. His body felt strange too. Somehow rubbery and elastic but aching, as though he'd spent five hours in the gym, and also deeply sated at the same time. He was naked too, which was standard for him during the summer months but odd at this time of year, when he would normally be wearing at least pyjama bottoms.

Most mysteriously, there was now a molten pool where his lower abdomen used to be, as though he'd turned into a chocolate pudding overnight, the gourmet kind with warm goo in the middle. If someone were to dip a spoon into him right now...

He sat bolt upright as everything came flooding back, mostly in reverse order.

'Betty!'

At his cry, there was a muffled groan of surprise, and his head turned, noting in the faint gloom the distinct outline of a female body lying beside him in bed. The light was off but there was still a light shining on the landing and the door had been left partly open. That no doubt accounted for the chilly nature of the room. Though not having a stitch to his body wasn't helping matters.

Murray resisted the urge to draw the duvet up over himself, roll over and go back to sleep, and slowly, gingerly, swung his legs out of bed instead.

He had to rescue Betty.

'Huh?' The feminine body in the bed rolled over to face him, only half-covered by the duvet. Susie Lovell. Her upper half, completely exposed, was so mesmerising, he found himself staring, dry-mouthed, unable to move. Memories came back. His hands, stroking those beautiful breasts. His lips there too, and lower. Her back arching beneath his mouth...

Her red curls were dishevelled, hiding her face, but her name was on his lips. 'Susie,' he mouthed silently, not wanting to wake her properly.

It had been wonderful. Mind-blowing. Far and away the best sex he'd ever had. He'd thought at one stage that he was going to die, and remembered thinking that at least he would end his days happily in her bed. Somehow he'd survived though, and fallen into a deep, dreamless sleep, and then woken to her touch, and it had happened all over again, their lovemaking sweaty and urgent in the darkness, accompanied by the constant flash of Christmas lights outside her bedroom window.

She shifted again, and he drew a sharp breath, his loins stiffening at the sight of her nude body. He was still good to go. She only had to say the word.

Except it was impossible.

Rescuing the dog from a night in the kitchen had to be his number one priority. Even if a more primal instinct was now rearing its enthusiastic head...

Quietly, trying not to make any noise, he slipped out of bed and began hunting among the clothing strewn across the dark floor for his suit trousers and shirt.

'Hey, where do you think you're going?' Susie slurred from under her mop of tousled hair and groped sleepily across his side of the bed. 'I haven't finished with you yet.'

He grabbed what he hoped might be his underpants. It turned out to be a soft, blue, silky bit of kit he vaguely recognised as her thong. It hadn't stayed on long after he'd been treated to his first view of her bottom...

'I can't, sorry,' he told her, grimacing as he dropped the thong. How women could wear something so restrictive up their butt crack he couldn't imagine.

'Is there somewhere you'd rather be?'

'I need to get home to Betty,' he explained, continuing his hunt in the gloom. 'She'll be anxious and waiting for me, you see.' He found a lacy bra and discarded it, frustrated. 'I've been gone for hours. She didn't even get a midnight snack or to stretch her legs.'

Maybe he could wear his trousers without

underpants. It wouldn't be the first time he'd gone commando after an interesting night out. But the green underpants he'd worn to the party had Santa's Sack written across them in garish red print – a jokey Secret Santa gift from a colleague last Christmas – and he didn't want her to find them later. He'd been too busy that week to do his usual laundry duty, and consequently had been faced with only the wacky underpants in his drawer when dressing for the party, the ones he almost never wore.

'Betty? *Betty?*' There was a growing note of outrage behind the repeated name. 'Who the hell is... Oh!' Susie exhaled slowly. 'Oh yeah, the dog.' She yawned then, and drew her knees up to her bare chest, looking utterly adorable. 'Okay, you'd better go then. Can't have Betty chewing her way out of the house in search of biscuits. You must be three hours late with her snack by now.'

'More like five and a half, actually.'

'It's *half past five?*' She stared at him through glinting red strands of hair, then groaned. 'That means I have to get up for work in two hours. Open the shop for Tom, walk up to the market stall, and stand there in my thermals and the freezing cold for the next eight or nine hours.'

'Yeah, I'm sorry. I tried not to wake you.'

Sod the underpants, he thought, giving up the search and pulling on his trousers. Now the grogginess of sleep had fallen away, he was genuinely worried. He had neighbours on both sides. He'd left the dog locked in the kitchen to avoid her destroying the new Christmas tree. Betty was usually okay when left longer than expected, but that was when she had the full run of the house.

Hopefully, Betty would be curled up in her basket like a fluffy little angel, having slept through his absence. Worst case scenario, she might have been barking hysterically all night and hurling herself against the kitchen door like Special Forces attempting ingress to a drug baron's compound. There would almost certainly be a puddle by now, and that would be his fault, and he would have to administer extra dog treats and apologise for being a very bad, inconsiderate owner, and suffer the dog glaring at him accusingly for days on end.

'I had a great time, by the way,' he added, reaching for his shirt.

God, that sounded so lame! What must she be thinking? He'd had a fantastic, brain-altering, body-morphing experience last night, and the only words he could find to express that to the woman who'd made it possible was... *I had a great time.* And yet, expressing anything more complex or in-depth right now would feel too unsettling, he considered. His body was still reeling, and as for his mind...

No, first he needed to process what had happened between them. And that could take some days. This wasn't the best time to start blathering on about his mind being blown, not to mention other parts of his anatomy. She would probably be freaked and run a mile.

Still, it hadn't been the most romantic thing to say.

Apologetically, he leant over the bed to touch her bare shoulder, still buttoning his shirt in a haphazard fashion. 'I'll, erm, call you.'

Susie didn't say anything but continued to stare at him through her hair like a cavewoman. A delicately scented, ultra-feminine cavewoman at this particular moment. Her silence left him suddenly unsure over what had just happened. They'd been to bed together. Yes, it had been amazing. For him, at least.

But maybe she'd been bored. Or underwhelmed by his sexual technique. And did going to bed together mean they were in *a relationship* now? And, if so, were they friends with benefits or serious boyfriend, girlfriend? Would he be expected to ask her out to dinner next? Send her flowers? Talk about his feelings?

'Or not, if you prefer,' he stammered, backing away.

Susie shrugged and rolled over to face the wall, the gleaming line of her spine like something Michelangelo might have painted.

'By the way, when you wake up, you may find some underpants...' Murray whispered from the doorway, but she remained silent, so he gave up and fled.

By eleven o'clock that morning, having snatched a few hours' restorative sleep after realizing he looked like Dracula in need of a blood fix, Murray was back at the desk in his chilly home office. With coffee in a thermal mug, he snapped on the electric heater and sat scrolling through WhatsApp messages and social media posts, between studying onscreen paperwork for the Christmas Market costs and projected final revenue, and making some due payments on the shop.

Occasionally, his phone rang, and he spoke chattily to the clerk of the council about an upcoming meeting, and also handled a call from an elderly member of the public who kept turning up at council meetings and waving his stick in a threatening manner, claiming they should all be in prison for having refused planning permission for him to convert his garden shed into a single-bedroom house and sell it on the open market. 'I understand your frustration, but the council is merely following the law,' he told the man soothingly, and held the phone at arms' length as the pensioner exploded into another tirade.

Betty lay beside him in her basket, watching him closely with her chin on her paws, still brooding after last night's failed promise of an early return from the party.

The dog hadn't had an accident during his long absence, thankfully. But she'd left scratch marks on the base of the kitchen door, and then refused to be drawn on how those had occurred when he pointed them out. Plus, she hadn't believed his excuses about needing to do his own thing for once. The dog had sniffed his hands and shoes when he finally released her, and then flattened her ears in disapproval, no doubt smelling Susie on him.

He still couldn't get to grips with how he felt after his night with Susie Lovell. It had happened spontaneously, and without his usual plan-everything-before-acting approach. And it complicated things.

Apart from anything else, she was essentially his employee. It was probably unethical for him to have gone to bed with her.

Then there was what-would-happen-next to consider.

Were they dating now?

Did he even want to be dating someone?

He was both excited and uneasy at the same time, an uncomfortable feeling that left him wondering if the milk was off in his coffee, which was not impossible. He hadn't been at home much lately and the carton had been open nearly a week.

Betty whined softly, her ears pricking.

Murray closed his eyes, leaning back in his leather chair. All he had ever wanted was a quiet, uncomplicated life. Was that so much to ask for?

These days, if it wasn't Genevieve causing him headaches, it was Betty sulking because he was out, seeing other females.

'Women,' he muttered, and jumped when the dog barked, his eyes flying open. 'For goodness's sake, you can't still be in a mood with me, Betty,' he complained, and then realised she'd jumped up and was standing to attention, staring tensely at the door as though expecting someone to walk through it. 'What is it, girl?'

Seconds later, his doorbell rang.

Shutting Betty into the home office, much to the little dog's disgust, Murray steeled himself for another unsettling throw-down with Genevieve. But when he opened the front door, he found his cousin Tilly on the doorstep.

Tilly looked awful, like she hadn't slept in days, her face pale and blotchy, her eyes red-rimmed. A navy-blue woolly hat with a holly leaf pattern had been jammed down over her unruly dark curls, a long matching scarf was wound twice about her neck, and she was hunched in a thick brown corduroy jacket with sheep's-wool trim.

'Tilly, what a surprise!' Frowning at her appearance, he gestured her inside. 'Come in out of the cold, I'll put the kettle on. What brings you to Penrock Downs? I hope it's our fabulous Christmas Market.' His voice tailed away as she looked up at him with forlorn eyes. 'Tilly…? What's the matter? What's happened?'

'It's Mum,' she told him, producing a tissue and blowing her nose. 'She went to the doctor last month, over some unpleasant symptoms, and was sent to the hospital for tests. Then the oncologist rang and told her the cancer's back.'

'Oh my God.' Swiftly, he ushered her inside and shut the door. 'That's dreadful news, I'm so sorry.' He followed her through to the kitchen. 'What's to be done? More surgery? More chemotherapy?'

'No point, apparently. All this time we thought she was clear of it, and instead it had spread through her body. There's no stopping it this time, they said.' She blew her nose again. 'She's dying, Murray.'

He was stunned, unable to process what she was telling him.

Aunt Alison, dying?

His late dad's sister had always been one of his favourite people in all the world. It was true that he hadn't kept in touch as much as he would have liked after his uncle had died and Alison had moved to live nearer his cousin Tilly and her husband, down in Truro. Still, they had exchanged cards and emails occasionally. Less frequently in recent months though, even his phone calls to her kept short, since she always seemed too tired to talk for long.

Now this news...

It felt as though someone had punched him in the stomach.

'I don't know what to say, Tilly. It's the worst thing imaginable.' He hugged her and they stood together through few moments in silence. 'You know how I feel about your mum. She was always so much fun when we were kids, wasn't she? It was hard to believe, at times, that she was Dad's sister, they were like chalk and cheese. Dad was so grim and taciturn, especially at family gatherings, and then Alison would bounce in and start tickling everyone.'

Tilly nodded, laughing and crying at the same time. 'She hasn't changed.'

'How long do they think she has?' he asked hesitantly.

'Less than two weeks, one doctor suggested.'

'*Two weeks?*' He shook his head, horrified. 'How is that possible? To have so little warning...?'

'She'd been ignoring the symptoms, they said. You know what my mum's like. Such a stubborn mare... She tried to pretend it wasn't happening again. And she kept making excuses not to see me so I wouldn't spot how ill she was and march her round to the doctor.'

He groaned. 'Did you try a second opinion?'

'I've seen the test results, Murray. They're conclusive. The cancer is everywhere, she's riddled with it. And she's so sick, far worse than before. Though now they've taken her into hospital and pumped drugs into her, she seems almost well at times. Sometimes I have to remind myself how little time she has left.'

He stood in a daze, not knowing what to say.

She filled the kettle herself and put it on while he watched dumbly. 'I'm sorry I didn't call and let you know sooner,' she added with an apologetic look, 'but we only found out ourselves a short while ago and I didn't want to tell you on the phone. It would have been too brutal. So I waited until Michael could take a day off work to sit with her, and then drove up to see you.'

'It's okay, I... I understand.' He remembered when his father had fallen sick and died over the space of a few weeks, how chaotic everything had felt.

'It's been ages since we saw each other, I know,' Tilly told him, biting her lip, 'and I wish I could be here now under better circumstances. I know you must be incredibly busy with this Christmas Market, and being Mayor and all, but are you able to... to come and say goodbye to her?'

'*Say goodbye?*' He buried his head in his hands, barely able to function, and then pulled himself together for his cousin's sake, saying grimly, 'Yes, of course I'll come. There's no question. Straightaway, in fact. I had a few meetings planned over the next few days, but I can cancel them. This is more important.' He took her hand and squeezed it gently. 'I'm so sorry, Tilly. How are you and Michael coping?'

While they drank a quick coffee at the breakfast bar, his cousin Tilly told him everything that had been happening in the past few days, how his aunt's diagnosis had shaken them all to the core. All except Aunt Alison herself, apparently. It seemed she hadn't been surprised by the death sentence handed to her by the consultant. But then, Alison had always been a cheerful, pragmatic soul. She had faced life's difficulties with a smile on her lips, and now she was facing death in the same fearless manner.

'Don't,' Tilly murmured, fetching a fresh tissue from her purse for him. 'Mum wouldn't want you to cry. She's already told me and Michael off for weeping buckets at her bedside.' She gave him a lopsided grin. 'And you're her favourite nephew. She'll hold you to a higher standard.'

'I'm her *only* nephew,' Murray pointed out unsteadily, dabbing at his eyes with a tissue. His petty difficulties with Genevieve faded into the distance. Though one thought did filter through his grief, and that was a memory of carrying Susie upstairs last night, the desire in her luminous green eyes as she kissed him back.

'You still living on your own, then?' Tilly asked, almost as though she could read his mind, glancing about the bare kitchen.

'You know me. I love the bachelor lifestyle.'

'Liar.' She mock-punched him in the arm. 'Hey, you were mad about some blonde once, weren't you? The one who ran off to join a convent. What was her name?'

'Genevieve,' he ground out.

'Did she become a nun in the end?'

'No,' he said wearily, and told her everything that had happened in recent days with Genevieve. Though he left out the part about Susie.

'Goodness me.' Tilly sipped thoughtfully on her coffee. She'd always followed Murray's amorous adventures with interest, though she herself had been married to Michael, a staid accountant in his forties, for the past twelve years. 'She sounds positively on the edge. Poor woman.' She peered at him from under her lashes. 'Only there's something here you're not telling me.'

'I don't know what you mean,' he said, rattled by her female intuition.

'The only reason a woman behaves like that is when a man is in danger of getting involved with someone else. Otherwise, she would just have bided her time.' When he refused to rise to that bait, Tilly finished her coffee and jumped down from the stool. 'Well, I'd better use the loo before heading back to Truro. Do you want to bring your own car or come with me?'

'I'll follow you in my car. I don't want you to have to drive me home again when...' He couldn't finish that sentence, swallowing and looking away.

'It's okay.' His cousin gave him another quick hug. 'My one prayer is that Mum suffers as little as possible.'

'Agreed,' he said heavily.

When she'd gone to the loo, he called his dog-minder and made arrangements for him to collect poor Betty and have her stay with him for the duration. It wasn't ideal but at least it wasn't an impersonal kennel. Then he packed clean clothes for a stay with his cousin Tilly, along with the carved wooden box he'd bought for her at the Christmas Market. He had intended to see her and his aunt over Christmas anyway, but now...

A tear trembled at his lower eyelid, blurring his vision before it spilled over and rolled down his cheek. Why did good people have such bad things happen to them?

On his way to Truro, following his cousin along the main A-road, he made a hands-free call to the clerk of the council. 'Cynthia, listen, I'm not going to be around for the next ten days, maybe longer. Someone else will need to chair the meeting on Thursday night, and there are various other things that will need someone else's oversight. I'll email you the details. It's unfortunate but something's come up.' He hesitated, feeling too raw to discuss his aunt's diagnosis. 'A family situation.'

'I hope you're well,' Cynthia sounded concerned.

'Perfectly well, thank you. It's a member of my family who's seriously ill. I have no idea when I'll be able to resume my duties. I'll try to keep up with the WhatsApp messages though. Can you manage without me?'

'We'll be fine,' she assured him. 'I'm so sorry, Murray. Best wishes to you and your family. You'll be in our thoughts.'

When he arrived at the hospital, he hesitated, his thumb hovering over the Call button, and then texted Susie instead.

Something's come up. I won't be around for a bit. No idea when I'll be back in town. But last night was amazing. Thinking of you.

He hesitated over leaving an 'x' as a kiss, and then decided against it. He still wasn't sure what their relationship was. Or if they even had a relationship. So far, it had been one night. Besides, he couldn't think about Susie. All that mattered now was his aunt and the terrible diagnosis she'd received. Yet his thoughts kept drifting back to her, and he longed to be lying beside her in the dark again, their warm bodies touching…

He ought to have told Susie exactly what was going on. But she didn't know anything about his aunt. She didn't know much about his family at all.

Everything felt so new, he feared ruining the bloom on this emotion by putting too much on her, overloading this delicate new thing between them with painful thoughts and feelings that seemed to have no place there.

'Michael's texted me,' Tilly told him on their way up to the hospital room. 'They've found a bed for her at the hospice. Apparently, she'll be better off there.' Her voice wobbled. 'A hospice... Oh Murray, everything's moving so quickly. I don't think I can bear it.'

Murray put an arm around her. 'I'm here for you, Tilly. I love your mum. We all love her. Even Dad, who was the grumpiest person in the universe, loved her to bits. So you won't be going through this alone. And if you need anything, just ask.'

He'd half expected to find his aunt unconscious and wired up to tubes. So he was surprised to walk in and see her sitting up in bed, chatting to Michael, Tilly's husband. He shook hands with Michael and then bent to kiss his aunt's cool, pale cheek, who looked delighted to see him.

'So that's where Tilly got to,' she said in a rasping voice, having been a smoker most of her life. 'Fetching my rascally nephew Murray. How are you, my lovely? As if I need ask…You look the picture of health, unlike me. Still surfing?'

'Not recently,' he admitted, drawing up a seat on the other side of her bed. 'I'm a summer surfer. Once the weather turns, I wimp out and hang up my surfboard until April at the earliest.' He glanced at the monitor beside her bed. 'I hear you're in a bad way, Aunt Alison.'

'These doctors... For years, they tell me I'm fine, that I'm imagining it all. Then I get a few funny symptoms, and apparently I'm about to pop my clogs. I'm sure it's a false alarm.' His aunt gave him a wink, which didn't quite convince, and then started coughing and couldn't seem to stop.

Michael jumped up to rearrange her pillows and pat her on the back, while Tilly helped her take a few sips of water. The coughing fit lasted several minutes.

'For goodness' sake...' Alison spluttered and collapsed against the pillows, limp and exhausted. 'Oh, you should go home. I can barely speak.'

Murray laid his hand gently on hers. 'I brought today's newspaper, in case you want to talk politics. Or we could watch a film together. Alternatively, you can sleep while I read a book. But you're not getting rid of me that easily.'

'You always were a lovely, thoughtful boy, Murray.' Aunt Alison's voice was weak, but she continued in her hoarse rasp, 'I never said it before, but your dad was a horrible man and he treated you very badly. I should have done more to stop him.'

Murray realised that he was crying again. Gruffly, he said, 'I always wished that I'd been *your* son, but that's life, isn't it? You do your best with the hand you've been dealt.'

'Exactly right. Now, I don't know if Tilly told you, but I'm unlikely to see out the end of this month.

Which means I need Christmas to come a little early this year. I'd like a small plate of turkey with all the trimmings, Christmas crackers with party hats inside, a bit of tinsel on the walls... But no presents for me, thanks. I wouldn't enjoy them for long, which would rather take the fun out of receiving them. I've bought a few gifts for you lot online though. Humour me, okay?'

'Oh Mum,' Tilly murmured, looking broken-hearted.

'There's a bed for me in the hospice, and I'll be moving there later today, with any luck.' She was whispering now, her voice almost gone. 'End of life palliative care, they call it. They've promised me a pain-free departure from this world, which sounds good to me about now. But once I'm drugged up to the eyeballs, I won't have a clue what's going on.' Aunt Alison patted Murray's hand, meeting his troubled gaze with a wan smile. 'So, how do you feel about celebrating Christmas the day after tomorrow?'

CHAPTER TWENTY

Just wondering how you are. Susie x

Susie threw aside her phone and put the shop delivery van into first gear, staring at grey skies ahead. Why, oh why, had she gone to bed with Murray? Oh yes, it had been marvellous. The most exciting night of her life. His lovemaking had left her delirious and eager for more. And then he'd got out of bed, pulled on his clothes, and gone home to rescue Betty.

It wasn't the most romantic thing in the world, being deserted halfway through their first night together... for a dog.

But the worst had been yet to come. Murray had left town abruptly later the same day, and had not yet come back. As the days passed with no contact, she'd sent him a few tentative texts, and he had answered each one with a generic response.

I can't talk right now, sorry.
I'll get back to you as soon as I can.

Sorry I've been away so long, please be patient.
'Be patient,' she muttered to herself.

Well, she'd been trying to be patient. But it was near impossible. And now it was Christmas Eve.

What was Murray Carew doing? Where on earth was he? And why couldn't he stop prevaricating and tell her the truth?

The simple fact was, she was angry with him, and disappointed with herself. He'd made love to her as though it really meant something, and then had simply disappeared, leaving nothing but a cryptic text message behind.

The inference seemed clear.

She'd misread the signals and put her trust in a man who wasn't worth it, bewitched by his smile and wrongly assuming they might have some kind of future ahead...

Instead, she'd sacrificed her dignity and emotional well-being for a one-night stand.

And now she couldn't get that night out of her system.

Ever since the party, she had been crawling into bed in a fever of unrequited desire, and then tossing and turning all night, wishing he was there with her. And every morning she had stumbled out again to leaden skies and a plummeting barometer, wrapped up in a sweater adorned with Christmas trees or cute festive penguins. For hours every day, she had stood in her stall at the market, forcing a smile for townsfolk and visitors alike, shaking hands with people and wishing them a merry

Christmas, trying her hardest to sell as many items as she could before the market closed on Christmas Eve.

But her head was in a mess, as she struggled not to think about Murray while simultaneously thinking about him the whole damn time...

There'd been a reduced rate for locals taking stalls at the big Christmas Market, but there was no denying that it was costing them an enormous amount to man the stall throughout December. And while they'd sold masses of Christmas stock, they needed to move the bulk of it to make even a small profit, once overall costs were taken into account.

In the past, she and Dad had simply drawn meagre wages from the store during lean times, to help balance the books. Sometimes she had worked for next to nothing. But now Dad was gone, and Murray would almost certainly expect sales to cover the wages for all these new staff. So she was stuck on the stall all day, constantly hoping for a sighting of Murray which never came, and having to look cheerful and festive when she was miserable and dejected inside.

There was a small car park at the back of the cat sanctuary in Penrock Downs, a large Victorian building gifted to the council by an elderly, childless cat-lover.

Susie pulled up there and checked her phone.

No reply from Murray.

She took a moment to shake off her gloom, and then pinned a bright smile to her face before getting out of the car.

'Your smile is your armour,' her mum had told her once, complaining that Susie never let people get too close.

Well, she'd let Murray get too close. And look what had happened there. Time to buckle on her brightest smile, Susie thought grimly, and keep marching forward.

Tansy was almost unrecognizable in smart navy-blue trousers and a cream blouse, her frizzy hair pulled back in a business-like ponytail, though the welcoming beam on her face hadn't changed a jot.

'Hello, hello, hello,' she cried excitedly, seeing Susie on the threshold of the cat sanctuary. Jumping up from her desk behind the reception counter, Tansy came round to usher her friend inside. 'Merry Christmas! I've been waiting for you to visit for ages. Come in and meet some of the cats. How are you? What have you been up to? I haven't made it up to the Christmas Market yet... What's it like?'

Susie found herself seized in a bear-hug, unable to respond to this barrage of questions as she was squeezed half to death.

'Don't mind the smell,' Tansy rattled on, releasing her. 'One of the new cats I was trying to comfort threw up half an hour ago, right behind the counter while I was petting her, and I had to bleach the whole area.' She wrinkled her nose. 'I hate the smell but it's regulations. There are so many regulations in running a cat shelter, you wouldn't believe it.'

'I probably would,' Susie assured her, only too aware of her own long list of health and safety regulations from managing the Christmas Tree Shop.

'Hey, a little bird told me about the launch party at the Cherry Orchard. Quite a few little birds, in fact. More like four-and-twenty blackbirds, to be honest, only not baked in a pie.' Tansy chuckled at her own joke, leading Susie through to the office. 'People said you ended up on the floor with Murray's ex on top of you, and then went home covered in red wine. But there were no photos to prove it. And no videos either, which is a shame, as I could do with a laugh.' She looked at Susie quizzically, her head tipped to one side. 'I texted you last week to ask if it was true. Only you didn't reply. Did you miss my message?'

She'd seen Tansy's message but hadn't felt up to replying. Not until she could see her friend face-to-face.

Susie flushed guiltily. 'Um, yes, sorry about that. I've been so busy on the stall at the Christmas Market, you see, and playing Mrs Santa since... since Murray went AWOL.'

Frankly, was she any better than Murray, ignoring messages because she couldn't bring herself to deal with them honestly?

'Anyway, it's true, more or less,' she added, seeing Tansy's expectant expression. 'But it was my fault, not Genevieve's. I... I took a tumble, that's all. Wearing heels that were far too high for me.' She managed a feeble smile. 'Silly me.'

She didn't know why she was covering for Genevieve. The truth was, it would be dangerously easy to let that incident at the party lead on to admitting that she and Murray had spent the night together. And she still wasn't ready to admit what she'd done.

Tansy looked unconvinced but didn't press the point. 'Well, let me give you a guided tour. There's a new volunteer somewhere... Paula. She'll be checking on the cats, I expect. I can ask her to look after the reception desk while I show you around.' Her smile broadened. 'I have my own digs upstairs; I can't wait to see what you think. Not much, just one bedroom and a bathroom, but I love it... It feels so safe and secure after years in a caravan.' She bit her lip. 'A bit claustrophobic too, but I'm getting used to it.'

Susie laughed, hugging her friend. 'I'm glad.'

She'd been meaning to visit for ages, and had kept putting it off, dashing about, flustered and inundated with work. But last week she'd finally recruited a seasonal worker to help her on the market stall, one of Tom's more politely spoken college friends who had come back to spend Christmas with his family and was pleased to be earning a little extra cash.

Meanwhile, Tom was playing Elf in the grotto, much to the kids' delight, and Tom's mum was working on the shop floor. As Susie had told Tansy on the phone last night, her business was fast becoming Tom's family business instead of hers.

The shop was busy even though it was now Christmas Eve, with a few people still belatedly buying their trees, though most were coming in for winter logs and kindling now, or for last-minute carved wooden gifts and unique decorations made for the shop each December by a local artisan. They sold centrepieces for dinner tables, made of ivy and holly wreathed beautifully about a Yule log or wire framework; traditional Christmas wreaths to adorn front doors; and gorgeous mistletoe bundles for strewing about a house or festive party.

She ought not to have left work during this all-important last sales period. But she had desperately needed to see Tansy and knew that her friend was equally keen to show her around the cat sanctuary. So she'd promised herself two hours off work that morning, and then her nose would be pressed firmly back to the grindstone again.

Room after room of the old Victorian house now housed cats, mostly in spacious, softly-lit single occupant pens of wood and wire mesh. Some cats crouched at their approach, silent and nervous, ears flattened against their skulls. Others were more playful and relaxed, two or three even purring as Tansy bent to stroke affectionately behind their ears.

Susie herself petted a few of the older cats, and even cuddled one sparky, mischievous-looking kitten, laughing when it became obsessed with her hair.

One irritable cat spat at her though, scratching her

hand, though luckily its claws did not manage to draw blood.

'Ow!' Susie exclaimed, jumping back.

'Sorry about him,' Tansy said with a grimace, drawing her hurriedly out of that pen and closing the door. 'Yeah, that's Elijah. He's had a difficult history. He was mistreated by his last owner, barely fed anything but scraps, and even beaten.'

'Poor thing!' Susie looked at the large, shambolic tabby through the pen window. 'He must have felt threatened by me. I shouldn't have tried to pet him.'

'No, it was my fault. I thought it would be all right. He's actually very sweet. But it did take him a while to get used to me. It's probably just because you're a stranger. Elijah finds most people frightening, so he puts on a big front, clawing and spitting and yowling. But it doesn't mean anything. Elijah likes a good belly rub, same as all the rest, especially when it comes with a handful of tasty kibble.' She sucked in a breath, grabbing Susie's hand. 'Let's get that cleaned up and put a plaster on it, shall we?'

After Susie's grazed hand had been wiped with antiseptic and covered with a plaster, they moved on to look at a mother cat who'd been brought in heavily pregnant and had given birth to her litter of kittens practically the next day. Seven tiny, smoky-grey kittens were now sleepily suckling on her while the mother cat lay in a contented stupor, seeming resigned to her fate as a parent.

It was wonderful, being shown around Tansy's proud domain. But Susie was soon sneezing, her eyes watering, and had to apologise as she backed away from the cat areas. 'It's nothing personal. They're all lovely. And that cute little tortoiseshell kitten is so gorgeous, I hope he gets a home soon. But my sinuses hate cats, and that's all there is to it. Sorry!'

'Don't worry,' Tansy told her. 'I know you're kind of allergic to cats. I'm just glad I managed to clear my own little gang out of your house before your nose fell off.'

'Yeah, it wasn't super comfortable sharing with all your cats. I was happy to help, of course... But I did start to wonder if I should buy shares in a tissue company.'

Tansy laughed and took her upstairs to see her cosy bedroom with an ensuite. Her own cats were housed up there in various cardboard boxes and on fluffy mats laid in corners, with a window left open on the landing so they could go up and down the fire escape if they wanted. Only Caesar stretched and yawned on seeing Susie, the other cats lay curled up asleep the whole time they were looking around.

'I have you to thank for all this,' Tansy told her as they made their way back downstairs. 'Honestly, if you hadn't known the mayor, and he hadn't suggested I apply for this job... Well, I'd probably be out on the streets right now.'

'You got this job on your own merits, Tansy, trust me.'

'I'm still very grateful. And to demonstrate it, I bought some Christmas cake for us to share. With a milky coffee? Unless you're sick of Christmas now, what with playing Mrs Santa for weeks, and then having to man that Christmas Market stall in the cold every day?'

'Me, sick of Christmas? Hell would freeze over first.' Susie laughed, but it rang false, and she looked away, shivering as though hell had done precisely that.

Tansy was interrupted by the sanctuary mobile phone ringing. 'Hang on a tick, this shouldn't take long.'

She answered the phone in quite a different voice, sounding polite and professional. 'Mrs Tilbury? Thank you for calling me back. How are you getting along with Stripey? Oh, that's good to hear. The first few days with a rescue cat are often the most difficult. But that sounds marvellous. Sorry? You've already renamed him? Well, Stripey was an odd name. I mean, he's not exactly a zebra, is he? So what's his new name?'

Tansy listened to a long reply, her head on one side, her gaze drifting ironically to Susie. '*Napoleon*? Well, I didn't see that one coming. Yes, I suppose he can be a bit aggressive at times. No, I don't think you should be feeding him French cheese. Or frogs' legs. Yes, dried kibble sounds perfect. Well, call me if you need anything else, Mrs Tilbury. Yes, goodbye.'

She turned to Susie with a groan. 'These people… Still, it was very good of her to give that problem cat a home. He's been here eighteen months. I just hope she doesn't bring him back when she discovers his unfortunate habit.'

'*Unfortunate habit?*'

'I did try to give her a hint about making sure she had a cat-proof bin. The last people he was housed with brought him back after a few days, saying he was constantly jumping into their swing bin and digging out the contents. He's a little rascal is our Stripey.' She tutted. 'I mean, *Napoleon.*'

Grinning, Susie took her arm. 'Did you mention cake?'

Paula was on desk duty, a middle-aged lady with a silvery bob and a lovely smile. After Susie had been introduced, Tansy sent the woman off on an early lunch break while they sat down for coffee and Christmas cake in the cosy area behind the reception desk.

'So,' Tansy murmured, casting Susie a meaningful look as she dusted Christmas cake crumbs off her festive cat jumper, 'no more distracting me with cat talk. I'm expecting all the skinny on Mr Mayor.'

Susie nursed her coffee, uncomfortable and caught off guard. What did her friend know? '*Skinny?* There's no skinny to be had. Or fatty, come to that.'

'You know what I mean. I want all the *gossip*. And don't pretend there isn't any. I can tell something's happened between you two.'

'Got a crystal ball, have you?'

Tansy shook her head disapprovingly. 'We've been friends for years, Susie. I know all your tells. And every time his name has come up today, you've *flinched.*'

'Indigestion,' Susie fibbed, and nodded at her plate of crumbs. 'Christmas cake... It's always been too rich for me.'

'Pull the other one, it's got bells on.' Tansy eyeballed her frankly. 'When we were talking about Murray and his ex earlier, your voice went high-pitched, and you got flustered and couldn't meet my eyes. Then his name came up again when we were talking about the Christmas Market... You folded your arms and shuffled your feet, and made a face like this.' Tansy screwed up her lips like she was sucking a lemon. 'I know you and Murray have never got on well. That's old news. But this is something new. Come on, I want to hear everything.'

Susie put down her coffee and burst into tears, unable to help herself.

'Goodness, what on earth?' Tansy jumped up and gave her a hug, looking horrified. 'Oh, Susie... I'm sorry if I badgered you. I didn't mean to tease you about the mayor. Please, don't cry.'

'I... I don't think I can stop.'

Tansy pulled multiple tissues out of her pocket like a magician pulling scarves from a top hat. 'Take these... Take all of them... Blow your nose. I shouldn't be let loose on people, should I? You've only been here an hour and I've already made you cry.'

Half laughing, half crying, Susie managed to shake her head, somewhere between dabbing her eyes and blowing her nose. She didn't know what was wrong with her. Or rather, she did, and it was mortifying to face it.

'It's not you. It's me. Or rather, him.'

Tansy sank back onto her seat, staring at her in consternation. 'Erm, okay. Maybe it is me. Because I didn't understand a word of that. Can you rewind to the beginning, please?'

'There isn't a beginning. Unless it was when Dad sold the business to Murray.' Susie thought for a moment, then shook her head. 'No, it was when Mum died. That's when everything changed for us. Dad was never the same after that. And nor was I.' She played with a clean tissue, shredding it as her chaotic thoughts tumbled helplessly over each other. 'After she'd gone, I felt... untethered. Like one gust of wind would blow everything away. And then it did.'

'Your dad selling up and leaving?'

Susie nodded unhappily. 'That was when I really understood what I'd lost. Everything that I'd thought would be in my life forever... All of it gone.' She paused, teetering on the verge of tears again. 'And then Murray came along, who was such an empty suit, a council bureaucrat with no finer feelings or understanding of what Christmas really means to people. And I *hated* him. I did at first, anyway...' she finished on a loud gulp.

'And now?' Tansy prompted her gently.

'Now, oh now, I...' Susie couldn't go on but buried her face in the shredded tissue instead, which promptly stuck to her damp skin in bits and pieces, so she had to peel fragments off like the remains of a face mask. 'Damn,' she muttered.

'That's an interesting look.' Tansy grimaced, watching this pantomime. 'Erm... You missed a bit.'

'Where?' Susie patted her face experimentally.

'To the left.' She blinked. 'No, more to the left. The *far* left. Think Communists.' Pointing helpfully, Tansy leant forward, peeled the last white shred off her cheek, and held it up. 'There you go.'

Susie met her gaze and they both cracked up laughing. Though it really wasn't that funny. But perhaps things had become so bad, everything was suddenly hilarious to her. And laughter was better than tears.

'You're right,' she admitted after a while, wiping her eyes. 'It's all gone badly wrong with Murray. I don't know what happened.'

'The party at the Cherry Orchard,' Tansy murmured wisely.

'Yes, maybe. After Genevieve gave me a red wine shower, I was a mess. Literally, I mean. People were staring. So I had to get out of there quickly. Murray offered to run me home. And then...' She blushed, leaving the rest to her friend's imagination.

Tansy smiled and leant back, definitely having filled in the gaps. 'How romantic.'

'It was incredible... Really, really hot.' Susie bit her lip, seeing Tansy's amused stare. 'But then he shouted, 'Betty!' in the middle of the night and walked out on me.'

'What the hell?'

'His dog,' Susie reminded her.

'Oh, of course. *That* Betty.' Her pet-loving friend shrugged. 'Understandable, in that case.' She caught Susie's eye and hurriedly added, 'But totally rude too. Only he rang you later to apologise, right?'

Susie shook her head silently.

'Texted you, then?'

'Yes, but only to tell me he'd left town. And he hasn't come back yet. No explanation, nothing. Just these…' Susie scrolled to his messages on her phone and handed it over for Tansy to study the screen.

I can't talk right now, sorry.

I'll get back to you as soon as I can.

Sorry I've been away so long, please be patient.

Tansy pulled a face, scanning through them. 'Oh dear.' She shot Susie a quick look. 'But maybe it's a family emergency. People can be funny about private stuff like that.'

'A family emergency?' Susie blinked.

She genuinely hadn't considered that possibility. She'd thought he must be regretting what they'd done and keeping her at arms' length. Which was fine, of course. If Murray wanted to pretend she didn't exist, she didn't care much about him either. She was happy that she'd found out early on how much of an idiot he was. Now she could spend the rest of her days counting her lucky stars that they hadn't suited after all. It wasn't as though she had fallen in love with him, after all…

'Oh for God's sake, I'm such a fool. Of course it's a family emergency. What else could have kept him away from the Christmas Market and his council duties for so long? Murray's obsessed with being Mayor of Penrock Downs. There's no way he'd neglect his work without a really, *really* good reason.' Tears rolled down her cheeks again, and she barely noticed them, staring down at the terse, uncommunicative messages on her phone screen. 'And instead of being understanding and supportive, I... I've been hating him all this time.'

'I doubt he noticed that,' Tansy put in helpfully.

'I'm in love with him,' Susie blurted out, and reached for another flimsy tissue to blot her wet cheeks, not caring if she ended up looking like an Egyptian mummy. 'And I don't think he even cares that I exist.'

Then her phone rang.

'It's Murray,' she gasped, and fumbled to answer the call, dropping her phone and diving under the reception desk to scrabble for it. 'Oh no!'

'You can do it,' Tansy told her encouragingly.

'Don't stop ringing, please don't stop ringing...' She finally answered the call on her knees, still crouched under the desk, tearful and breathless. 'Hello?'

The silence on the other end was deafening. Terrifying too.

Had he given up and rung off?

'Hello, are you still there?' she whispered. 'Murray?'

CHAPTER TWENTY-ONE

Murray hadn't thought Susie was going to answer his call, the phone had rung for so long. And he wouldn't have blamed her. He hadn't spoken to her since leaving town and had barely responded to her texts either. Yet what could he have said? He'd been denying reality for days now, pretending the worst wasn't happening, and ignoring all calls and texts had been part of that fantasy.

Admitting to Susie that his aunt was dying would have meant admitting it to himself too… And he hadn't been ready to do that. Not until yesterday. Not until the end.

'Yes, I'm here,' he agreed, leaning against his car and staring down at his trainers. 'I'm sorry I haven't been in touch. I couldn't speak to you. To anyone, in fact. The thing is…' He swallowed, battling a desire to cry. 'I'm outside the cat sanctuary. I rang Tom at the Christmas Tree Shop and he told me you'd be here this morning. So I turned up on the off-chance that I might be able to catch you in person.'

'You're here? At the cat sanctuary? *Right now*?' She

sounded astonished.

'I'm standing next to your car in the car park.' He took a deep, painful breath. 'I'll understand if you say no, but do you mind if we talk? I mean, face-to-face?'

She said nothing, but he could hear her relaying in a hoarse whisper what he'd just said to someone else, presumably Tansy.

'I don't want to hurry you for a decision,' he added, shifting uncomfortably against the cold metal door panel of his SUV, 'but I'm kind of freezing.'

Even as he was saying that, a solitary snowflake drifted past him on the icy wind. It looked cold and lonely and miserable, as though it had no idea where all the other snowflakes had gone, leaving it to find its own way to final oblivion, swirling aimlessly about on the chill Cornish air.

Murray watched as the snowflake hit the ground near his feet and melted clean away. Gone forever, in a nanosecond, like it had never existed.

Just like that.

Murray cleared his throat before wiping the back of his hand across his damp cheek. He couldn't stand the idea of crying in front of her. 'The temperature just dropped below zero,' he rasped.

'I'm on my way,' she said, and rang off.

Susie appeared barely a minute later, looking vibrant as always in her typical jeans and Christmas jumper, a sparkly green clip in her hair that matched the glint of her green eyes.

She stopped dead as she rounded the corner into the car park, staring at him. 'Good God, Murray... Why didn't you wait in the car for me? Or come inside? It's perishing out here.' Hurrying on, she halted again a few feet away, as though unsure whether to hug him or slap him, then compromised by simply folding her arms and glaring at him. 'All right... We're face-to-face. So, where have you been all this time?'

'I'm sorry,' he began in a hoarse voice, but Susie didn't seem to have heard him, her words simply ploughing straight over his.

'I've been trying to keep the shop afloat at the busiest time of year,' she rushed on, 'it's been all hands on deck for days on end, and no sign of you. Which is crazy, frankly. I mean, you're only *the owner*! You might want to consider showing up at some point, if only to make sure the place is still open and earning you money. And what about the invoices I've been forwarding you? I hope they've all been paid on time, otherwise we're going to have some disgruntled suppliers come January. Everyone in Penrock Downs has been wondering where you are, by the way, it's not just me. I've had councillors coming into the shop, asking if I know where you are, as though they suspected me of murdering you and burying you under the tree nursery. You haven't even been up to the Christmas Market since it opened, and that was your pet project from the start.' Susie shook her head, an impressive fury in her bright eyes, her face flushed in the cold air.

'Tansy reckoned something must have happened to you, some kind of family emergency, but I think –'

'My aunt passed away,' he said.

Susie put a hand to her mouth. 'What?' Her tirade of angry words died away as she took in what he'd said. 'I had no idea,' she whispered at last, her eyes widening. 'So Tansy was right. I'm so, so sorry.' She hesitated, coming nearer. 'What... What was your aunt's name?'

'Alison.' He swallowed, gritting his teeth. 'That's where I've been... In Truro at her bedside in the hospice, along with my cousins. We didn't want to leave her alone, you see.' He ran a hand over his face. 'Aunt Alison passed away late yesterday evening. There was no pain, the doctor made sure of that. She just slipped away in her sleep.'

'Oh, Murray.'

Her sympathy almost undid him. 'I'd been steeling myself to face it for days, but it was a shock all the same. I still can't believe that she... that my aunt's gone. We were close, you understand. Very close. Alison was like a second mother to me, especially after my own mother died.' He heard the gulp in his voice and folded his arms tightly, pushing away his grief. 'Anyway, I came to say that I'm sorry I didn't contact you before today. I wanted to, but... it was out of the question. I couldn't focus on anything else.'

Susie bit her lip, looking horrified. 'Please, there's nothing you need to apologise for. Honestly, I'm the one who should be apologising. I'm really sorry to hear about your Aunt Alison, and I should never have spoken to you like I did just now. It was an incredibly insensitive thing to do.' Her wide eyes pleaded with his. 'Say you forgive me?'

When he muttered, 'Don't be ridiculous,' under his breath, she reached out a hand but didn't quite touch him, perhaps not yet ready for them to be friends again after such a prolonged absence. He couldn't blame her for that either. Not given what they'd done before he left. He'd made love to her and then essentially disappeared without a word. She had every right to be furious.

'How are you?' she asked tentatively. 'And your family? You said… cousins.'

He nodded with difficulty. 'Tilly and her husband. We took turns being with Alison this past week, just chatting and sitting with her, though she became increasingly unable to speak. She was on strong pain relief, you see. Then, when the nurse said she was ready to go, we all sat around her bedside and talked to her until…'

He ground to a halt, finding he couldn't go on. Everything was still so raw.

'You poor thing.' Her eyes sparkled with tears.

He had to look away, not trusting himself not to start crying again too. 'I wanted to stay on in Truro afterwards. There are so many things for them to arrange, I didn't want to leave my cousins to cope alone. But Tilly insisted that I go home. She said she's got it all in hand. Alison was her mum, you see, so they'd discussed beforehand what she wanted at her funeral. Tilly told me to come back to Betty... Yes, I didn't take my dog with me to Truro. It would have been impossible. I left her with the dog-sitter all this time instead. She'll probably never forgive me for abandoning her like this. I seem to have abandoned everyone, don't I? Betty, you, the Christmas Market folk...'

He was rambling incoherently, he realised, and groaned. 'Sorry if I'm not making much sense. I haven't slept properly in days.'

'Of course you haven't. Why don't you go home? Get some rest.' Susie hesitated, then added with deceptive lightness, 'I could come with you, if you don't want to be alone.'

Her suggestion struck at him like the bitter tail-end of a whiplash, hitting somewhere raw and tender deep inside. He wanted to say yes. *Yes, please.* To be alone with Susie again was a dream he'd come back to again and again on the long, cold, lonely drive home from Truro. And yet his primary instinct was to recoil from that sweet invitation too. From what it might mean...

Restlessly, Murray drew his car keys out of his pocket, studying them instead of her face. 'I can't, not yet.'

'Right,' she muttered.

'Sorry, but I have to pick Betty up from the dog-sitter, settle the bill, and take her with me up to the Christmas Market. It's their last day, and I've been neglecting the place ever since I heard...' He shook off that thought, desperate to return to calm and normalcy, to the space in his brain where work existed instead of this devastating emotion that he simply couldn't handle any longer. 'Plus, there's a Christmas Eve presentation by the council in a couple of hours. Best festive stall display, that kind of thing.' He glanced at his watch, and grimaced. 'Less than two hours, actually. I should go.'

Her brows had drawn together, and he could see her worrying away at some problem. It didn't take much imagination to work out what.

'Why did you come here first, then?' she threw at him as he shuffled, playing with his car keys. 'Why not go straight to the dog-sitter and the Christmas Market instead?'

'I don't know.' He frowned. 'To... apologise, I guess,' he added unsteadily.

'Well, you've apologized,' she said with a rush, and he felt her burning gaze on his face but still couldn't meet it. 'So, you'd better go.'

'Yes.' Murray turned to his car, and by the time he'd got the door open and climbed inside, she had already vanished back inside the cat sanctuary.

Curiously numb, he pulled out onto the busy main road, thinking ahead to seeing Betty again – she would be wildly ecstatic as well as accusing, no doubt – and the Christmas Market presentation where he was due to give a short speech. He wasn't thinking about anything else. His aunt's last few moments of consciousness, blessedly painless, her grip relaxing in his... Or Susie's expression, a blend of disappointment and sympathetic understanding, and that note in her voice, telling him to go. The finality of it all.

There was no time to consider. And he lacked the strength, anyway.

Hadn't he just wrung his heart and soul out over his beloved Aunt Alison? The last few days had left him utterly poured out, depleted, empty... He had no emotion left inside. At any rate, none for anyone but Betty, who by all accounts had missed him dreadfully and would need him to be there for her, close by her side, until she felt secure again.

Betty had to be his priority now.

And what about you? a voice asked inside his muddled head. *What do you need, Murray?* The voice sounded uncomfortably like Susie's. Only he wasn't ready to listen to it.

He adjusted the mirror, peering at swirling snowflakes in his wake...

'Time to get back to work,' he told himself, and thrust out his chin, squaring his shoulders. 'Back to work and back to normal.'

Which meant slamming the door on all this raw, uncontrollable emotion, once and for all.

Betty, of course, had other ideas.

As soon as he rang the doorbell at the dog-sitter's house, he heard her familiar, muffled bark from somewhere deep inside, and caught his breath on a half-laugh, half-sob.

Keep it together, Murray.

He had a professional smile ready by the time the

door opened.

After the inevitable handshake and murmured condolences, he was finally ushered into a bright kitchen space, where Betty leapt up at him repeatedly, ears flying, tail wagging so fast it was a blur. She was yapping at a high pitch that made his ears cringe, her wide, excited gaze fixed on his.

Laughing, he crouched to hug her. 'Yes, I'm back, I'm back…'

Having paid what was owed, collected all her favourite toys and bedding, listened with a crooked smile to tales of her adventures while he was away, thanked the long-suffering dog-sitter and his partner, and somehow clipped on her lead, he managed to persuade Betty out to the car, though she was still yapping hysterically and dancing about him on her hind legs like a circus dog. The dog-sitter had fastened a warm red coat about her that morning, decorated with a border of silver snowflakes and designed to keep out the December frosts. He thought Betty looked very festive and smart in her finery as she hopped athletically into the front of the car.

'Sit down and stop barking, that's a good girl,' he told her, finally closing the passenger door and hurrying round to the driver's side, where she whined with anticipation as he pulled on his seatbelt. 'Yes, it's amazing, isn't it? Daddy's back and we're going home at last.'

He started the engine, laughing unsteadily at her wild yaps. Betty didn't seem to have lost her enthusiasm for life during his lengthy absence.

Checking the time, he pulled away into slow traffic. 'Though we need to make a quick stop first. The Christmas Market... You like that place. Lots of interesting smells and people who'll want to pet you.' He spoke more sternly when she tried to crawl onto his lap. 'No, get down. Naughty girl, Betty. You know that's not allowed when Daddy's driving.'

Apparently happy to be told off for once, Betty retreated at once to her side of the car, turned three times in a tight circle and dropped into a semi-tense reclining position, head on paws, her unwavering gaze on his face.

The Christmas Tree Shop had all its display lights on, the flashing Santa and reindeer cluster lit up outside, looking bright and festive in the crisp December air.

The car park was surprisingly busy, given that most people must have obtained their trees by now. But the shop didn't only sell trees, of course, and there was a sign up, advertising that the grotto itself was open until 5pm Christmas Eve, presumably for any latecomers still wishing to see Santa's Chief Elf, AKA Tom, before tomorrow's presents arrived.

Slowing as he passed the car park entrance, he felt a jolt of disappointment on the children's behalf, aware that some might have badly wanted to see Santa himself instead of an elf. Then he recalled that the guy who'd originally agreed to stand in for the missing Santa had filled in with a few afternoon slots since Murray had left the grotto. So hopefully all bases had been covered and no kids had been left feeling shortchanged by an encounter with a skinny, beardless elf or a sharp-eyed Mrs Santa instead of the jolly big guy himself.

His brain flashed back to the huge man in a red suit with bushy beard and twinkling eyes who'd accidentally dropped him off his bony knee, so that Murray had broken his collarbone instead of whispering his Christmas list into the man's ear...

Maybe that had been the *real* Santa.

He laughed.

'I'm losing my marbles,' he told Betty, who sighed gustily. Perhaps she was worried he would now buy the wrong dog food or forget to take her for walks. 'I just caught myself wondering if Santa might be real.'

Betty whined, her expressive eyes still fixed on his face.

'What would I ask for if Santa *was* real, though?' He pulled into the jam-packed car park at the Christmas Market and carefully negotiated his way to the reserved section, set aside for market workers and VIP visitors. As mayor, and there to make a presentation speech soon, he felt it was within his rights to bag the last available slot for himself. 'A better surfboard? A bigger house? To get elected to Cornwall Council?' He chuckled, turning off his engine, and then winced as Betty leapt to her tiny feet, yapping excitedly again. 'Ear-defenders?'

Murray reached into the back for what he laughingly called his 'mayoral football,' the special briefcase where all the highly valuable accoutrements of office were kept safely locked up, and adorned himself with the long, heavy golden chain he always wore to perform his official duties as mayor.

'There... Now you'd never know I was an idiot,' he told her.

Grabbing the dog's trailing lead, Murray walked her up the field to the Christmas Market entrance. Betty sniffed everything she passed, and pranced along in cheerful, wide-eyed anticipation of something fun ahead, like another dog to chase. Many people exclaimed on seeing him, asking where on earth he'd been, to which he gave a carefully neutral reply, while others balanced armfuls of shopping to shake his hand in a jovial fashion and wish him, 'Merry Christmas!'

The air was cold and frosty, everyone's breath steaming, and there were heavy snow clouds gathering in gloomy, leaden skies. A snowflake or two drifted past him, reminding him of his ill-judged conversation with Susie in the car park at the cat sanctuary.

Why on earth had he spoken to her like that? He had basically ended things between them before they'd properly begun.

Susie must hate him now. All this time away, with no explanation, and then he'd come back and treated her as though she meant nothing to him. A one-night-stand, and not a particularly memorable one. Which was not true, not even remotely. He had pushed Susie Lovell out of his thoughts, yes. But for a good reason.

His feelings over what had happened between them had been wild, chaotic, inconvenient... They had not fitted the sombre mood of his aunt dying.

His memories of their night together had not obeyed and gone away, of course. This 'thing' that was Susie-and-him had still been there, shadowy and threatening to his peace of mind, like an iceberg hidden under the water.

Yet, stupid and indefensible though his comments might have been, he couldn't help feeling it might be for the best to let her go. He shouldn't pursue her any further. Not for another few years, at least. Not until he had himself completely and utterly under control. Which he didn't. Not by a long shot.

Because he didn't think he could stand even to tap with one fingertip the wellspring of raw emotion churning just below the surface...

'Or perhaps I should ask Santa for a new heart?' he muttered, bending to untangle her lead, the excitable dog having somehow contrived to wrap it around all four of her legs at once. 'Because mine seems to be defunct.' Betty yapped in agreement or perhaps derision, he could no longer tell the difference. 'You don't mind either way, do you? Not so long as you get fed and walked on time, and I always have a milk-bone treat in my pocket.'

Except when he made a chukking noise and dug into his pocket, Betty standing on her hind legs again to beg for the expected treat, there was nothing there.

'Sorry, Betty... I must have forgotten to replenish the biscuit hoard.'

But of course he had. This suit had been to the cleaners, hadn't it? And then his aunt had died. And now...

'Ah, there you are. We're about to start.' The clerk of the council tapped him on the shoulder. She held out a Santa hat. 'To make things more festive.'

He grimaced. 'I thought I'd finished being Santa,' he grumbled.

'Sorry?' Cynthia looked puzzled.

'Nothing.' He pulled on the Santa hat, which promptly flopped over one eye. 'Ho ho ho.'

'Perfect.' The clerk smiled and held up a hand. 'Give me five minutes to check the sound system, then we'll get everyone gathered for the big presentation.'

Murray watched her go, sighing.

The last thing he wanted to do was make this presentation. His heart was too heavy, every smile was an effort, and frankly he felt more like curling up at home with Betty and drowning his sorrows for a few days while everyone else was celebrating Christmas.

Why had he ever thought that being mayor would be fun?

Wearily, he bent to unwind Betty's lead again, which had somehow wound its way between his legs once more, and was still adjusting it when another female voice, only slightly more strident, interrupted his thoughts.

'Murray! I was beginning to think you'd left town forever.'

He straightened, his heart thundering, to meet Genevieve's sardonic gaze.

His ex was looking fit and alluring in what could only be described as a Christmas Fairy outfit, all stiff white net and lacy bodice, with gold sparkles and gold high heels. She was even wearing a tiara. He must have been staring at her in a daze, his mouth open, because she laughed and tapped him on the cheek lightly with her wand.

Yes, she even had a wand. A long, slender fairy's wand, topped by a golden star.

'Cat got your tongue?' Genevieve asked with a malicious smile. 'Can't believe your eyes, I'm guessing. You need very long legs to carry off a skirt this short, of course.' She did a little twirl for him, and a group of teen lads wandering the market together stopped and stared across at her, clearly entranced. Genevieve beamed at them with her perfect, ultra-white teeth before looking back at him. 'Magical, aren't I?'

He wanted to ask what on earth she thought she was wearing, then realised she was standing in front of a glittering, tinsel-festooned float, and recalled someone on the committee suggesting a pageant for Christmas Eve, a festive float doing the rounds of the stalls before heading into town, featuring seasonal tableaux: Santa with some penguins and reindeer, a man in a Christmas pudding outfit, an elf, and the obligatory Christmas Fairy...

No prizes for guessing who'd got the role of fairy.

'Hello, Genevieve,' he said, restraining a growling Betty as she attempted to jump up at his ex-girlfriend's puffed-out skirts. 'Yes, you look, um... very festive.' Then added, unable to help himself, 'Shouldn't you be on the pointy end of a Christmas tree somewhere?'

Ignoring him, his ex crouched to fondle Betty instead, who bared her teeth. 'Aww, she's gotten so cute... And look at those teeth! How have you been, Betty sweetie? I'm sorry I went away. I missed you so bad...' Genevieve shot him a sharp look. 'You haven't forgotten she's actually *my* dog, have you, Murray?'

The truth of that realization hit him hard.

Yes, he had forgotten.

'No, but since you've never even so much as asked after her,' he began unsteadily...

But Genevieve interrupted, straightening to take the dog's lead out of his hand.

'Well, I'm asking now,' she said.

CHAPTER TWENTY-TWO

With careful expertise, Susie wrapped three delicate gold-and-silver filigree-decorated baubles in soft lilac crêpe paper, slipped them into the box at her elbow and sealed it, before turning to her customer with a grateful smile. 'Is that everything?'

'Yes, thank you. Bit late to go on the tree this year but they'll do me for next Christmas. Wonderful to see such great value reductions on Christmas Eve.'

The lady handed over her credit card and Susie tapped it on the mobile reader before handing it back with another smile.

'That's gone through, thank you so much. Did you need a receipt?'

The lady checked her phone to make sure the transaction was as expected, and shook her head. 'No, that's fine, thank you.' Gingerly, she lifted the heavily laden box in both hands, stacked with price-slashed decorations for next year's festive season. 'I'll take these straight to my car. And may I wish you a very Merry Christmas?'

'Thank you. And a very Merry Christmas to you too.'

With a jingling shake of her festive multi-coloured hat, which sported tiny golden bells at each corner, Susie turned to the next person in line. 'And how may I help you?'

She had been working hard all afternoon, making sure she had no time to think about Murray, and definitely no time to brood.

Even when there were no customers waiting in line, she had been carefully packing away surplus stock, ready for the cabin to be cleared and dismantled on Boxing Day. There was always something to do, a job or a tweak to block out unwelcome gloom and the ever-present threat of tears. Not that he deserved a single drop of salt. Yes, he'd left to be at his dying aunt's bedside, and nobody could fault him for that. Indeed, she would have been horrified if he hadn't gone. But to have come back, and then spoken to her so coldly and dismissively...

Susie winced, not for the first time that afternoon pretending it was the cold wind that had prompted her physical flinch and the bright sheen to her eyes. There might have been a moment for her and Murray, immediately after that fateful party. When she recalled how he had held her, the romantic sweetnesses he'd whispered in her ear as they made love, none of them quite making sense but sounding wonderful all the same, her body still thrilled, and she could have soared up into the cold December air.

But that moment had passed, and now his heart was elsewhere.

So her own heart needed to be packed away too, not left on display for all to see. Packed up like these unsold decorations, ready for next Christmas instead. Or maybe the following Christmas, or the one after that...

'I'd love one of those gorgeous table decorations for my Christmas Day lunch tomorrow. The one with the cute robin sitting among the holly berries.' The next customer, a well-built lady with a striking red beret and lipstick to match, was pointing to a large table decoration on the shelf display behind her. 'I saw your Big Christmas Eve Sale sign and couldn't resist coming over. You've got some incredible bargains here!'

'Yes, some of the older stock has been knocked down by fifty percent today, so we can make room for next year's goodies.' Determined to sound cheerful too, Susie turned to fetch down the beautifully decorated Yule log and wrap it in crêpe paper, but was interrupted in this task by a deep, familiar voice on the other side of the counter, saying loudly, 'I can't believe the prices either. How on earth are you making a profit? Up to fifty percent off old stock? I hope you're not trying to put yourself out of business.'

Her head jerking up with a cry, Susie abandoned the acres of crêpe paper she'd been wrestling with, thrust open the side door and ran round to the front, arms wide.

'Dad!' she cried out and was instantly enfolded in her father's warm embrace. 'I had no idea you were back in the UK.' She drew back to stare at him as he released her, overjoyed to see her dad again but concerned by this surprise visit. 'Last time we spoke you were working in Australia and had no intention of coming back, or not before next summer at the earliest... What happened? Are you unwell?'

Beaming down at her, looking deeply tanned from the Australian sun, her father shook his head. 'I'll explain everything in a minute. First though, you still have a customer waiting.' He smiled at the bemused lady, adding, 'I'm so sorry. My daughter will be with you right away.'

Also stammering an apology, Susie ran back inside to finish wrapping the customer's table decoration. Safely cushioned in crêpe paper, she then slipped the whole package into a thick paper bag for extra protection against knocks. But with her head still whirling with shock, it was all she could do to work out the reduced price and take payment.

As soon as the cheery lady in the beret had wished them both a 'Merry Christmas!' and gone on her way, Susie opened the side door for her dad to come inside the cabin. Outside, snowflakes had begun to fall again, and the chill was deep, each sharp blast of Cornish wind cutting to the bone.

'Get in here,' she told her father, 'before you freeze! I have a mini-heater under the counter to keep my toes warm. Otherwise, I'd probably have lost one or two by now.'

He grinned. 'It was scorchingly hot in Australia,' he admitted. 'Coming home has been a bit of a shock.'

Inside the chalet-style cabin, she hugged him again, and then dragged out a second stool for him to sit on.

'So, why are you back so soon?' she demanded, pouring them both a half-cup of coffee from the heavily lagged cafetiere she'd made up earlier. 'Creamer? I don't have any fresh milk, I'm afraid.'

'As it comes will be fine.'

'Don't get me wrong, I'm thrilled to see you.' She handed her dad a warm black coffee. 'And thankful too. I'd got used to having Tansy in the house with all her cats, but she's living at the cat sanctuary now and says she'll be madly busy tomorrow, celebrating Christmas with the rescue cats and two of her volunteers, so can't join me for lunch. Basically, I was facing a rather lonely Christmas Day.' She managed a quirky smile, hiding her depressed mood. 'In fact, I was half-tempted to take Tom's mum up on her kind offer of joining their family for Christmas lunch. But now you're back, I'd better grab us a last-minute turkey and some chipolatas.'

She frowned when he didn't say anything, staring down into his coffee mug instead, and became convinced that her father was hiding something from her. But what?

'All right, come on, what's happened?' she demanded.

'It didn't take,' he said heavily. 'I gave Australia my

best shot, love. But I guess I'm too old to start again in a new country. Truth is, you can't teach an old dog new tricks.'

'You're hardly an old dog, Dad.'

'*Woof*,' he said, laughing feebly, and then shook his head. 'Look, the job I had lined up when I first applied for a temporary work visa… Well, it wasn't all I'd expected. I was meant to be a regional rep for a Christmas tree grower. Sounds like a match made in heaven, right? But the truth is,' he added, pulling a face, 'I got the sack.'

She stared, unable to believe her ears. 'I hope you mean Santa's sack?'

He laughed again reluctantly. 'I wish it were that simple… No, they let me go a couple of weeks back. I didn't see eye to eye with the boss. Or, more accurately, the boss's son, Jacob. He was a real jerk. Hated me from day one and made my life a misery. Kept calling me a 'limey'.'

'A *what?*'

'It means someone from the UK… Apparently, early British sailors ate limes to stop them getting scurvy on the long sea voyages. Anyway, Jacob's mother was English, only she abandoned him and his dad when Jacob was a baby and came back to the UK alone, so he has a real chip on his shoulder when it comes to us *limies*.'

'He sounds bitter.'

He smiled appreciatively. 'Eventually, we had a row over it, and his old man gave me the push. Since the visa was tied to that specific job, I had no choice but to leave the country. So here I am, back in Cornwall and unemployed, and not sure what to do with myself.' Her father sipped his coffee. He looked despondent, hunched on the stool. 'But at least I still own the house. So that's something.'

'Yes, it's lucky you didn't sell our *house* to Murray as well.'

'I deserve that.' His eyes twinkled as he studied her face. 'On first name terms with him, are you? I never thought that would happen. How are you and the mayor getting along these days?'

She didn't know what to say, hiding her unhappiness by shrugging and sipping her coffee.

Luckily, her dad didn't seem to notice her hesitation. 'I saw Mayor Carew just now, by the way, wandering around with his dog and gold chain, looking like he owns the place.'

'Well, he kinda does,' she pointed out. 'Or rather did. You sold him this land, remember? And then he sold it to the council.'

'Is that how he managed it? A clever move.' Her dad gave her a shrewd look. 'I couldn't believe my eyes when I rolled into town and saw this gigantic Christmas Market in our old fields. I wasn't sure about it at first. You know how I feel about commercialising Christmas. About the same as you, I expect. And your mother would have hated all this too.' He peered over the serving counter at row upon row of Christmas stalls, many still lit up with lights and glittering tinsel, canned carols blaring throughout the market. 'Christmas by numbers.'

'Mmm,' she said, not trusting herself to use words without bursting into tears.

'However,' her dad went on slowly, 'having walked around all the stalls, and seen all the crowds and how well the retailers seem to be doing, I have to hand it to Murray Carew. He's done a good job here at Penrock Downs.' He paused. 'Don't you think?'

Putting down her coffee, Susie pretended to look out across the market too, hugging herself as a chill gust blew through the open counter, a few dancing snowflakes accompanying it. She was overjoyed to see her father home again. But he couldn't have come at a more complicated time, frankly. And she didn't know how much or how little to tell him about her and Murray, assuming there was anything to tell.

It was all rather uncomfortable and embarrassing.

'The mayor's certainly bought a lot of new trade to the town,' she said carefully, feeling her way through the subject, and trying to keep her voice neutral. 'When I first heard about this project, you're right, I hated it. Commercialising Christmas... It's about as far from our cosy little family business as you can get.' She chewed on her lip, not looking at him. 'My original objection was that local businesses would suffer. But Murray got around that by offering stalls at reduced prices to local business people. So it's worked out in the end. Though it's had its downside. We've been very stretched at the shop during December.'

He nodded. 'I know... I called in there before

coming up to the market. Spoke to Tom and his mother. Everything looks amazing at the shop. You've made the old place shine. And Tom thinks the shop's had its best Christmas ever. Big sales across the board.' He shrugged. 'I would never have foreseen it myself, but it looks as though having this outdoor market adjacent to the shop has brought new customers in.'

'Yes, I can't complain about sales. Though it's Murray that sweeping the profit, of course.'

Her father met her gaze directly. 'And that's my fault.'

She began to protest but he held up a hand.

'No, let me finish... You were right to be angry when I sold the business to Murray. I should have had more patience and faith. But I was going crazy in here. Couldn't think straight.' He tapped the side of his head. 'Getting away helped clear my head. I'm not saying I'm over my grief at losing your mum. That will never happen. But I can see that loss in perspective now, and I'm not going to let it overwhelm what's left of my own life.' He paused, looking at her deeply. 'Or yours, Susie.'

'Oh, Dad.' She reached for his hand and held it.

'That's why I came up here today. To apologise for having wrecked your life.'

'*Wrecked*? Oh no...' She shook her head, refusing to let him take the blame for everything that had gone wrong since Mum had died. 'Honestly, you don't need to apologise. It was your business to sell, not mine.'

'True, but you'd poured your heart and soul into the business for years, not to mention all your time and effort since you were the same size as a baby Christmas tree. And I didn't even consult you. Just sold up and abandoned you to your fate.' Her dad put a hand on her shoulder. 'I'm sorry, kid.'

Susie swallowed, blinking away tears. 'That's all right, Dad. It's not all bad. I... I've been coping on my own.'

'But not brilliantly?' He held her gaze probingly. 'Tom told me you've been a bit manic lately. Behaving erratically? Run off your feet, I daresay. And that's my fault. No, let me own this one. I just dumped everything and left you to hold the business together, with the mayor on your back.' He must have caught her flinch, for he added gently, 'I suppose he's been riding you pretty hard.'

Oh God... This was not a conversation she wanted to be having with her own father. Yet here they were.

'Um, yes, you could say that,' she muttered, bending her head to avoid his gaze.

'I thought as much. Which is why I imagine a proposal wouldn't be entirely out of order.'

Her head jerked up and a hot blush spread across her cheeks. '*P-Proposal?*'

Good grief, what the hell had he heard on the town grapevine?

She hadn't supposed anyone knew about her and Murray. Not the gritty details, at least. But perhaps Murray had told someone, or they'd been seen leaving the party together, and rumours had spread.

'Look, me and the mayor... We haven't... That is, we have but it wasn't...' She saw his widening stare and demanded flatly, 'What on earth are you talking about, Dad? What proposal?'

'*My* proposal, of course.'

'Huh?'

'Okay, I seem to be missing something here.' Her dad studied her more closely. 'What are *you* talking about, Susie? *You and the mayor*?'

She bit her lip and said nothing, too embarrassed to find the right words.

Thoughtfully, Louis Lovell rubbed his chin, which was rough with grey-white stubble. Her father might be tanned but he looked generally unkempt, she realised in dismay, his greying hair in need of a cut too. She felt guilty that she hadn't kept closer tabs on him after he left for Australia.

'Is there something I should know about you and Murray Carew?' he pressed her.

'No, absolutely not!'

His brows rose at her emphatic snap. 'Then why are you blushing?'

'Because... Because I'm *cold*.' Horrified by the way this conversation was going, she jumped up and peered desperately out of the hatch in search of fresh customers. But there was nobody in sight. Indeed, everyone seemed to have disappeared. 'And something's going on. What am *I* missing?'

'Seems that's what we'd both like to know,' her dad said drily, but stood and cocked an ear to an announcement being made on the loudspeaker system that usually belted out carols. 'What's that man saying? It's utterly garbled.'

'It sounds like...' Her infuriating blush deepened, quite against her will. 'I think it's the mayor. He's saying something about...' Frowning, she leant out of the hatch as a fellow stallholder passed in a hurry. 'Rob, what's going on? That speaker's on its way out, I can't understand a word.'

Rob, who sold festive jewellery three stalls down, halted briefly and threw back over his shoulder, 'It's the big Christmas Eve presentation before the market parade. Come on, you're one of the stalls up for a prize. Didn't you hear your name called?' Then he hurried on.

Susie sank back onto her stool and looked at her dad, bemused. 'I... I'm up for a prize?'

'That's good news,' was all her dad said, beaming. He leant forward to close and secure the serving hatch for her. 'Let me help you lock up the stall, then we'll go to the presentation together, shall we?'

It was gloomy inside with the hatch closed. She shivered, grabbing up a woolly scarf and winding it about her neck. 'I suppose so.'

They trudged up the muddy field together to the raised area where she could already see a large crowd of shoppers and stallholders gathered, various local dignitaries standing in a row on the platform. Murray was there, hogging the microphone as usual, telling some festive joke about penguins that had the onlookers in stitches. Especially since at least one of the onlookers appeared, bizarrely, to be dressed as a penguin...

Murray was wearing a Santa hat again. For the kids' benefit, she guessed.

'What... What was your proposal, Dad?' she asked, wishing she didn't have to look at Murray again or listen to his deep, charismatic voice, or dwell on everything that had happened between them. But it would have made her dad suspicious if she'd refused to go. And right now she couldn't bear to have to fend off questions about Murray. With any luck, she'd never need to talk to anyone about what had happened between her and the mayor – except Tansy, of course.

But best friends didn't count, did they? Best friends were always there for you and would never walk out on you. Except when there was a cat in need...

'I was hoping you might agree to go into business with me again,' her dad said. 'Only this time as equal partners.'

She stared round at him, too distracted to really take in what he was suggesting. 'Sorry? What kind of business?'

'Same as before. Christmas trees.' He put an arm about her shoulder, hugging her. 'You've got the greenest fingers, just like your mum. You'll grow the trees, and I'll handle the sales and accounts. Only this time we'll make it an online business. Sell the house and downsize, then use the surplus revenue to invest in land for a new nursery and stock, free of Carew.'

Susie didn't know what to say. 'Dad, I...'

'Take some time over Christmas to think about it,' he urged her. 'There's no hurry. Though we'll need to get the house on the market by early spring if we want to be sure of selling it quickly. Unless you think the mayor might want to buy it? Maybe for warehousing excess stock? Or as a holiday rental? Folk love staying in Cornwall for their holidays.'

They were nearly at the platform, and people were turning to look at them in a wave of applause.

'For those at the back,' Murray was saying into the microphone, his gaze on Susie's face, 'the Prize for Best-Dressed Local Stall goes to the Christmas Tree Shop, put together by Susie Lovell.'

'Isn't that your business, Mayor?' someone yelled from the crowd.

'It is.' Murray cleared his throat at the uproar that followed, adding above the cheers and jeers, 'To be clear though, this competition was voted for by market visitors, not the council. So no complaints about nepotism, please. The best stall won and I'm just here, as mayor, handing out the prizes.' He beckoned to Susie. 'Miss Lovell? If you wouldn't mind joining us on stage?'

'Go on, silly.' Susie's dad shoved her forward when she hesitated.

Still protesting, Susie lurched up the steps to the podium, hot-cheeked and wishing herself a thousand miles away as those nearest the front looked her curiously up and down.

Murray shook her hand. 'Congratulations.' Under

his breath, he added, 'Stop looking so terrified.' As she glared at him silently, he spoke into the microphone again, addressing the crowd, 'Here she is, ladies and gentlemen... the Winner of our inaugural Christmas Market Prize for Best-Dressed Local Christmas Stall, Miss Susie Lovell.'

A few cheers rang out, along with sporadic clapping.

'Come along, ladies and gentlemen, that's not a big enough cheer for a green-fingered local girl.' Murray was still shaking her hand. 'Turn and face the crowd,' he whispered in her ear, adding into the booming microphone, 'Okay, how about we try that again? Please, let's hear a big hand for our Penrock Downs winner!'

The applause grew louder. She could hear whistles now.

'Stop encouraging them,' she hissed, dragging her hand free. 'No nepotism my backside. I bet you wrangled it so I'd win and you could bring me up here to humiliate me.'

His eyes widened. 'Humiliate you? Why on earth would I –'

'Just give me the prize and let me get out of here.'

A muscle worked in his jaw. He turned her to face the crowd, a fake smile once again tugging at his lips. 'To present the prizes to our winners, I'd like to introduce one of the chief sponsors of our first annual Christmas Market, Mrs Pennyweather of Pennyweather Saddles and Leather Goods.' More applause. 'Ah, Mrs Pennyweather... How are you?'

Murray was shaking hands with a tall, angular woman in late middle-age. 'Thank you for being one of our most generous sponsors. Your company isn't only restricted to Cornwall, is it? Though your company began life as a proud Cornish-based business, you now export saddles and other equine leather goods across the globe.'

While the other two chatted into the mic, Susie stared out across a sea of faces, stricken with nerves. Oh God... She'd always hated being the centre of attention for anything at school, and now Murray had dragged her up onto this platform in full view of everyone.

Her frantic gaze flicked through the faces gazing back at them... Customers, townsfolk, the clerk of the council, her dad, and... Good grief, even Genevieve, Murray's ex, was among the front row of onlookers, staring back at her with a fierce expression of dislike.

For some reason, the mayor's ex was dressed in a stiff white tutu and spangly tights like the Sugar Plum Fairy. And she was holding Betty's lead.

Betty yapped and stood on her hind legs in a cute red coat, dancing about like she was part of the spectacle, and Genevieve bent to pet her, cooing, 'Who's Mummy's ickle doggy then?' Her malicious smile seemed intended for Susie though, not the dog, as she added loudly, 'Yes, you're Mummy and Daddy's ickle *baby* doggy.'

Watching this saccharine performance with a jolt of disbelief, Susie felt herself stiffen, her heart beginning to thud with hurt and fury.

Was it possible that Murray had simply asked his ex to look after the dog while he was up on stage? Or had he lied when he insisted the two of them were no longer an item?

Not that it was any of her business, she told herself, wishing her teeth would stop grinding painfully together as she watched Betty tug on the lead. The dog was dragging Genevieve towards the steps up to the platform as though desperate to get back to her master. But Genevieve merely laughed and scooped Betty up, cradling the small dog in her arms like a baby. A furry, ungainly baby who kept struggling and turning to nip at its mother's hands, while Genevieve's tinkling laughter rang out, growing more stilted by the second, until at last she stopped laughing and bared her own teeth at the dog instead, perhaps snarling back at her...

'So it's with great pleasure that I present to you this handsome leather riding crop,' Mrs Pennyweather was saying, turning proudly to Susie with the riding crop in hand, its working end topped with a scarlet First Place rosette.

It was at this moment that Betty snapped her teeth straight into Genevieve's face, who dropped the dog with an ear-piercing shriek. 'Oh, you beast!'

Free at last, Betty legged it through the crowd, perhaps too guilty and shaken to stay and be chastised for what she'd done. Or nearly done, as it didn't seem to Susie that Genevieve had actually been bitten. That snap had been more like a warning shot across the nose...

Some onlookers jumped aside, while others laughed and tried to dive on her trailing lead, but Betty evaded them all, zigzagging between the strangers' legs.

Then she was off, running full tilt across the field, a red streak in her cute little coat.

'Betty!' Murray called, sounding panicked, and stuck both fingers in his mouth to whistle after his dog almost as loudly as Genevieve had shrieked.

Betty must have heard him but didn't even break stride. The little dog seemed to be heading for the exit onto the main road, where cars could be seen whizzing to and fro at their usual insane speeds.

Murray pelted down the steps after his dog. 'Why *the hell* did you let her go?' he demanded of Genevieve, his voice shaking, but then set off after Betty at a run without waiting for an answer.

'Because your mad dog tried to bite me, perhaps?' Genevieve shrieked wildly in his wake, gesticulating after him with what appeared to be a long, golden wand. 'Did you... Did you *train her* to do that to me, you bastard? I'll never take her back now, not after she *snarled* at me.'

Her arm flailing, she struck the young guy next to her with her wobbling wand. The man, who was the one dressed as a penguin, presumably for the North Pole float in the pageant parade, glared round at her in amazement, putting a hand to his reddening nose.

'I'm so sorry, I didn't mean to hit you,' Genevieve

wailed, adding hurriedly, 'But did you see what just happened? Oh my God, I'm shaking. I've never been so scared... That dog's *dangerous*, it ought to be put down.'

The penguin said nothing, still staring at her and rubbing his nose.

'For First Place in the Best-Dressed Local Christmas Market Stall competition,' Mrs Pennyweather had continued in an uncertain tone, holding out the prize, but with her gaze now on the fleeing mayor, 'our hearty congratulations to Susie Lovell and the Christmas Tree Shop Stall.'

To Susie's relief, nobody except her enthusiastic dad applauded this time, the crowd's full attention on the rapidly disappearing figure of Murray Carew.

'Thanks.' Susie grabbed the riding crop with its First Prize rosette, threw it to her father, and dashed down the steps after Murray.

There was only one thing that might stop Betty before the little dog was crushed to death under the wheels of a passing juggernaut, and that something was lodged in the dusty lining of her old jacket pocket.

A tasty, bone-shaped biscuit treat.

CHAPTER TWENTY-THREE

Murray knew he had to reach Betty before the dog could slip through the busy exit gate from the Christmas Market and out onto the main road.

The traffic was lethal there at the best of times, and today was Christmas Eve, one of the busiest days of the year, with a steady flood of cars, vans, and even agricultural vehicles sweeping in and out of Penrock Downs, not to mention visitors to the Christmas Market, who were mostly leaving at this late stage of the day. Except for those who had stayed specially to watch the prize presentation and special Christmas parade, intended to tour the market before heading through back lanes into the town itself. One last ditch-effort to engage additional interest in the town before the end of the Christmas season.

All his big idea as mayor, of course. His grand vision for the Penrock Downs Christmas Extravaganza, still bringing in extra revenue for the town, extra visitors, extra traffic, extra cars to kill his runaway dog…

It was gloomy, the light already failing in the early afternoon, and snow was falling, the ground icy and slippery. His dog was tiny. Even with her red coat on, she would barely be visible to a harassed motorist, he guessed, especially one with their eyes more on the satellite navigation screen than on the road ahead.

Betty wouldn't stand a chance.

People turned to stare at their mayor as he thudded down the field after his dog, whistling and calling her name periodically. "Excuse me,' he muttered, diving through and around bemused family groups and wandering shoppers. 'Pardon me, coming through.'

He was a fit man, but in his suit and mayoral chain, moving at speed while attempting to whistle and call at the same time, he was growing more breathless with every stride.

'Betty! Heel, girl!' he yelled, his voice lost amid the noise of the Christmas Market crowds. Behind him, he could hear the clerk taking over proceedings as she continued to announce the best-dressed stallholder awards, and honourable mentions. 'Come back here, Betty, damn you!'

At the back of his mind was Susie's face, almost stricken as she realised she'd won.

Why?

The only reason he could come up with was that she hadn't wanted to speak to him again, let alone shake his hand and stand next to him in front of that large gathering.

He had spoken coldly to her at the cat sanctuary. Not only spoken coldly but turned away from her as though she didn't matter. Which wasn't true. Susie mattered. She mattered deeply. But she hadn't forgiven him.

Did he deserve to be forgiven?

Probably not, was his bleak thought.

He had slept with her, not got back in contact with her, and then turned up only to abruptly change his mind about their relationship. And he still didn't really know why.

Because you're afraid, a voice jeered at him inside. *Afraid of investing all your emotions in one person only for her to leave, to walk away or maybe even to die, for that relationship to be shelved and your heart shattered into a thousand pieces.*

Okay, ridiculous. But also potentially true. What if Susie didn't find him interesting enough, after all? Or attractive enough? Or good in bed?

What if they started up together in earnest and then she left?

What if she died?

What if she was abruptly and irrevocably run over by cars whizzing past on the main road?

'Betty, for God's sake, you crazy dog! Heel, heel, heel!'

His mayoral chain of office had become an intolerable weight about his neck, violently clanking up-and-down on his chest with a repetitive clunk for every step he took. It was like performing jumping jacks in an armoured breastplate. He'd probably have bruises there tomorrow. These mayoral accoutrements might look good in official photographs. But they were not designed to be worn while thundering over uneven ground after a tiny dog who seemed determined to commit suicide...

Panic assailed him.

He'd never make it in time to rescue Betty from the perils of the main road, not with this hefty gold nonsense bouncing up and down on his chest, like someone trying to resuscitate him ahead of him even getting a heart attack.

A friendly face swam up out of the crowds.

'What on earth...?' Gus stared at him. 'Where are you going, Murray?'

'Gus... Thank God! No time to explain.' Fumbling with his shiny golden chain of office, Murray dragged it over his Santa hat and thrust it, priceless gold pendant and all, into Gus's astonished hands. 'Look after this for me, would you? Sorry, can't stop.' He flung out an arm, pointing. Or perhaps just flailing for air. 'Dog!'

As he pounded on breathlessly, he was vaguely aware of Gus shouting after him, but there was no time to stop and have a conversation. And he knew that Gus would take care of the mayoral chain. Perhaps he ought to have taken a few extra seconds to explain that it was worth a small fortune.

Frankly though, his dog's life was worth more to him than that bloody chain, and he might need those extra seconds.

Betty was at the exit gate. He was never going to make it in time to stop her.

Terror lent him new speed, despite the tearing pain in his lungs.

'Hey, Fido, where d'you think you're going?' Thankfully, one of the marshals on the entrance had seen what was happening, and dashed after Betty himself.

To Murray's intense relief, the marshal managed to wrestle Betty to the muddy ground. Snow was falling more thickly now, those first errant flakes now turning to a flurry of white.

As he pelted through thickening flakes, the air misty before his eyes – though it could have been sweat rolling off his forehead and blurring his vision – Murray saw Betty snap and snarl at her captor, struggling to get free again. Perhaps she was having a flash-back to Genevieve cradling her like a baby...

'Betty, stay, stay!' he gasped.

But it was no use.

Betty had broken free from the marshal's grasp. Giving herself an angry shake, she bolted out of the exit gate, leaving her red coat behind in the hands of the marshal.

As Murray watched in horror, his dog paused at the side of the busy main road, her gaze on the flashing lights of the shop on the other side.

So that was where the dog was headed.

To the Christmas Tree Shop.

But why?

It must be a place of familiarity now, he guessed.

She'd been spooked by Genevieve's crass inexpert handling, and perhaps the crowd itself too, all that noisy applause and cheering… So she'd made for the only place of safety she could see. Which meant the Christmas Tree Shop, where she'd spent so many happy days this winter, sitting quietly in a corner of the grotto while he played Santa, or asleep on a chair in the staff office, or yapping cheerily out of the window of his SUV while he helped Susie with some outside task such as clearing logs or carrying a Christmas tree to a customer's car.

'Betty, no!' he bellowed, but in vain.

This was it. He was going to lose her. He was going to lose his beloved dog.

And he'd almost lost her back there, when Genevieve had reclaimed Betty as her own dog. The bottom had dropped out of his world in that moment, and he'd felt so alone, stripped of everything, as his ex cuddled and cooed over Betty.

The thought of going home to his empty house and sitting with a stiff drink in front of the flashing, tinsel-clad Christmas tree, completely alone, without even his dog to keep him company, had provided such a bleak picture of his future that he'd felt quite desolate.

Until that second, he hadn't realised how much it meant to have Betty in his life.

His little dog, cuddled against him on the sofa, her head on his lap, or trotting alongside him on their daily walks beside the canal or through the busy town or over frosty Cornish fields.

'Betty! Here, girl, *please!*' His voice was hoarse and sick with terror. 'Heel!'

At last, Betty turned her head, perhaps hesitating at the fear in his cry.

But as his heart leapt with hope, and he held out both hands to her, pleading with his naughty little dog to come back, Murray tripped over a large muddy tuft of grass at the entrance to the field, and fell flat on his face in frozen slush and mud.

Gasping, he struggled to his hands and knees, spluttering and spitting out icy mud, and heard rather than saw the quick thunder of footsteps behind him.

That was when Murray realised he was not the *only* person in pursuit of his dog.

'Betty! Betty!' He recognised that voice, wiping mud and snowflakes from his blurred vision. It was Susie, whistling and calling to his dog, 'Look what I have here, Betty! A lovely, tasty biscuit… *Nom nom nom.* Don't you want it?'

The words were cajoling, rather than strict and commanding as his had been. Until he'd disintegrated into mere abject begging, that was. And, big plus, they had a biscuit attached.

Could this new ploy work?

But Betty had already scampered into the road.

His heart seemed to stop.

The tiny dog paused in the middle of the road, turning to stare at oncoming traffic, and then froze at the sound of a car horn, cowering and looking confused at lat.

Murray lurched to his feet and stumbled forward through spinning snow, still dripping with mud and dirty water. 'Betty, no!'

Another motorist, or perhaps the same one, leant on their horn. Tyres sloshed through slush, a few cars braking, but not quickly enough.

He held his breath, half-bent over in sickening agony, waiting in despair for the crunch that must surely follow.

Then he saw, with astonishment, a lone figure standing in the centre of the road. It was a woman, with a bell-adorned, red-and-gold Christmas cap on her head, holding his dog in her arms, both lit up by the headlights of cars crunching towards them through the whitish-grey slush.

It was Susie, he realised.

She had dashed out after his dog into thick traffic and was now facing oncoming vehicles on both sides. But the road was so busy...

A horn sounded again.

Susie turned a scared face towards the large truck headed her way, seeming frozen in place, just as the dog had been.

Drivers were braking everywhere. More horns sounded, urgent and irate. A car on the other side of the road slithered in the slippery snow, zigzagging towards the lone woman and dog in the middle of the road.

'Hang on, one second, I'm coming!' Murray yelled, running out into the traffic too.

He stood sideways beside Susie and Betty, holding

up a hand in both directions at once, commanding the traffic to, 'Stop!' as loudly as he could.

As though backing him up, Betty gave a frightened yap.

Susie gasped, hiding her face in the dog's fur.

Her Christmas cap jingled faintly.

To his relief, the cars were slowing now, though still oncoming.

'Stop!' he yelled like a madman into spinning flakes lit up by car headlights in the gloom of that late December afternoon. 'Stop right there.' He thrust both hands higher. '*All. Of. You.*'

Somehow, miraculously, one by one, the cars stopped safely just a few inches short of their position, the stream of traffic finally motionless in both directions.

A few car horns still sounded, but most people just seemed to be staring through their windscreens, a few motorists yelling at them to, 'Get out of the road!' They had even attracted a small crowd at the Christmas Market exit too, the mud-covered marshal raising a congratulatory hand.

'Come on, this way.' With an arm about Susie shoulders, Murray steered her across the road, right in front of the other line of traffic, until they were standing safely in the entrance to the Christmas Tree Shop car park. 'That's it. Now we're good.'

He had them safe at last. But shock was setting in... He was shaking and, despite his relief, his heart felt like it was going to thunder right out of his chest.

Between them, a terrified Betty shivered, dirty with mud and snowflakes as she peered up at her master. 'Erm, have I been very, *very* naughty this time?' her guilty look seemed to ask, before she went back to crunching on the bone-shaped biscuit Susie had used to entice her.

A stream of furious words chased through his head, gazing down into those naughty eyes. But he didn't bother chastising her, merely hugged Susie and Betty at the same time, holding them close and closing his eyes against the horrible vision he'd just endured, of losing them both under the wheels of an unstoppable juggernaut.

'Don't ever, ever, ever, *ever* do that to me again,' he muttered roughly.

'Are you talking to me or the dog?' Susie's laugh was shaky.

'Both of you, dammit. I nearly had a heart attack just now. And not just from having to chase halfway across the duchy after that idiot hound.' He sucked in a harsh breath. 'Anyway, what the hell did you think you were doing, running out in front of moving traffic like that?'

'Again, is that question aimed at me or Betty?'

He shook with laughter. Or was it tears? He didn't know and didn't much care. He had them safe. Betty and Susie. That was all that mattered.

'Both, like I said,' he growled, doing a good impersonation of Betty with a bone she didn't intend to share.

Susie pulled back to stare at him, her cap bells

jingling. Her body felt so warm and vital against his. So alive. And rather like a Christmas elf in that jingling cap...

'Where's your chain of office?'

'Gus.'

She blinked, staring up at him in surprise. Like Betty, who was wriggling and looking more cheerful now, having guessed she wasn't about to be yelled at for running away and ignoring multiple commands to stop.

'You have... wind?'

'Gus, not gas.' He jerked his head towards the Christmas Market. Traffic had started moving again, not without a few angry gestures from irritable motorists they'd held up for all of thirty seconds. 'Somewhere over there is a large man carrying around a mayoral chain worth a few grand with absolutely no idea why.'

She glanced down at Betty, who was sniffing at her jacket. 'Sorry, doggy... No more biscuits left. I only had the one in my pocket.'

'And thank God you did.'

Her gaze raised to his face. 'Why did she run? Because of Genevieve?'

'You saw her?'

'Dressed as the Sugar Plum Fairy, yes.'

'That's her Christmas Pageant outfit. Though I suspect she was going for Wicked Fairy rather than Sugar Plum,' he admitted, recalling Genevieve's manic response to his repeated refusal of her proposal. 'Especially when she suggested the two of us should get back together.'

He'd thought for a moment that Genevieve was going to tear his head off, she'd been so incandescent with rage at that moment. Poor Betty had looked terrified to be in her arms. If he could have extricated his dog from her long, glitter-tipped fingers without exciting attention from the various member of the press who'd been invited to the presentation, he would have done so.

But he'd decided it would be more discreet to wait until *after* the ceremony before retrieving his dog and explaining to his ex – as politely as possible – that she didn't seem stable enough to be looking after an animal.

Besides, all other considerations aside, Betty was his dog now. Heart and soul.

'Genevieve decided, after all this time apart, that she wanted to take her dog back,' he told her. 'To spite me, I should imagine. Only it seems Betty had other ideas.'

Susie had felt her heart stand still at Murray's throwaway remark that he and Genevieve might be getting back together. But then his grim expression and the rest of his words filtered through the horror of that possibility and restored her to reason. It was hard to concentrate after the ordeal she'd just suffered, breathlessly grabbing up the dog and then finding herself staring down a large oncoming truck... But it had all been worth it to save Betty's life.

'To *spite* you?'

'Yes.' As he nodded, his snow-flecked Santa hat flopped over his forehead. There was distaste in his voice. 'I wasn't terribly polite in my refusal. But she told me, not for the first time, that we ought to make a go of it again. Get back together. With Betty as our... our *baby*. And I couldn't help my reaction.'

Susie stared at him, chewing on her lower lip. What did that mean? 'So you... you turned her down?'

'I did.'

Her brain whirled. 'Oh.' She sucked in a breath, her heart thumping with sudden delight. 'Why?'

'Because of this.' Murray bent his head and kissed her.

Oh my! she thought dizzily.

Her Christmas cap bells jingled as though in response to the kiss.

Closing her eyes, Susie leant into Murray's warmth and masculine strength, feeling her steadiness return after the trauma of standing in front of oncoming traffic, sure that she was about to be hit.

She should never have done it, of course. Rushed out into the road after a dog, waving a bone-shaped biscuit all she was worth. Was she crazy? Perhaps... But she couldn't have lived with herself if Betty had been killed and there was even the slightest chance that she could have saved her.

His kiss was a miracle, bringing her back to life and warmth where she had felt so cold and alone before, devastated by the knowledge that he no longer wanted her. If he had ever wanted her, beyond their one amazing night together. But it was also a minefield of confusion where, every second their lips were in contact, tiny parts of herself were being detonated into oblivion. Parts she might have preferred to keep intact, like integrity and commonsense.

There were snowflakes on her cheeks, quickly numbing her lips as she pulled away with a jingle and a murmured protest. 'Good grief, Murray. Your mood swings...'

'Sorry?' His eyes opened more slowly, studying her with a new awareness on his face.

'They're giving me whiplash.'

Betty whined and wriggled between them, no doubt objecting to having been crushed by their kiss. With a muttered apology, she placed the dog gently on the ground, hoping the icy tarmac of the car park wouldn't be too cold for her paws, and handed the lead to Murray.

'Keep hold of her lead this time, okay?' she told him. 'I'm all out of puff for running.'

Had that kiss been a reward for catching the dog? Because if so, she'd rather he had just said, 'Thank you,' in his usual cool manner, and walked away.

'I won't let go,' he breathed.

His gaze was on her face though, not on the dog.

She struggled against a mounting sense of frustration, searching his expression like a detective hunting for clues and finding it impossible to read his thoughts.

What did Murray *feel* for her? Did he feel anything at all? Or was this kiss, this sudden flurry of romantic interest, just a typical male reaction to having nearly lost his dog? For God's sake, where did she even rank in his list of interests: higher or lower than Betty?

'What is it?' he asked, his gaze narrowing.

There was no point hiding her confusion. 'Why did you kiss me just now?' she blurted out. 'You do remember what you said this morning, don't you?'

This morning?

It felt more like a hundred years ago that he'd driven away from her and the cat sanctuary, she thought with a jolt of disbelief. Not a mere three or four hours.

'I remember.'

'Well, so do I,' she snapped back, her frustration boiling over. 'You made it obvious you weren't interested in a relationship with me. Oh yes, you were very polite. Pure Mr Mayor. And I know you're still grieving for your aunt.'

She saw his jaw harden as he looked away, and felt abruptly awful. Talk about insensitive…

'I'm really very sorry for your loss,' she added in a stutter, 'I know things must feel hard for you at the moment.'

'Thank you,' he muttered.

'But you can't keep blowing hot and cold like this,' Susie finished, and took a step back from him, needing to highlight the distance between them.

His jaw looked like it was made of pure steel now.

Bending to scoop Betty up, he held her close, apparently oblivious to the paws smearing mud over his smart suit. Though, she realised, looking him up and down, Murray seemed to have dragged himself through several acres of mud, and possibly under barbed wire too. A smattering of dirty pawprints were unlikely to make much difference to his suit now, she thought.

'I'm blowing more cold than hot at the moment.' Murray exhaled, puffing snow away from the muddy Santa hat dangling over his eyes. 'Look, it's properly snowing now. You're freezing, Betty's freezing… Let's nip into the shop and talk there instead. Or your house, if you'd prefer the privacy. I could probably do with washing my hands and face as well.' He grimaced. 'I fell in the mud.'

'Really?' She bit her lip.

He saw her sweeping look, glanced down at himself, and winced. 'Wow, okay. I do seem to be rather muddier than I realised.'

'You look like a chocolate Santa.'

'I doubt this mud would be as tasty as chocolate, so I wouldn't advise you to have a nibble.' His gaze hooked on hers, growing steadily more intense. 'Or a lick.'

'Santa!' she gasped, blushing.

'And, um, the shop might be a better choice than the house. I'd be far less tempted to kiss you in public, you see,' he said unsteadily, 'in front of Tom and his mum, and any little kids still queuing for the grotto, if there are any at this time on Christmas

Eve.'

She looked him up and down. 'Because of the state you're in?'

'Because being a chocolate Santa right now is dangerous.' His voice was husky. 'If we were to kiss for too long, I might just melt.'

She gave a half-laugh that turned into a sob. 'But earlier you said –'

'I didn't say anything.'

'Murray, you walked away from me.'

'Technically, I drove away from you. So I could rescue Betty from the dog-sitter.'

She shook her head stubbornly, and her festive hat jingled. Belatedly, she realised how ludicrous they both must look, standing in a snowy car park on Christmas Eve, an elf and a Santa. Though since he hadn't mentioned it, maybe he hadn't noticed what she was wearing.

'Pull the other one, Santa,' she said huskily. 'It's got bells on.'

'It's not the only thing around here,' he said, gazing pointedly at her head.

Okay, maybe he had noticed.

'You weren't just leaving to collect Betty.' She gulped. 'You were ending it. Ending *us*.'

He stroked Betty's ears, who whined softly, looking extra-smug and comfy in his broad male arms.

'Yes,' he agreed slowly, 'you're right. I was ending it.'

'Then why do this?' Susie hugged herself with a

sudden chill that lanced right to her bones. 'Why put me through this charade? Why *kiss me* again like that?'

'Because I'm an idiot,' he admitted, raising his eyes to her face. 'Because I was scared.'

'Of me?' Her voice was high with disbelief.

'Of whatever this is, of the way you make me feel... Of love.'

She swallowed. '*Love?*'

'Love,' he repeated, holding her gaze.

Susie didn't know what to say, her breath snagging in her throat. 'Oh, Murray,' she whispered, shaking her head.

'The truth is, I was afraid of letting myself feel anything for you. Of even admitting that my emotions might be involved. Because if I did, and then you kicked me to the kerb later, or somehow I lost you...' His voice trailed off and he blenched. 'I couldn't have handled that. It would have killed me.'

Susie picked her way through what he was saying, very slowly and delicately, and with growing amazement, like someone picking jewels out of mud and blinking at the hoard of precious gems unearthed in such an unlikely place.

Murray was right. He was indeed a prize idiot.

Though she wasn't much better, was she? She'd taken one look at Genevieve in that ridiculous spangly fairy outfit, cradling Betty like the two of them were a couple again, and had been happy to chuck Murray Carew back into the sea like a pointless sprat and sail on merrily, braving the ten-foot waves of life in her precarious little boat, convinced that she didn't need anyone, let alone Murray Carew, that her life was complete, that baby fir trees were everything she had ever wanted for Christmas.

Only it wasn't true.

She loved baby fir trees. But baby fir trees couldn't love her back. And this Christmas, and all future Christmases, what she really wanted was *to be loved*. Loved for herself, for who she was when nobody else was looking, for being plain old Susie Lovell, smelling of fir and the outdoors, and with dirt under her fingernails.

And just anybody loving her back wouldn't do either. She craved *his love*, specifically.

Murray Carew's love.

But how to express that without admitting she was an idiot too?

It wasn't possible.

'But isn't that how it's supposed to happen?' she asked, her tummy turning somersaults as she realised where she was going with this. 'I mean, falling in love with someone, telling them how you feel and hoping you don't get kicked in the teeth…?'

'To the kerb,' he corrected her gently. 'I like my smile the way it is, thanks.'

'It's a lovely smile.'

'And it's all yours, Susie Lovell.'

'Very kind of you to say so,' she told him. 'Though I suspect you may have overlooked a few thousand members of the public who get treated to the mayor's smile every day.'

'Not every day. Sometimes I just go surfing.'

There was a thin blanket of snow on his shoulders and on the dark, shoulder-length hair peeping out from under the Santa hat. She wanted to freeze-frame this moment, his muddy, snow-covered figure and crooked boyish grin. Capture that crooked smile of his forever, hide it away, and maybe only take it out to look at it from time to time, to wallow in her feelings and wish things could have been different between them. Except then she would never discover how it would feel to grow old with this man and see that charming smile change and develop, to become the smile of a lover, a husband, maybe even a father one day...

'I think I'm in love with you,' she whispered.

'Sorry? What?' Murray cleared his throat, staring into her face. 'The traffic's so noisy... Did you just say –?'

'There you are at last,' a voice interrupted them, and Susie jumped violently as a hand came down on her shoulder. 'I've got something for you.'

'You h-have?' she stammered, staring round into her father's mocking face.

'Of course. You left your prize behind. Threw it at me, in fact.' Dad handed her the leather riding crop she'd won for having a great market stall display, still adorned with a scarlet First Place rosette. 'Though since you don't ride, I don't know what you'll use it for.'

Susie caught an enigmatic expression on Murray's

face and cast him a quelling look, tucking the riding crop under her arm. 'Erm, thanks.'

'Me and this fella have been hunting high and low for you,' her dad said, jerking his thumb towards the man crossing the road in his wake. 'I should have realised you'd come back to the Christmas Tree Shop, Susie... Like a homing pigeon, eh?' Her father laughed. 'But what on earth are the two of you doing out here in the car park in the freezing cold? Haven't you noticed it's snowing?'

Murray frowned at the other man. 'Gus!' he exclaimed, and then clapped a hand to his forehead. 'My chain of office. I'm so sorry... I'd forgotten all about it.'

Gus handed over his mayoral chain. 'Bloody heavy, this thing.'

'Tell me about it.' Murray threw it over his Santa hat and arranged it haphazardly on his chest. 'Erm, thanks for looking after it. I couldn't have run another inch with this weight around my neck.'

'Happy to help. I'm just glad you got your dog back safely.' The man was looking Murray up and down dubiously. 'Not sure that gold chain goes with all the mud though. Or the Santa hat. Down-and-out festive mayor?' He rubbed his chin. 'Not your usual look.'

'Yeah, I'd better take the chain back to the car for safe keeping, before someone reports me for stealing it.' Murray's gaze returned to hers, reluctant. 'Not yet though. I've a few things to finish up here first.' He paused, and then turned to shake her dad's hand.

'Hello, Lovell. Good to see you again, and Merry Christmas. I thought I saw you in the crowd up there... When did you get back?'

Interrupting this exchange, Susie said loudly, 'Dad, Gus... We were just in the middle of a very important conversation.'

'Oh,' her dad said blankly, glancing from Murray to his daughter. 'I take it you haven't had a chance to think over my proposal yet, Susie?'

'Proposal?' Murray echoed, frowning. 'What proposal?'

Susie's dad pursed his lips. 'Well, it's quite a complex matter to explain. Perhaps we should all go inside and discuss it over a cup of coffee?'

But Susie had had enough by that stage, about ready to stamp her foot in frustration. 'Dad wants to sell our house and use it to fund an online Christmas tree business.'

'Not that complex, apparently,' her dad murmured.

Murray stared at her. 'And you, Susie? What do *you* want to do?'

'I want us to continue our previous conversation,' she said sharply, with a significant glare at her dad, who blinked in surprise.

Gus scratched his head, then grinned. 'Aha, gotcha.' He slapped Susie's dad on the back. 'I think that's our cue to make ourselves scarce.' He nodded to the shop, beautifully lit up in the dark of the snowy Christmas Eve, festive lights flashing. 'You told me that used to be your shop? How about we take a look inside, give these two a bit of privacy?'

'Um, yes, all right.' Her dad turned away, still looking bemused.

'And you could take the dog with you,' Susie suggested. 'Betty's lost her coat and is very muddy, and I don't want her to catch cold.'

'Of course.' Gus relieved Murray of the dog's lead. 'Come on, Mr Lovell... Why don't you show me those Christmas trees you were boasting about? Firs, did you say? Or was it spruce?'

The two men trudged away through the snow with Betty trotting happily alongside them, no doubt as keen to get out of the cold as they were, while Susie's dad enthusiastically launched into a description of the key differences between spruce, pine and fir Christmas trees.

As soon as they were alone again, Murray looked at her longingly. 'Despite this chain, I'm not always the mayor, you know. Or Santa Claus. Sometimes I'm just Murray.'

He was holding out his hand.

She took it, smiling mistily through the thickening snowfall. 'Hello, Murray, pleased to meet you. I'm just Susie.' She met his gaze shyly. 'Shall we go into the house rather than the shop? It's a bit nippy out here and I think there's snow wedged down the back of my collar.'

'We'd better get you out of those wet things, then.'

'And maybe later we could find a use for this?' Innocently, she held up the riding crop, and saw his eyes widen...

EPILOGUE

Penrock Downs, three years later

'Perhaps another strand of golden tinsel here,' Murray murmured, leaning perilously far to his left as he draped the glittering strand of tinsel as far around the Christmas tree as he could reach. 'And some more silver on this side? What do you think?' To the accompanying sounds of chortling and creaking, he repeated the movement with a long, silver strand of tinsel. 'Okay, how about this fat red tinsel? Wow, it's so thick, it's practically a garland. This one would look very jolly on our tree, don't you agree, Jack?'

Jack gurgled his approval, kicking his short, stubby legs with such violence that the bouncer chair he was fastened in *boinged* up-and-down with ever louder creaking noises.

'Oh no, it's dancing on your head!' Murray exclaimed, holding the red tinsel garland above his son. 'And now it's trailing down your chest... And over your bare toes... Oh, my goodness! This tinsel is *alive*!'

Still dressed in his Santa costume, Murray dangled the tinsel over his son until Jack exploded into laughter, kicking and gurgling, his bright eyes following the tinsel's glittering flourishes.

'I think that's meant to go on the tree, not on the baby,' a woman's voice told him with quiet reprimand.

He turned to find Tansy watching them, a wire basket full of Christmas goodies on her arm, grinning at him and the baby.

Tansy looked quite presentable these days, Murray thought, turning to greet her. If they didn't have dinner together every few weeks, he would barely have recognised her as the same hippyish, disorganized cat obsessive who'd been rescued from that flooded-out caravan by the river. Working as Director of the Penrock Downs Cat Sanctuary had given Tansy purpose and determination as well as a smart new wardrobe. At dinner last month, she'd even been talking about running for a place on the council next time there was a vacancy.

'Shopping for the cats?' he joked, but his smile faded when she nodded.

'Of course.' Her lips pursed. 'Rescue cats deserve a Christmas too, you know.'

'I... I'm sure.'

'I've already put a tree up for them in the recreation room. I just needed some more of these special cat-proof baubles.' She showed him a set of carved wooden balls made for the Christmas Tree Shop by a local artisan. 'No dangerous paint, no plastic or glass to hurt them if they get pulled off the tree… They're perfect for cats. And when they do pull them down, the baubles roll in a highly enticing way. I bought a trial pack of six a couple of weeks back. They've been so successful, I came back for more.'

'I'm glad the cats at the sanctuary are in for another brilliant Christmas with you at the helm.' Stringing the red tinsel around the tree in a haphazard fashion, he glanced towards the till. 'I can't leave Jack unattended, I'm afraid. If you're in a hurry, Mr Lovell looks free to serve you.'

'Thanks,' she said, but didn't move away. 'How's Susie? I saw a story about her yesterday in the Penrock Downs Gazette. She's doing marvellously, isn't she? You must be so proud.'

Murray smiled slowly. 'Yes, I am incredibly proud of my wife. And she's in fine form, thank you. Personally, I think she could have taken more time off after Jack's birth. Now we've expanded our range of pet foods, the shop's pulling in enough revenue alone to cover all the bills. But she was eager to get back to work, and it was her choice.' He smiled down at his son. 'Luckily, I'm happy to stay home with the baby. It's a nice change of pace.'

'Did you manage to get any surfing done this summer?'

He grinned. 'Two days only. But Susie and Jack are worth it.'

'I'm sure. That's how I feel about my cats.' Tansy looked him up and down curiously. 'You know, you were a blinkin' good mayor. But you make an even greater Santa.'

'It's mostly stuffing, honest. Though not surfing hasn't helped.'

'And you don't mind not being mayor?'

'Being mayor is a lot of hard work and responsibility, you know. I don't miss it one little bit.' He winked at her. 'Perhaps one day you'll be mayor, Tansy. Then you'll find out what it's like on the other side of the table.'

'Me? Mayor of Penrock Downs? That'll be the day!'

'I managed it.'

'You make a good point.' Tansy laughed with him, and then hesitated. 'Did you hear about your ex, by the way?'

'Genevieve?' He frowned.

'She's marrying Mike Reevers, one of the penguins from last year's pageant floats. Actually, I think he's been a penguin several years on the trot.'

'Sounds like a match made in the North Pole.'

'Apparently, he's minted too.'

'My all-time favourite flavour.' Murray grinned. So Genevieve had finally found a wealthy man to call her own. Not that she'd been around the place much since his rejection at the Christmas Market three years ago. 'She'll be happy, then.'

'Well, Merry Christmas!' Tansy gave him a wave, muttered some incomprehensible baby talk to Jack, something along the lines of 'Goo-goo gaga doo-doo,' and made her way merrily to the till, where Susie's dad seemed thrilled to take her money.

Watching them in conversation, Murray smiled to himself before turning to remove his Santa hat and unhook his beard, and close up the grotto for the day.

It had worked out brilliantly, bringing Susie's dad back into the fold as manager of the Christmas Tree Shop once Susie was heavily pregnant and ready to put her feet up. The man was a good manager and had an impressive instinct for moneymaking, despite all his protests that he preferred to keep things small-scale and local. Plus, he knew every single return customer by their first name, and seemed to know the trees by their first names too.

Assuming Susie hadn't been fibbing when she'd claimed that all her trees had names.

Besides, at this time of year, with the commercial Christmas Market in full swing again, they needed all hands on deck, both at the shop and on the market stall. Jim was on the stall again today, helped by his mother, though soon they would be packing away the market cabins after another successful December.

Jack cooed and dribbled, thumping his legs again to get his dad's attention.

The tactic worked.

Murray crouched, using a tissue to wipe away drool from the corner of his son's mouth. 'This teething lark isn't much fun, is it? Poor Jack... Still, you seem happy enough at the moment.' He grimaced. 'I daresay we'll be hearing more about it in the middle of the night though.'

'I'm glad to see the two of you getting along so well,' his wife said, surprising him as she strode across the shop floor towards them, briefcase swinging violently at her side. 'You seemed rather grumpy at five o'clock this morning when I mentioned that he was crying again and it was your turn.'

'Well, I'm not at my best at five in the morning. Am I, Jack?'

With a lopsided grin, he wiped away more drool before touching the tip of his son's nose affectionately. He still couldn't get over having become a father. A real-life miracle, every day bringing new revelations and stinkier nappies. But he was happy at last, nappies aside. And it was the kind of happiness that made him smile on rolling out of bed in the mornings, instead of staggering about with a frown on his face, feeling stressed and constantly on the alert for problems, as he'd done in the old days. The before-Susie days, as he mentally referred to them.

'Especially not after two nights of being awake at five in the morning,' he added. 'Not to mention *three* in the morning a few nights back, as I recall. That was a doozie.'

He stood to kiss his wife, his arms slipping about her wonderfully soft and shapely body as their lips met. Several seconds of pure joy ensued before Murray reluctantly raised his head, murmuring, 'Mmm, I've missed you. How was the council meeting?'

'A cross between herding cats and breaktime at a kindergarten,' she said frankly, handing him the car keys. 'Talking of cats, I saw Tansy in the car park. She's asked us to Boxing Day lunch with her at the cat sanctuary.'

'Is Betty invited?'

'What do you think? I'm sure Betty can handle a few hours alone on the sofa until we're back.'

'We'll have to strip the chocs off the tree,' he reminded her. 'I volunteer to eat any excess.'

'You are developing a sweet tooth, Mr Lovell. I may have to take steps.'

'Time for the riding crop again?' he asked hopefully.

'I should take it to council meetings. Things might go a little quicker.' Rolling her eyes, Susie balanced her briefcase on a stack of boxed Christmas lights, unlocked it and flung open the lid, before removing her gold mayoral chain of office and arranging it carefully inside. Then she locked the briefcase again. 'I wish I'd known how much diplomacy was involved in being mayor before I let you talk me into standing for election. Not to mention the long hours... Being a simple council member was a doddle by comparison. No wonder you were happy to stand down.' She gave a deep and thankful sigh. 'Still, no more mayoral meetings now until January. I can't wait to pull on my wellies and spend some time outdoors with the trees.'

'And there I was, thinking the festive break would mean us spending more time together.'

'You can always put on your wellies and join me. You do own *several pairs*, after all, as I recall you telling me once.'

'You old romantic, you. Anyway, I think you make a superb Lady Mayoress. But there's no escaping the fact that it's a tough job, as I was just telling Tansy.'

'You still miss it though, don't you?' Susie threw him a skeptical look when he denied it. 'Come on... All the cut and thrust of council meetings? Though you wouldn't have loved chairing today's meeting. It was more cut than thrust. Ted was at his absolute worst. I thought he'd never shut up. First, he complained about our plans to encourage more affordable housing, then he started going on about the impact of the Christmas Market on local infrastructure and how we need to stop hosting it at Penrock Downs. Never mind all the revenue it's brought to the town.'

'Hark at you!' Murray threw back his head, heartily amused. 'Once upon a time, that was *you*, back when you were still Miss Lovell and a right royal pain in my mayoral backside. You would have approved of affordable local housing, it's true. But you were always blogging about the impact of this and that on Penrock Downs and blaming it on me... The way you were spitting fire over the Christmas Market that first year, I would happily have seen you barred from the council chamber.' He grinned. 'Exiled from Cornwall, even better.'

'But then we would never have fallen in love,' she pointed out demurely, 'and never had our lovely little Jack.' Susie bent to remove their son from the bouncy chair, grinning as he gurgled at her. 'My goodness, you're getting heavy, my boy. Do you have a nuclear core? No need to ask if daddy's been feeding you properly today.'

'That boy could eat for Britain, I'm telling you. He's going to be a big lad. Just like his father.' Murray reached for a Christmas tree chocolate, unwrapped it and popped it into his mouth while his wife shook her head at him disapprovingly. 'Next year, he'll be eating tree chocs with the best of us. After that, it'll be downhill all the way.'

'I see you're working on your festive paunch. Have you been a good Santa today?'

'Of course. I told all the children they would probably get what they wanted, but if they didn't, to address any post-festive complaints to the Lady Mayoress.'

'Why you...!'

As her eyes sparked, he put his arm around his wife and kissed her on the lips, while Jack was still in her arms, the three of them locked in a warm embrace. Meanwhile, Jack kicked and burbled noisily between them until drool ran down his chin.

Backing off with a grimace, Murray nodded to their son. 'Erm, your turn, darling. I've had him all day. He even sat in the grotto with me earlier while I was playing Santa. Let's hope he's forgotten about that by next Christmas, or there may be awkward questions...'

As Susie tidied up their son's drool, a series of

high-pitched yaps heralded Betty's arrival in the shop. The little dog came bounding towards them and danced about on her hindlegs, delighted to see them after all day at the Christmas Market, cooped up in the stall with Tom and his mother.

Murray patted his dog guiltily, though he knew that Tom always took her out for a quick run every hour or so, and it was far more fun for Betty to be running about the Christmas Market, barking at all the visitors and stallholders, then to be stuck indoors at the shop. Though she was getting into middle age now, in dog terms, and finally seemed happier to spend time lying about in her basket and dreaming rather than always bothering him for attention.

He scooped up the playful dog and let her lick his face, then laughed. 'Looks like someone's had a good day, at least. Good old Tom. He took you out for a few walks, I see. You've got mud all over your paws. Bathtime for you tonight.'

'Haven't you finished dressing that tree yet?' Susie demanded, studying his handiwork. 'Come on, I'd better help you. I'd like to take Jack home before midnight.' She murmured with a wink, 'I hear Santa may be coming later.'

'Ho ho ho.'

Betty wriggled in his arms and Murray let her jump down, watching as she pelted across the store to wreak havoc with Mr Lovell's newly arranged display of dog treats.

Going home after their long day did sound

wonderful though, he realised. They lived at his place in town now, while Susie's dad lived in the house beside the shop, opening and locking up the premises for them. It was an arrangement that had proved very handy, especially now the festive season was upon them again. Murray couldn't now imagine spending Christmas without his wife by his side, sitting on the sofa with her in the evenings, watching lights flash on the tinsel and listening to carol singers working their way around the town. And his father-in-law would be having Christmas lunch with friends, so it would just be the three of them this year… Him, Susie and baby Jack, enjoying his first Christmas.

He recalled with a jolt when he'd dragged that tree home, the year they'd met, and dressed it with tinsel, and then sat there feeling utterly alone and depressed…

How times had changed.

Placing Jack in his pushchair ready for home time, Susie turned to the box she'd given Murray that morning, containing the last of the tree decorations that had once belonged to her mother. He'd only left a few at the bottom, she realised. Tears pricked at her eyes as she fastened on a delicate glass reindeer, a hand-painted Christmas Pudding, and a soft knitted penguin, before stepping back to admire the tree. 'There, that's perfect.'

'Thank you.'

'I just meant, not bad for a novice.'

'Hey, this is my fourth attempt at dressing a Christmas tree, I'll have you know,' Murray pointed out. 'I'm practically a Grandmaster now.'

'That's chess, not tree-dressing.'

'Treemaster, then.' About to laugh, he stopped and peered at her face. 'Susie, love? What is it?'

She wiped away a tear, horribly self-conscious. 'Don't you remember?' She nodded to the homely family decorations adorning the shop tree. 'I saved these last few for the tree here at the shop, but the rest went onto our own Christmas tree at home.'

'Your mother's decorations?' When she nodded, not quite able to speak in case she began to sob, he put a comforting arm about her waist. 'Oh Susie… Of course I remember you telling me. These are very dear to you, aren't they? Your mum hand-painted some of them, didn't she?'

'The Christmas Pudding,' she muttered indistinctly.

'It's very good. Looks almost edible.' He paused. 'Not sure about the penguin though. It's lost some stuffing. To be fair, I could do with losing some stuffing too. Maybe in the New Year. Back to the gym for Santa!'

'Idiot.'

'Sorry.' But she knew he was only doing it to distract her from the sad memories. Thoughtfully, he looked down into her face. 'Hey, did you hear about Genevieve and the penguin? And no, that's not the start of a dirty joke.'

'They're getting married. Tansy told me last week.'

'You never mentioned it.'

'I thought it might be a sore point.'

His brows rose. 'I was never in love with her, you know. Not *really*.'

'Of course not. But I saw you look at that penguin sideways a few times.' She waggled her eyebrows at him. 'Mike, wasn't that his name?'

'Yeah, he always makes such a cute penguin in the Christmas pageant.' He laughed at her expression. 'Seriously though, I'm thrilled that Genevieve has found someone at last, and we no longer have to worry she's sitting outside the house with a shotgun.' She nudged him in the ribs, and he grinned, hurriedly returning to the safer subject of Christmas trees. 'Okay, I'm the first to admit it, I'm no big expert on decorating trees. Not like you. But I had special help this year.' When Susie frowned, he nodded to their son. 'Jack.'

'Jack is seven months old. He can't even talk yet, let alone dress a Christmas tree.'

'Ah, but we worked out a system. Didn't we, Jack? I would hold up a strand of tinsel and say *here*? Or *there*? And I would interpret his intentions depending on the various noises and leg movements he made. Honestly, it was very scientific.'

She shook her head, laughing. 'What on earth are you talking about? I swear you never used to be like this when I first met you.'

'That's because you changed me, Susie. Once upon a time, I was a rational human being. I always made sense and I had my whole life planned out. Surfing, politics, making money. Then I met you, and now...' He sighed and shook his head. 'Now I'm a father.'

Her tears forgotten, Susie chuckled at the dreamy look in his face. 'Yes, you do tend to spout gibberish these days, but I love you all the same.'

'Thank goodness for that, because you've ruined me for all the other ladies out there.' Murray snaked a strong arm about her waist, pulling her close. Too late, she realised he was dangling a fresh sprig of mistletoe above their heads. 'Did I already tell you how much *I* love you?'

'Only about a thousand times.'

'And did I wish you a Merry Christmas yet, Mrs Carew?'

'Roughly as often.'

'Then, for the one-thousandth-and-first time, I love you to the ends of the earth and for ever and ever, and I wish you a very, *very* Merry Christmas, darling.' And he kissed her.

AFTERWORD

Thank you so much, dear reader, for choosing this fun and festive Christmas romcom by Beth Good.

If you've enjoyed this, please know that Beth Good is a prolific writer and has a whole STACK of other delightful romcoms to choose from, from summer beach reads to festive stories like this one!

She also writes romance as Pippa Summers and Elizabeth Moss, WWII sagas as Betty Walker, and bestselling thrillers and suspense as Jane Holland.

Printed in Great Britain
by Amazon